KILLER TIME

Bill Edwards

FriesenPress

One Printers Way
Altona, MB R0G 0B0
Canada

www.friesenpress.com

First Edition — 2022

ISBN
978-1-03-912880-4 (Hardcover)
978-1-03-912879-8 (Paperback)
978-1-03-912881-1 (eBook)

1. FICTION, THRILLERS, CRIME

Distributed to the trade by The Ingram Book Company

To Lies,
for her enduring love and support.

PROLOGUE

Wednesday, April 15, 1987

WEDNESDAY SEEMED LIKE a lucky day for Rico Sanelli. He'd cut short his sales calls to watch the dogs run at Lincoln Downs and had won big by hitting the Exacta. Now he was at his favorite watering hole, regaling a crowd of mostly regulars with the story of his win. Most of those gathered around him in Sal's Bar had already heard the story at least twice, but since Rico was buying, they didn't mind if he carried on a bit.

Rico was a small guy, with no fashion sense—the plaid of his red sport coat clashed with his houndstooth trousers, and the color made his florid complexion even more so. Still, at the moment, nobody was paying much attention to those details—least of all Rico. Most days, his luck was lousy, and he probably owed more drinks to the regulars than even his Exacta winnings could cover.

"So, how much did you score?" Sal, the bartender and owner,encouraged him, since Rico's celebrating was good for business.

"Eight hundred and twenty bucks!" Rico exclaimed. "Man, for a change, Lady Luck was really smiling at me!" He took another swig and frowned suddenly. "Oh, shit!"

"What's the matter?"

"My old lady! If she gets wind of it, this pile will never make it to Friday's poker game!" He frowned again. "And if I'm late for dinner, she'll smell something, sure as hell!" He pushed back his sleeve. His watch (fancy-looking but actually a cheap knock-off) showed five past six. "Sonofabitch! Gotta go!"

"Aw, come on, Rico! You can stay a little longer!" said Sal. There was a chorus of agreement from the regulars gathered around. Nobody was eager to lose their source of free drinks.

"No, no. I gotta go. If Angie finds out, it's goodbye bankroll!" He gulped down the last of his Scotch and headed for the door. Amid the shouted goodbyes that followed him, nobody noticed the stranger who left shortly after.

Rico was stumbling slightly as he headed onto the sidewalk. The Scotches—was it three or four?—were affecting him more than his usual two or three beers. He paused, trying to remember where he'd parked his car, then recalled that it was in the alley around the corner.

As he lurched in that direction, he was unaware of the man who'd followed him out of the bar. Rico headed into the alley, and was about ten feet from his car when he heard a noise behind him. He stopped, suddenly very aware of both the wad of bills in his wallet and the rapid pounding of his heart. Only five foot six, and not what you'd call a fighter, he sighed, reached for his wallet, and slowly turned. As he did so, he got a glimpse of a taller man—and the blur of a moving arm just before something solid hit him in the temple. He was unconscious when his head hit the pavement, but given the impact of the first blow, hitting the pavement scarcely mattered.

The attacker stood over Rico's crumpled body for a moment and looked around to check if anyone had seen. There were no windows in the alley, just metal loading doors for various stores. He dropped the brick from his gloved hand as he knelt beside the body and looked intently at the still form. Almost as an afterthought, he took the money from the wallet, which was still clutched in Rico's hand.

"So, how's your luck now, asshole?" he muttered with a thin smile.

There was no one around in the gathering dusk to offer an opinion as he sauntered out of the alley.

ONE

ED UNDERWOOD PAUSED at the bottom of the stairway. His body was here, but his mind wasn't. He took a slow, deep breath, trying to clear his head. His personnel job at Barton Jewelry hadn't been particularly rough that day, but he still felt distracted, and knew he needed to focus. Exhaling, he began climbing to the entrance of Yoshikawa's .

The steps from the ground floor were clean but bare, as were the walls. He paused again in the doorway, still trying to calm his mind. The entrance opened onto a large room whose floor was covered with straw *tatami* mats. Bowing, he called out, "Good evening, *sensei*," and crossed the floor to the changeroom of the *karate dojo*.

As he entered the dressing room, he came face to face with Yoshikawa-*sensei*. (The term was roughly equivalent to calling him "Master Yoshikawa" in English.) Yoshikawa was a small man in his fifties; slightly built but with well-defined musculature, he exuded an air of vitality. Seeing Ed, his face lit up.

"Ah, good evening, Underwood-*san*! It's nice to see you!" The greeting was genuine, a reflection of the joy he took in each moment. It didn't matter that he saw Underwood two or more times a week.

"Good evening, *sensei*. Thank you!" Outside the school, the two men were on first-name terms—in fact, were close friends. However, it was a tradition of the martial arts that in the *dojo*, one acted with proper regard for etiquette, a reminder of the discipline and concentration the training required.

After donning his white *gi* and black belt, Underwood went back into the training area, where several students were practicing or doing warm-ups.He began doing some leg stretches, watching a pair of students spar. Suddenly, he sensed movement behind him; something told him to shift his position—but too late. The next moment, he was lying on the floor, while Yoshikawa looked down at him with a look of mild disapproval.

"I have told you many times, Underwood-*san*. Never let your mind get caught on one thing—especially in the *dojo*! You make too easy a target for me!" Yoshikawa began laughing.

"Yes, *sensei*!" Underwood frowned, annoyed at his lapse—and as a result, he almost didn't block the kick that Yoshikawa suddenly launched at him.

"Better," said Yoshikawa, nodding slightly. "But you are still not present. Why?" Now he was the one frowning.

Underwood hesitated, trying to frame an answer. Before he could speak, Yoshikawa continued.

"I think tonight you should practice *kata*. No *kumite*." He stared intently, seeing a student, not a friend. "You cannot be a danger to others—or yourself." So saying, he walked off, already focusing on another student.

I can't spar. Great. Underwood had known his awareness was off, but he'd hoped, foolishly, that Yoshikawa wouldn't notice. The tone of the brief encounter carried through his training session, as he tried to focus on the choreographed movements of *kanku sho kata*. Angry with himself and still unable to restore his equilibrium, he cut his workout short after only forty-five minutes.

As Ed Underwood was leaving Yoshikawa's school, Sgt. Mike Langan of the Providence Police Department was leaving the alley behind Sal's Bar. The call had come in at about six o'clock, and Langan had been sent from the homicide squad. Sometimes called "Hangin' Langan" by others on the force (though rarely to his face), after a dozen years in homicide, he still had an intense drive to catch killers. The fact that the whole state saw fewer than forty murders most years meant that each one mattered even more.

The scene in the alley was not the worst he had faced, but over the years, he'd found it never got easier, either. The body had been found by a regular from the bar, and by the time the police arrived, there was a small crowd in the alley. Most of them had known Sanelli, and more than one, after some initial staring, had gone back into the bar to fortify themselves. One of the patrolmen had taken statements, but they all said they'd been inside when it happened. *Except for the killer*, thought Langan.

It was, of course, possible that the attack had had nothing to do with the bar, though the preliminary comments from the forensics team suggested that robbery had been the motive: Sanelli's wallet had been found near the body, but only the cash was missing. His credit cards and watch had been left behind. It appeared Sanelli had been hit in the head with a broad, flat object, though it looked like he'd also hit his head when he fell. A brick with what might be bloodstains had been found and would be analyzed by the lab. From Langan's viewpoint, it didn't make a lot of difference which blow was fatal; either way, Sanelli was dead.

A chance mugging by a street punk with no fence? Or does it relate to Sanelli bragging about his winnings? And if so, was it one of the regulars, or a stranger?

For the moment, Langan dismissed any further thoughts about possible suspects. There would be time later to go through the statements and look for motives. Forensics had finished their work in the alley and the body was being taken to the morgue, but Langan still had one more chore. It was the one he always liked the least: he had to tell Angela Sanelli that her two kids no longer had a father.

Stan Osiewicz, a reporter for the *Providence Journal-Bulletin*, observed the crime scene as Langan prepared to leave. For the past ten years, Osiewicz had mostly covered the crime beat for the paper, though he preferred doing feature stories that required more research. In the present case, he also realized that the camera crew from Channel 10 would scoop him, since they could make the eleven p.m. news and his story wouldn't appear till the morning paper. Still, it was his job, so he spoke to one of the officers manning the perimeter, a patrolman named Joe Walsh. The Providence PD was small enough that many faces had become familiar as the reporter covered stories. He knew Walsh well enough that he could usually count on getting at least the basics from him (aided by the occasional thank-you of a case of beer). Now, though, neither Walsh nor anyone else at the scene would confirm the victim's name. Osiewicz suspected it was due to the presence of Detective Langan, who was known to dislike reporters.

Seeking more information, Osiewicz went into the bar. He ordered a beer and started talking to the bartender. Sal was willing to confirm that the dead man was a regular, that he had won a big bet at the Lincoln Downs dog track that afternoon, and that he had celebrated by buying rounds for the house. Putting things together, Osiewicz decided it was likely a robbery where the mugger hit his victim a bit too hard. Unless or until he heard more, that would be enough for a write-up in the morning edition. He finished his beer, thanked Sal, and left a ten-spot for the beer and information. It had already been a long day, but he still needed to file the story.

Rhode Island's small size meant it took Ed Underwood less than fifteen minutes to get from Yoshikawa's *dojo* in North Providence to his girlfriend's place on the East Side.

He parked his car on the street outside the large old house, setting the handbrake on the steep hill. He glanced at his watch: seven fifty-five p.m., which meant he was early. Liz Reynolds taught nearby at Rhode Island School of Design, an art school more commonly known as RISD, but she often worked late. Given he'd cut his workout short, he was ahead of their usual Wednesday routine, so she was probably not yet home. Climbing the steps to the front door, he considered using his key, but instead knocked, in case her housemate, Karen Durant, was home. The door opened.

"Oh, hi, Ed!" said Karen. "How are you? Liz isn't home yet—but come in. Would you like something to drink?" As usual, Karen's words came in a torrent. She was dressed in a robe and had curlers in her hair, but seemed totally at ease.

"Thanks, Karen." Underwood stepped in and headed for the kitchen. After five years, it was as familiar as his own. "I'll just help myself to some juice."

"How are things in the jewelry business?" She continued talking as she followed him through the house. "You know, Ed, I keep meaning to visit you at work. I mean, I need some new jewelry, and you've said you can get me a discount, right?" Without waiting for his reply, she continued, "I'm going to that new club on Thayer Street tonight—"

At this point, there was the sound of the front door opening. A woman's voice called out, "Karen? Are you home?"

"Hi, Liz. I'm in the kitchen with Ed."

"Well, I hope he isn't eating, because I'm starving!" This was said as she entered the kitchen. She saw Underwood and smiled, and then, seeing Karen in a half-open robe, her face took on a mock scowl. "Look at you, Karen, with no clothes on! If I didn't know you better, I'd say you were out to steal Ed!"

Karen couldn't resist the bait. "Actually, I was trying, but I guess not hard enough!" She smirked at Liz, and then beat a retreat. "But I can take a hint! Bye, Ed!" With that, she was gone.

Underwood smiled broadly at the pair of them, but as Karen left, his grin disappeared and he rose to embrace Liz. They shared a lingering kiss, and as they broke off, she pulled back to look at him. "Is everything okay, Ed?" He said nothing, and his dark eyes darted away. She looked at him for a long moment and decided to let it go. Instead, she said, "As you can see, I haven't made dinner. So where shall we go?"

Dinner ended up being Italian, at Carmen's on Federal Hill. Underwood's mood over-shadowed the otherwise pleasant meal; he gave a vague apology for being "busy at work," but no details. Liz knew him well enough to realize pressing him to talk was pointless. Given the evening's downward trajectory and the fact that they both worked in the morning, after dinner she asked him to drop her off, while he continued on to his own place.

The eleven o'clock news on TV that night carried the usual assortment of national and local politics, interspersed with reports about a volcano erupting in Peru and the murder of a local man. Sandy Rivera, the "action-camera reporter" for Channel 10, gave a report from the scene.

“At approximately six o’clock this evening, a man’s body was found in an alley just off Gano Street. The victim was a male in his forties, and was apparently bludgeoned to death. Robbery is suspected as the motive for the murder, but police are not releasing any details until the investigation of the scene is completed. The victim’s identity is being withheld, pending notification of next of kin. This is Sandy Rivera for Channel 10 news.”

Most of those watching had little reaction, having viewed countless similar reports over the years. The late news was just something that preceded the *Tonight Show*. A few people felt a small shudder, thinking it could be a friend or family member—or even themselves—on some future crime report. That was life in the city these days.

One of those watching sat idly swigging a beer, and stared intently at his TV on hearing the word “murder”. Though few details were given, the camera did catch the body being taken away in the ambulance.

The viewer smiled and silently toasted the screen with his bottle.

TWO

Friday, April 17, 1987

MIKE LANGAN PULLED his car into the lot behind the Providence Police Department on Washington Street. The old brick building, centrally located downtown, had stood there for decades while the city changed around it. Now, Interstate 95 was a block away, and the pedestrian mall and the Civic Center arena were each about two blocks away. Like the PD building, Langan had seen many changes in his twenty-eight years on the job, which he started as a patrolman in the newly built University Heights area (public housing erected to replace a quasi-slum area). Eventually he made detective, and now, at forty-eight, the twelve years he'd spent in robbery-homicide had been the most fulfilling part of his career. In truth, the robbery cases were less interesting than the homicides, but the Providence PD was small enough that the two areas were combined, and Langan accepted that reality.

He made his way up to the third floor, where his desk sat in its usual disarray. Langan had a good memory and was never big on compulsive order. As long as he placed something on or in his desk, he knew he could find it later. At the moment, Betty Cavendish, who had been a fixture in the department even back when Langan joined, tossed an envelope squarely onto the center of his desk.

"Hey, Betty. Is that what I think it is?" Langan said by way of greeting.

"It is, if you're thinking it's the Sanelli report, Mike. Good luck to you, from what the doc tells me." After untold years in the department, Betty probably knew more about what went on than the chief did.

"Yeah, that's about what I figured." Langan sank heavily into his chair, opening the lab report before adding it to his binder on the case. In Rhode Island, homicides mostly fell into one of three categories: domestics, drugs, or mob. *Which one is this?* he wondered.

The report confirmed what he had already guessed. The medical examiner had identified two skull fractures. One was in the right occipital region, from a large, flat object; small fragments of clay in the wound had been sent to forensics to compare to the brick found at the scene. The second skull fracture was in the left frontal region, likely sustained when the victim fell after being rendered unconscious by the blow from the rear. There were signs of concussion and massive hemorrhaging; it was unclear if the first blow had been fatal on its own, but it was certainly contributory. The angle and force of the first blow indicated that the attacker was at least two inches taller than the victim, and quite strong. Langan checked the description of Sanelli in the medical examiner's report and concluded the attacker was about six feet tall. Six feet and strong enough to wield a brick—the two factors almost certainly ruled out a woman as the attacker. In addition, the direction from which the blow came—from behind and on the right—strongly suggested the attacker was right-handed. Nothing in the report suggested a struggle—no secondary bruising, no fragments under the fingernails, and so on. The medical examiner, like Langan, had concluded that Sanelli had died when a big guy came up behind him and crushed his skull with a brick.

Langan gave a sigh. He hated these cases. Some poor bastard gets done in because he's carrying too much dough and is foolish enough to let others know it.

The preliminary report from the forensics lab was not encouraging, either. The clay fragments from the first wound matched the brick, while the hairs, skin, and blood found on the brick matched the victim. No blood spots were identified that didn't match the victim's type. No fingerprints were found on either the brick or the wallet, though both were challenging surfaces for lifting prints. Mike speculated that the attacker might have worn gloves, but they hadn't found any identifiable fibers to confirm this possibility. A full report on the victim's clothing and the items from the scene would still take another week. When they'd spoken, Doc Yoshida had told him not to hold his breath expecting much.

So, at the moment, the evidence was a dead end. That left Langan with checking witnesses. He'd talked to everyone who'd been in the bar when he'd arrived at the scene. Being a neighborhood bar, it was mostly regulars, more than a dozen. However, the tally on who had been present was approximate, since about half an hour had elapsed between Sanelli's exit and the discovery of the body. Consequently, by the time the police arrived, several people had come and gone. The bartender and a couple of patrons had reported seeing one or more unfamiliar faces in the bar earlier, but reports on what they looked like, and even whether they'd left before or after Sanelli, were contradictory.

Initially, Langan had not pursued this aspect further, pending anything the lab results might tell him. In truth, tracking down a stranger from such reports was almost like chasing a ghost. Besides, some regulars had also come and gone, and nothing said the killer couldn't be someone who knew Sanelli. In any case, Langan would pay a return visit to Sal's Bar to talk to the bartender in more detail. If it still led nowhere, he could contact each patron to review what he'd already been told. Check and double-check, looking for gaps and contradictions. It was a tedious process, nothing like the drama of TV crime shows, but Mike believed the truth was always in the details. And seeking that truth was what kept him going.

Henry Cohen, the president of Barton Jewelry, was at his desk, going through the day's mail and pondering a rather cryptic item. A large manila envelope had arrived, labeled "Confidential" and addressed to him by name. The lettering was very childish, and there was no return address. Inside was a sheet of newspaper, taken from the classifieds section of the *Providence Journal*, that was pasted over with letters that were obviously cut from other parts of the paper. The result was a crudely laid-out message:

Just you watch. The time for payback is coming.

Cohen looked at it, his brow furrowed. He looked again at the envelope, confirming that it was in fact intended for him. He turned the page over, but there was nothing more. The page had been torn from the job ads of a paper that was a week old. (He checked, but saw that Barton's ad was not included.) The postmark was from Providence, sent the previous day.

Cohen leaned back in his chair, an old-fashioned leather high-back swivel chair with wooden armrests, the finish worn by years of use. He sighed, rubbed his eyes, and gazed across the room at the picture of his father-in-law, Nathanial "Ned" Barton, the company's founder. Barton, who had been dead for several years, still seemed to oversee—and judge—his life.

Henry Cohen had been in business school when he'd met Emily Barton. Initially classmates and casual friends, they'd married before his graduation. To his dismay, the marriage was greeted with hostility by Ned Barton. Thus it had been a surprise when, after Cohen had completed his degree, Ned pushed him into the Barton family's jewelry business. Ostensibly it was because Ned had no sons, only three daughters, but it sometimes seemed to Cohen that Ned felt that if you were going to have a Jew in the family, you'd better keep him where you knew what he was up to. When Cohen had entered business school, he'd never imagined he would end up running a global jewelry company. Now, as he looked at the strange note in front of him, he wished that he wasn't.

"Just you watch. The time for payback is coming." What could it mean? Was it merely a prank? Neither April Fools' Day nor Halloween was near. And besides, weren't pranks only fun if you could see the person's reaction? *No,* he decided, *not a prank.*

Cohen thought about other possibilities. *If the message was a threat, what was it referring to? Payback for what? A soured business deal? A personal insult? Maybe some paranoid raving with no basis in reality?* He briefly considered turning the note over to the police, but decided it was premature. If it turned out to be a prank, he would look pretty foolish. And if it was serious, the wording implied that more information would follow. Uneasy, but unwilling to dwell on the matter, Cohen carefully refolded the sheet of newspaper, put it back in the manila envelope, and placed it in the bottom drawer of his desk. From across the room, the portrait of Ned Barton continued to stare down at him.

Late that afternoon, Ed Underwood was in his office at Barton Jewelry, struggling with the staffing issues that came with being Personnel Director. Glancing at his watch, he decided it was time to put aside the challenge of finding new hires and cleared off his desk. The martial arts had taught him that clutter was mentally distracting, so keeping his office well-organized had become a habit. As he prepared to leave, he mentally calculated how long it would take to get to the *dojo*, and also what time he was meeting Liz for dinner. Both *karate* and Liz were passions in his life, though thankfully not in competition.

Underwood had started in *judo* at age twelve, as a scrawny kid who'd sometimes had to cope with schoolyard bullies. After three years, he'd switched to *karate* when he realized that, contrary to popular opinion, *judo* depended as much on weight as skill. By contrast, he felt *karate* (literally "empty hand") emphasized technique over size, and its choreographed *katas* offered a form of solo practice lacking in *judo*. Now, at age thirty-four, he had been doing *karate* for nearly twenty years, and at six feet tall, was far from the scrawny kid who had started in *judo*.

Climbing the stairs to the dojo, he paused and bowed, calling out a greeting to Yoshikawa-*sensei*. To his relief, he recognized that he was less distracted than at his previous session. He sensed Yoshikawa's presence without seeing him—a kind of intuition called *haragei* in Japanese. Despite his background in psychology, Underwood still couldn't explain it, and the English translation ("stomach art") didn't help much. In any case, he'd experienced the sensation enough times to know it was real.

At that moment, Hisao Yoshikawa appeared from the small cubby that served as his office. After a quick glance at Underwood, he smiled and said, "Ah, Underwood-*san*! So nice to have all of you here today!" He laughed and turned away to help a green belt student.

After a solid workout, Ed headed to Liz's house, feeling both physically and mentally refreshed. As always, he looked forward to spending time with Liz. Her background in art, and particularly pottery, gave her a worldview that was far different than his training in psychology. Despite—or maybe because of—their differences, they were a well-matched couple, and had been almost from the beginning, five years ago. Liz seemed to understand his commitment to the martial arts, and accepted the occasional compromises that were required in making plans with him—though this had nothing to do with being weak or compliant. Instead, it reminded him of *judo*, where the basic principle is to redirect the opponent's force, rather than to oppose it head-on. Doing so meant you often didn't end up exactly where you originally intended, but neither did your opponent. Balance and compromise: despite training in art, not martial arts, Liz practiced her own form of *judo*.

For his part, Ed appreciated Liz's willingness to compromise—but he also knew that compromise should work both ways. Checking his watch, he realized that the slow traffic meant he was at risk of being late to meet her. Fortunately, as he turned off Smithfield Avenue onto North Main, the traffic thinned, and he headed up the hill towards her house with a few minutes to spare.

Liz opened the door just as he was about to knock and greeted him with a warm smile, followed by their usual embrace. Before he could speak, she held him at arm's length, and then spoke.

"Hey, Ed! Looks like you had a good day today!"

Not for the first time, he marveled that Liz could read him almost as well as Yoshikawa could. "Um, yeah. Pretty good. How was yours?" Before she could answer, he continued, "Hmm—from what I'm smelling, I'm guessing dinner is almost ready?"

"Veal parmesan and spaghetti. I hope you remembered to bring wine."

Underwood had been holding the brown bag with the bottle of Chianti at his side, and now lifted it with a flourish. "Take me to your corkscrew!"

Late that evening, a solitary figure sat in a modest, somewhat bare apartment. He didn't mind being alone—in his view, most people were fools, and when he had the choice, he didn't suffer fools. Here, in his home (hardly a castle, but it was still his private domain), he could do as he wished, and think without being interrupted by banal chatter.

Killing that guy Sanelli had made quite a splash on the news. Though the attack had not been pre-planned, the publicity confirmed that the situation was actually unanticipated good fortune. At the bar, his frustration at having recently been fired had been a simmering fire in his belly—but picking Sanelli as a target had actually been an impulsive act. Sanelli's bragging and waving the wad of bills, his arm upraised to show the whole place, his watchband flashing as his sleeve slid back—all of it had turned the simmering resentment into a white-hot rage. Observing Sanelli, he experienced a sudden cascade of ideas, an adrenalin-like surge that carried him forward, so that he almost felt like a spectator to the actions that followed. After leaving his victim lying in the alley, the energy had faded and he'd had a moment of worry that someone had seen the attack. By the time he'd gotten home, that concern had faded and was replaced by anticipation: after days of doing little, with no job or other goal, he suddenly had something to focus on. Getting revenge on Barton became his prime motivator.

In the bar, he'd remembered that a few years ago, somebody had put cyanide in a bottle of painkillers in a drugstore, and the resulting panic almost bankrupted a major pharmaceutical company. He'd realized that he could hurt Barton in a similar way Killing Sanelli, followed by quickly making and sending the note, had been accompanied by the thrill of impulsive action. but he knew his actions should not be done on impulse. That wasn't his style, and it was too risky. Now, he needed to carefully work through his next steps. He sat in the armchair, his eyes staring absently as he thought.

After several minutes, he stirred and picked up the issue of *Soldier of Fortune* magazine he'd been reading. For most readers, much of the magazine's appeal (whether acknowledged or not) was fantasy. But now he found one article of specific interest: it described the principles behind handgun silencers, and different ways of implementing them. In the same issue, at the back, were the usual ads for assorted weaponry, from Bowie knives to army surplus rocket launchers. One was a display ad featuring handguns, with the caption, "Prompt delivery for all makes and models! We ship the same day (with valid credit card or certified check)!" Listed were a variety of types, from .22 caliber pistols to .45 caliber Mac-10s. After browsing through the whole issue, he tore out the silencer article and the handgun ad.

THREE

Wednesday, April 22, 1987

NINE-YEAR-OLD JOEY GONSALVES was excited. Just this morning, he'd received a new two-wheeler—not a tiny little-kid bike, but a real one, with ten different speeds!

For what seemed like forever, he'd been after his parents for a new bike. More than once, his dad had raised the seat and handlebars on his old bike so Joey could continue to ride it, but it was still dismally small. Silently, Joey watched his friends get new bikes, his heart sinking a little more each time it happened. Finally, only he was still riding a small one. His father, struggling on a janitor's pay, tried reminding him how happy he'd been when he first received his old bike, but for Joey, his father's words missed the point.

And then, this morning, he'd gone out to the front porch after breakfast, wondering what to do today. He'd let the screen door slam, knowing it would provoke his mother, but not really caring—and then he'd seen it. He'd let out a yell that even Gina Gonsalves couldn't match. A new bike!

The bike was a delayed birthday present, its arrival (unknown to Joey) disrupted by shipping problems. Its appearance now overshadowed even the watch he'd gotten from his grandparents on his actual birthday, the week before. It was a shiny Timex with a real expansion band, the kind you could twist in a knot. The watch had already earned Joey a lot of attention among his friends—but it wasn't a new bike.

Now, in the late afternoon, he was still full to bursting with joy; even his mother's request to go to the store was okay, because he could continue riding. Gina shook her head in bemusement, thinking it was a rare occasion when she didn't have to ask Joey three times. The market was over on Mineral Spring Avenue, with its busy traffic, but Joey had made the trip many times before on his old bike. As he headed off, Gina called from the porch, "Remember, Joey, you watch the cars! And don't forget the cheese!" But Joey was already halfway down the block. *Kids*, Gina thought, shaking her head once more.

Joey turned onto Weeden Street, taking side streets past his school as he headed toward the supermarket on Mineral Spring Avenue. He was just approaching the school when a car pulled alongside and a man called out to him. Joey had always been warned about strangers, but he figured he was safe on his bike.

"Say, son, do you know where Rice Street is?"

"Huh?" Joey stopped the bike, his feet barely reaching the ground as he straddled it. He thought for a moment, puzzled by the unfamiliar name. "Gee, I dunno, mister. You sure you got the right name?"

The driver gazed at him intently, his eyes taking in the shiny new bike and flashing watchband. "Oh, I'm sure, all right." He continued staring at Joey.

Something about him, his eyes or his voice, gave Joey the creeps. "I . . . I've never heard of it," he mumbled, looking down at the handlebars.

"Well, I guess I'll keep looking," the stranger said, his eyes still fixed on Joey. Finally he said, "Thanks anyway, kid. . . ." He shifted the transmission back into gear, and the dark blue car moved slowly off.

Joey watched him go and saw the car turn left two blocks up. The chill he'd felt while talking to the man passed, and he shrugged, pedaling his bike once more. He passed the school and started to turn right onto the side street that was his shortcut to Mineral Spring Avenue.

To the left, just outside Joey's vision, a blue car careered out of a side street, ignoring the stop sign at Weeden Street. It continued across the intersection and hit Joey's bike just as he was completing his turn. The bike lurched forward as it bounced off the front of the car, and the boy struggled to control its wobbling motion. Then the front wheel caught the curb, and the jolt sent Joey hurtling over the handlebars. As he did so, his body upended, his head striking the pavement before his back did.

The driver stopped the car momentarily but did not get out. When he saw the boy wasn't moving, he looked quickly around. No other vehicles were passing by, and no one was walking on the street. He turned the steering wheel, carefully detouring his car around the bike and fallen boy, and drove on.

The accident, so late in the afternoon, did not make the papers that day, and for once, Sandy Rivera and her "action camera" were too slow to catch video footage, but the story still made the six p.m. broadcast. Predictably, the story also made the front page in both the *Pawtucket Times* and the *Providence Journal* the next day. (As Joe Houle, city editor at the *Journal*, put it, "pathos sells papers.")

Ed Underwood approached the clapboard house belonging to Liz, as familiar as his own apartment. As he walked up the worn wooden steps to the front porch, he heard a cardinal sing in a nearby tree. Its song, staccato and melodic at the same time, reminded him of a Japanese flute. Instead of knocking, he paused to listen to the bird, but the door opened anyway.

"Hey, Ed!" Karen exclaimed. "I *thought* I heard somebody on the steps!"

"Hi, Karen." Ed smiled briefly. "I was just listening to—"

But before he could finish the sentence, Karen had left the doorway, calling back as she headed toward the kitchen, "Liz is upstairs. She should be down in a minute. Why don't you come in and make yourself comfortable?"

Left alone at the open door, Ed entered; the bird had moved off, anyway. After a moment's deliberation, he decided to rejoin Karen in the kitchen rather than wait for Liz at the foot of the stairs. Sometimes, estimates of "a few minutes" were less than accurate.

"So, what's new, Karen?"

"Not a great day. I'll be glad when Friday comes. It's been one of those weeks that seem three weeks long."

"Anything in particular?"

"No, not really . . ." Her voice trailed off momentarily. Underwood wasn't sure if it meant she didn't want to say, or was just concentrating on the pot she was stirring on the stove. She paused to taste the contents, made a face, and began rummaging through the spice rack beside the stove. Finally, after several shakes and stirs, she turned back to him. "Did you hear about that poor boy? I mean, it's just awful!"

"Oh, you mean that accident? I think I heard something on the radio as I was driving here." In fact, Ed seldom listened to news broadcasts, and made it a general rule to avoid the daily papers. Most of the content was sensationalist, or at least depressing. He always heard about major events, anyway—as in the present case. "What was it, a drunk driver?"

"They didn't say, but the report gave the impression it was a hit-and-run. The kid got hit and the fall broke his neck. Imagine—somebody hits a kid on a bike, and then just drives away. I mean, what kind of monster could do that? It makes my blood boil!" She stomped across the open expanse of the kitchen.

"It sounds like one of those one-in-a-million accidents." Ed tried to imagine the scene. "Probably the driver got rattled and took off, figuring the boy was just knocked out."

"Yeah, sure," said Karen, tensely stirring the pot. Then she pointed the spoon at Ed. "If you hit someone, would you just take off?"

"I don't know. . . . I'd like to think I wouldn't. But I suspect it's one of those situations where you don't know how you'll react until you actually face it." This was a curious response on his part. For over twenty years, he had been studying the martial arts, in which words and actions are supposed to be synonymous, and actions are supposed to be spontaneous rather than a product of analysis. To say that he was unsure was to admit he still didn't know his own nature.

"What situations?" asked Liz as she entered the room. Without waiting for an answer, she came up behind Ed's chair and bent down for an over-the-shoulder kiss. The embrace lasted for several moments.

Karen, who was accustomed to their displays, waited a suitable interval, then said, "God, do you guys ever come up for air?"

Liz broke off, laughing. "Look who's playing Miss Manners!"

"Is that so?" Karen responded in mock outrage. "Well, we were having a serious conversation until you came in!"

Ed nodded in agreement. "She's right, Liz. This time Karen was being serious."

"Oh?" Liz's expression changed immediately. "About what?"

"That boy who was killed," Ed continued. "The hit-and-run case."

"Oh . . ." Liz reflected briefly. "Can you imagine how his parents must feel? Did I hear something about it was a new bike, too?"

"Yeah," Karen interjected. "Talk about a birthday present. If I were them, I'd want to see the driver dead."

"Karen! What a thing to say! Don't you know that—" Liz stopped herself. She and Karen had frequently discussed capital punishment, and each knew how the other felt. "Well, anyway, it's an awful thing." She turned to Ed. "And speaking of which, if we don't get some food soon, I may be ready to kill!"

"Right." Ed took the cue. "We'd better get going. We've got a reservation at Castelli's, and they don't like holding tables." He nodded to Karen. "Have a good evening, Karen!"

"You too!" Karen waved her spoon at them as they headed towards the front door. "And don't eat too much calamari!"

Calamari was unlikely to be on the menu for Mike Langan. He was heading home for supper, and Clare, while a good cook, was a traditional meat-and-potatoes type. In general, that suited him just fine; his ulcers didn't take well to fried foods, anyway. While seldom fancy, the dishes she made were tasty, and there were always homemade desserts to finish the meal. In their twenty years of marriage, Mike had put on about twenty pounds, which he figured was OK—each pound was sort of an anniversary present.

In general, Mike had no complaints about his marriage. He and Clare had met a few years after he joined the force, at an accident scene while he was on traffic duty. She had been a passenger when a girlfriend had had a fender bender, but it was Clare who had captured Mike's attention. Clare had been a redheaded colleen, her fine features a contrast to Mike's brown hair and pug nose. Both Irish, they'd connected quickly, and less than a year later, they'd gotten married.

While the job was usually the biggest hazard in cops' marriages, for Mike and Clare, the real challenge had come with the death of their first son, Mike Jr., from aplastic anemia at age ten. The loss had hit Mike even harder than Clare. Though death was familiar on the job, this pain had blindsided him. It had left a gaping hole that threatened to swallow his entire being. For months, he went through the motions of being alive, while Clare, despite her own grief, kept trying to connect with him. In the end, she'd succeeded by suggesting what Mike had considered unthinkable: that they should have another child. Now, James Matthew Langan was almost four, and the joy of Mike's life.

As he drove, Mike mentally reflected, wondering what had led him to dredge up these memories once again. In the same instant, he knew. It was the phone call he'd gotten just before leaving the department, from Charlie Bickert over in Pawtucket. Almost against his will, the conversation replayed itself.

"Sergeant Langan." Langan rarely wasted words on the telephone—or, for that matter, off it.

"Mike? It's Charlie." The two men, both working homicide for their respective forces, had had many contacts during their investigative careers. Though they rarely met face to face, on the phone, no last names were needed. Many times, if he was in a jocular mood, Bickert would simply ask, "How're they hangin', Mike?", a line that managed to be both a dirty joke and a pun on Langan's name. Today, Langan sensed no such easy humor.

"What's up, Charlie?"

"Just checking in, Mike." His response seemed overly casual, almost evasive. In fact, while Bickert had served in homicide for seven years, and had seen his share of sad deaths, he knew this one would resonate for Langan. "Actually, I just came back from one you'll be hearing about. It's a nine-year-old kid. Hit-and-run."

"Oh . . ." Langan felt the bottom drop out of his stomach. Since Mike Jr., he'd felt an intense mix of pain and empathy whenever a child was the victim. Though they'd never talked about it directly, they'd known each other when Mike Jr. died, and, like the others around Langan, Bickert had seen the pain it caused.

"Yeah." Bickert hesitated, not quite certain how to proceed, wanting to share, but knowing Langan's vulnerability. "Er, look, Mike, maybe I should call you later." It was a question, not a statement.

"No, no, it's OK. What happened?"

Bickert went on to relate the details, covering points quickly. The death itself had been caused by a broken neck, the result of a fluke landing. In Langan's mind, he saw a small body tumbling in slow motion. *Shit.* Probably hundreds of other kids had taken spills from bicycles, even going over the handlebars, and at worst ended up with a broken arm. Joey Gonsalves hadn't been so lucky.

In terms of cause, the evidence was circumstantial. While accidents can happen, the scratches and damage to the rear fender suggested that the bike had been hit from behind by a car. Dark blue paint chips found on the bike's fender seemed to confirm this. No skid marks had been found, suggesting that the driver had been slow to react, or didn't care. Given the car had left the scene, it was too early to speculate on the role of alcohol or state of mind.

"Were there any witnesses?" Langan was asking the obvious, but his mind and stomach were both still churning.

"No, not that we've found. The kid was dead by the time it was phoned in; some woman out with her dog found him. We checked the neighboring houses, but nobody saw it happen." He paused, probably dragging on a cigarette. Bickert was a chain smoker, Langan knew. "We found one old lady who thought she heard a kid cry out and looked out her window. She says she saw a blue car going by, but since she didn't see the kid and bike, we can't assume it was the right car." Another pause. "Besides, we showed her pictures to try to ID the car, and she said it was either a Ford Tempo or a Toyota Tercel." He let that sit with Langan.

"But hell, those cars don't look alike!" Langan's brain was beginning to function.

"Right. In other words, the old broad's almost as blind as a bat. We don't even know for sure if she was wearing her glasses when she saw the car. That's why only the color seems to jibe."

"But the forensics boys should be able to identify the make from the paint samples," Mike noted. Every manufacturer had different paint formulations, even for seemingly similar colors, and the chemical composition could be used to trace any manufacturer's color and most after-market paints.

"True. But let's say the old lady is half right, and it's a dark blue Tempo . . ."

Langan could anticipate Bickert's direction. "Shit, those are pretty common. There's probably two or three hundred of them in the state, and of those, a lot could have some fender scratches." Based on the nature of the accident, looking for blood stains or other evidence on the car would be pretty useless.

"Yep. And we don't even know that it was a local car."

"Yeah, I see," said Langan, considering the case from various angles. "You've got your work cut out on this one."

"Tell me about it. And the heat's building real fast." There was that pause again, another drag on the cigarette. "Apparently the mayor and the chief have already been talking to the press, telling 'em about 'all available resources' and all that crap." Another drag. "I've already been in touch with the Troopers, and the chief is talking to the feds. Might as well share the heat."

"I know what you mean." Langan was sympathetic. The worst nightmare for a homicide detective was a case that became political. Not that any homicide was ever low-profile, but some became full-blown media spectacles, hindering the real work involved.

Langan could still remember a case in Pawtucket some years before, where three women disappeared over several months. The press was low-key until the killer turned himself in, then they had a field day. He was your typical all-American boy—a straight-A high school student, captain of the football team—except he was also insane. “Psychopathic,” the doctors called him; the cops who had to deal with the bodies, including one that had been shoved through a hole in the ice of a reservoir, had other names for that type of killer. In that investigation, the media had not been involved till after the case broke, which made life easier. Today, of course, at the first scent of anything, they’d be jabbering about a “serial killer” on the loose, getting people panicked and screwing things up for the authorities—that is, for guys like Langan and Bickert. Langan turned his attention back to the phone. “So,” he continued, “what can I do?”

“Not much, old buddy, unless you got a crystal ball. Just thought I’d touch base with you on this one.” Again, the pause. “But if you do get anything, like maybe somebody stops a blue Tempo for speeding, you lemme know, OK?”

“Sure thing.” Langan knew as well as Bickert that there was little to do in that regard. Listings of stolen cars, for example, were regularly updated, and any suspect vehicle could be checked through the police dispatch system. Mostly, it was acknowledging the common bond of their work. “I’ll put the word out.”

“By the way, how you doin’ with that guy who got mugged?” Langan knew he was referring to the Sanelli case.

“Nothing yet. Lab reports don’t have much. And there are a few witnesses to still check out. You know how it is. . . .”

“Right. I sure do.” Another break as Bickert took another puff. “Well, you keep in touch, Mike.”

"Sure thing." Langan groped for something more to say, as the thought of the dead boy hit him once again. "Oh, and Charlie . . ."

"Yeah, Mike?"

"Someday you ought to quit smoking."

There was a sound somewhere between a snort and a laugh. "Yeah, right, Mike. You take care too." The line went dead, and Langan hung up the phone.

Now, as Mike Langan approached his neighbourhood in Cumberland, it hit him once more. *A nine-year-old boy. Fuck* . . . He saw a colorful blur out of the corner of his eye, as the Graham boy, himself only ten, dashed down the sidewalk. He pictured Mike Jr. and a wave of sadness flooded over him. He pulled into the driveway and parked. As he walked to the front door, his large frame felt too heavy to carry.

"Hi, Daddy!" At the sound of the car pulling in, Jamie Langan had stopped his playing to greet his father.

"Hi, big guy!" Mike swooped him up into his arms, hugging him close. Momentarily, the dark thoughts he'd been carrying were washed away by his son's enthusiasm and affection. It often seemed to Mike that the years between two and five were the best years from the point of view of a parent: There was a degree of interaction that babies could not offer, and more than that, there were the outbursts of love expressed freely, before the inhibiting effects of school intruded. Together, he and Jamie went to the kitchen to find Clare, with the boy rattling on about his day's adventures.

Later that night, as Mike and Clare were going to bed, she turned to him.

"What is it, Mike?" After twenty years and the trials they'd been through, Clare Langan knew her husband's moods.

"Oh, you know." He shrugged, his dark eyes seeming even darker as he felt the too-familiar heaviness return.

"Oh, darling, why? What happened today?" She moved closer to him, massaging his shoulders. Although he hadn't said it directly, she knew from long experience that these dark moods almost always had something to do with the death of Mike Jr.

"I got a call from Charlie Bickert today." The words came slowly, tinged with a deep sadness. "He's working on a hit-and-run case. That kid who got killed today."

"Oh!" Clare let out a startled cry. *Of course!* she thought. She'd heard it on the radio, but hadn't made the connection. For her, Mike Jr.'s death had been a tragedy, but early on, she had resolved to go forward with her life. She still had difficulty understanding the terrible hold it had on Mike, periodically propelling him into a black mood because of some chance event. And she still remembered how it had nearly wrecked their marriage. Mike would withdraw into stony silence, to hide the emotions from himself as much as Clare. Other "fixes"—infidelity, therapy—were not options open to a working class Irishman like Mike, and he'd seen too much devastation from alcohol to consider booze an answer. For reasons she herself didn't fully understand, Clare had stayed rather than bail.

Now, here they were, middle-aged, having started over with the business of family when most people were looking forward to getting the kids out for good. It certainly wasn't what either of them had imagined when they'd met, but then, very little was. Love meant something very different now than it had twenty years ago. Oh, true enough, the new version wasn't always thrilling. It required compromise and forbearance, and it never seemed to reach a final state. It certainly wasn't rapture, but it also wasn't despair. For Mike, his love for Clare was based on what they shared—from making love to planting the garden, the dozens of minor intimacies of being together. In some ways, it was like police work, where the risks of the job made your ties to others that much closer. In both cases, there was the connection to another person, another life. In a world filled with anonymous others and unforeseeable tragedies, such contact was a saving grace.

Lead stories always attracted attention. Some people liked the feeling of knowing what was happening in the world, while some just had a momentary curiosity.

For one listener, the evening news that day was personal. As he watched the story about Joey Gonsalves, he was reminded that even careful plans do not always turn out exactly as intended. Oh, he'd worked it right in terms of avoiding witnesses and not leaving hard evidence, but his intent had been to find a pedestrian target and execute a hit-and-run. The fact that it had ended up being a kid on a bike, and hence was generating lots of publicity, was just an unexpected bonus.

FOUR

Monday, April 27, 1987

HENRY COHEN LOOKED down once again at the paper on his desk. It had arrived in a large envelope, addressed to him personally, but mailed to the company's offices. In some ways, it was a duplicate of the note he'd received earlier, which still lay in his bottom drawer. Both had arrived in manila envelopes with a childish printing. Both were cut-and-paste jobs: newsprint letters arranged on newspaper. But the other note had come about a week ago, and this one had arrived today. Cohen read it again.

You'd better start counting; the time is near.

What did it mean? He thought of the earlier note, with its equally cryptic message: "Just you watch. The time for payback is coming." While he had been uncertain before, Cohen was convinced now that the earlier note was not just a joke. Whatever else it was, it wasn't funny.

Comparing the notes, he tried to decipher their meaning. The references to "payback" and "counting" made it likely that this was a blackmail scheme. But if so, blackmail for what? Was it directed at the company, or at him personally? He looked up at Ned Barton's portrait. *Well, Ned, this is one time I wish you were here!*

Since Barton Jewelry was a privately held company, it made sense that corporate blackmail would be aimed at the company owner. But why? It wasn't like they made some high-risk or illicit product; what was there to blackmail in a jewelry company? In Cohen's experience, protection rackets by gangsters were no threat to his business. Neither was it likely that someone was fingering an internal scandal: Cohen tried to keep a close watch on company operations, and ran the company honestly. He was equally sure that old Ned had been as square as his Protestant background.

On the other hand, if it was a personal threat, it still made sense that it would be sent to the company address. After all, to send it to his home might risk it being revealed to his family, when presumably the blackmailer thought that Cohen would pay to ensure his family did not find out. The only problem was, find out what?

Cohen thought about his life and realized that, mostly, it was distressingly ordinary. His only sexual indiscretion had been almost five years ago—a secretary at his lawyer's office with whom he'd had a brief affair. Surely she was not the source of blackmail? He thought further, seeking other moral lapses, but was almost disappointed to recall none.

The more he thought about it, the more perplexed and concerned Cohen became. After all, there was a third possibility: this wasn't a rational attempt at blackmail, but rather the crazed act of a madman. And that possibility scared Henry Cohen most of all. He seriously considered calling the police at once, but decided to first seek a second opinion. He picked up the phone to his secretary. "Joan, would you get me Ed Underwood, please?"

Ed Underwood was in his office, reviewing the latest quarterly report from the company's benefits officer, Sharon Falco. It was not what he considered stimulating reading, and he welcomed the interruption when the phone rang and he was summoned to Cohen's office.

The administrative offices for Barton Jewelry were spread over the top floor of a thirty-year-old building, one of three in the Providence area. (The company also had production facilities in Georgia, Hong Kong, and, more recently, the Mexican maquiladora zone.) The building was functional but hardly ostentatious, reflecting the preferences of Ned Barton. Whatever else he was, Barton hadn't been a man who favored a flashy image—which was ironic, given that the jewelry business is all about image.

As he approached the president's office, Underwood paused to take a deep breath, his diaphragm dropping in a type of controlled breathing called *sanchin*. Long years of training had made the practice almost second nature to him, and it had practical benefits, in terms of both relaxing the body and clearing the mind. Still, he often reflected that if his mind didn't try to race ahead so often, he wouldn't need to control it. And that was something his years of training had not succeeded in changing. Sighing at his shortcomings, he opened the door to Cohen's office.

In the outer reception area, Underwood was greeted by Joan Davis, Cohen's secretary. She had been a fixture in the company even before he'd joined eight years ago. Word was she had started at the bottom as a clerk, had eventually become secretary to Cohen when he was still second to Barton, and had moved up the ladder with her boss. At this point, it was said she knew nearly everything that happened in the company. She certainly knew most of the administrative staff, from clerks to controller, and all the senior production staff. When he'd started as personnel manager, Ed had found her an invaluable resource in learning about the company's staff.

"Hello, Ed! I haven't seen much of you lately! How are you?" Joan, just shy of fifty, was as full of enthusiasm as most twenty-year-olds.

"I'm fine, Joan. How about you?"

"Oh, I'm doing well, thanks." She fixed him with a mock-serious look. "And how's your art teacher friend? Do you two have any plans yet?"

"Er, she's fine too." Ed was occasionally startled by how much Joan knew about people. "And no, we have no immediate plans, if you're talking about marriage." He smiled. "But you never know . . ."

Joan smiled in return. "Oh, yes, I do. You just grab her before she gets away, Ed!" As she spoke, she punched the intercom to the inner office. "Ed Underwood is here, Mr. Cohen."

"Thanks, Joan. Send him in."

Cohen rose to greet Underwood. "Joan still after you to settle down?" he asked, shaking hands. His handshake was firm and his gaze direct—just like his character

"Oh, you know how it is. Bachelors make good targets." He was smiling, even as he shook his head resignedly.

"Yes." Cohen nodded in agreement. "But she's a gem. I don't think I could function without her!" He sat down again and gestured to a seat across from him.

Cohen shuffled some papers that were sitting in front of him, and then folded his hands over them. Underwood watched in silence, letting him take the lead.

"As I recall, you majored in psychology in college, didn't you, Ed?"

"Uh, yes. At Wesleyan." As he answered, Underwood was thinking, *Does he remember that from the interview when he hired me? That was years ago! Or has he been reviewing my personnel file? And if so, why?*

"What made you pick psychology? Did you want to become a clinician before you decided on personnel work?"

"Something like that. I was curious about people, why they acted as they did—sometimes, wanting to understand my own actions." Underwood's dark eyes looked away, following a private line of thought, then reverted to meeting Cohen's gaze. "But by the time I graduated, I knew I'd never be a therapist. So, the shift to business in grad school was pretty natural. I prefer the real world to the ivory tower."

"Well, even so, I guess you've retained an interest in human behavior?" It was as much a statement as a question.

"Sure. After all, a large part of my job could be considered applied psychology-interviewing, personnel relations, all of the people-oriented aspects."

"Good. Then maybe you can tell me what to make of these." Cohen's tone altered, becoming crisp and slightly hard. He handed over the two notes.

Underwood's eyes widened as he saw them. Before even reading, it was obvious this was not routine correspondence. He read the two messages, then examined the paper they were pasted on. From what he could see of the ads and story contents, they were from local newspapers, though no title was visible. He turned them over, then back again to reread the messages. Finally, he looked up at Cohen.

"What are these, Henry? Blackmail notes?" Ed felt concerned, and his face showed it.

"I was hoping you could tell me, Ed. I received one about a week ago and the other today. I can't make any sense out of them. I was thinking you could interpret them."

"Well, I'm no clinician . . ." Ed paused, thinking. To buy time as he reflected, he asked, "Did you keep the envelopes they came in, by any chance?"

"I did." Cohen passed them across the desk.

Underwood examined the crudely stenciled lettering and the common manila envelopes. Still thinking about their contents, he noted the postmarks.

"That's interesting."

"What?"

"They were mailed from different places. See, this one was sent from here in Providence, but the other one is from North Providence." He handed them back to Cohen.

"Hmm. You're right. I hadn't noticed that." Cohen looked at Underwood, thinking he'd been right to seek his opinion. "What do you make of that?"

"I'm not sure. It seems likely it's not just a bad joke, though. Somebody went to a lot of effort to send these."

"Do you think I should call the police?"

Underwood thought for a long moment before answering. "I'm not sure . . ." He looked again at the two sheets, reading the words aloud. "'You'd better start counting; the time is near.'" Then the second, "'Just you watch. The time for payback is coming.'" He looked across the desk. "Which one came first, Henry?"

"The one about payback . . ." It hadn't occurred to him that the order might not be obvious from the contents. But on reflection, he realized Underwood was right—the order did seem ambiguous. "You're right, Ed, they could be read in reverse. So what does that mean?"

"It's hard to say, precisely, but maybe the sender isn't really sure what they want. The fact that each note is vague, and that there is no clear sequence, suggests the writer doesn't have a clear focus."

"Does that mean it's just a prank of some kind?"

"Possibly. Or that the person is frustrated at something and doesn't really know how to deal with their frustration." He paused, wishing to be tactful in his next remark. "I assume you've considered blackmail and decided there are no grounds?" Cohen had avoided a direct answer when he'd asked the question earlier, but Underwood wanted to eliminate blackmail as a possible motive.

"No, there's nothing like that." Cohen grabbed the papers impatiently. "If I thought I was vulnerable, do you think I'd be talking to you about it?" He stared at Underwood, his eyes intense.

"No, I realize that, Henry. I just wanted to be clear that we're both thinking in the same terms." *Does he protest too much?* Shakespeare, Underwood had often reflected, was no slouch as a psychologist.

"So, where does that leave us? Should I call the police?" Cohen's brief moment of anger had passed.

"Well, it's up to you, of course, but I don't think so, based on just these notes. I mean, has there been anything else? Serious vandalism at a plant, or phone calls in the night? No strangers bothering your family?"

"No, not that I'm aware of," Cohen replied. "I mean, the second note just came today, so I haven't been thinking in those terms. And I haven't spoken to Emily—I don't think I will, either. Unless it looks like there's some danger to her or the kids. What do you think? Is that a risk?"

"I can't say for sure, Henry, but given there are no specific threats in the notes, it seems unlikely. The real psychos aren't usually reluctant to state their intentions." Underwood paused, thinking back to his limited training in psychopathology. "And what can you do right now, anyway? Even if you call the police, they'll probably just open a file, or at best send the notes to the crime lab. And who knows? If it's actually a prank, this may be the end of it."

Cohen sat in silence, thinking things through. Finally he rose. "Yes, you're probably right. It's been a disturbing experience, but it's likely harmless." They shook hands. "Thanks for your advice, Ed."

"Anytime, Henry. Glad to help." As he left, Underwood found himself thinking about the comments he'd made, and his conclusion. An old cliché came back to him: *Famous last words.*

That night, Ed and Liz were scheduled to go to a play at Trinity Square Playhouse. The eight-fifteen curtain meant he had just enough time for a session at the *dojo* beforehand, and he headed there right after work.

As he bowed at the door of the *dojo*, Ed was reminded how this ritual gesture was also a cue to clear his mind—what psychologists call a conditioned response. Still, on some occasions, his mind was preoccupied by other issues. Tonight was one such case. *What about those notes Henry showed me? What do they mean? And did I give the right advice?*

He consciously pushed the questions aside and headed for the dressing room, pausing en route to bow once again to Yoshikawa-*sensei*, who was in the midst of teaching a class.

As he changed into his *gi*, Ed found his breathing settling into a slow, steady rhythm, but his mind was still racing. Dismayed, he took several more deep breaths, determined to put the notes out of his thoughts. The breathing helped, and he headed into the training area.

The next hour went quickly. After the formal class was over, Ed continued to train, doing some sparring with Jim Pulaski, a brown belt. His intention had been to help Pulaski with the finer points of timing; instead, Ed found his own timing was off. They clashed repeatedly in a series of abrupt, graceless attacks. It was martial, but it wasn't art. Frustrated, Ed began to rely on speed, not finesse, to score on the brown belt. After about ten minutes, Yoshikawa interrupted them, calling him aside.

"You are acting like stone, not water, Underwood-*san*. What is wrong?" Like much of the language of Zen, the comment was expressed as a metaphor. In this case, it referred to a classic Zen observation that stone is strong, but flowing water is stronger, for it can wear stone away.

"Yes, *sensei*." Ed bowed, hoping his face did not reveal his own inner frustration. "Someone at work had a problem and I guess I'm still carrying it with me." There was no point in apologizing. "Sorry" had no value in the martial arts, since most accidents were human error, and saying sorry could not undo damage once done.

"I see. . . ." Yoshikawa looked at Ed for a long moment, feeling as much as seeing the other's turmoil. "You seem to be carrying many problems lately. Maybe if you go now, your problems will not be with you next time." However mild the words, the rebuke was harsh. Unspoken was the message: *Get control before someone is hurt.*

Ed bowed and went off to tell Pulaski it was time to finish. They bowed to each other, and then the brown belt grinned, clapping Ed on the back. "Rats! Just when I get the jump on you, you quit!" Ed laughed along with him, though the words stung.

"Well, don't get too cocky, my friend. Next time I won't be so easygoing!" It was a fairly lame comeback, but the best Ed could manage. Glancing at the clock, and suddenly thankful for his date with Liz, he headed for the locker room.

As he exited the building, it was approaching sunset. Still sweating slightly, Ed glanced at his watch again; it was just after seven o'clock—too late to head home to change. *Oh, well. It won't be the first time I've had to take my shower at Liz's!*

Ed made it across town to Liz's house in ten minutes, showered, and grabbed a bit of cheese from her refrigerator. This sequence was not new to Liz, and she let him proceed without feeling a need to comment. They were downtown at Trinity Square just after eight, making the curtain without difficulty.

The play was an adaptation of Chekhov's *Uncle Vanya*, based on a new translation. Chekhov was one of those rare playwrights who seemed to tap into the basic wellspring of the human condition—like Shakespeare or Sophocles. While no serious English writer would tamper with Shakespeare, the notion of revising a foreign author, in the guise of translation, sometimes posed an irresistible temptation. Yeats, for example, had done a version of *Oedipus Rex*.

In this production, Chekhov's storyline was undamaged, but the context had been shifted into a modern setting, with matching colloquial language. Ed found the result less than convincing, despite sincere efforts by the cast. His disappointment was visible to Liz, who queried him as they exited.

"You seemed a bit absent tonight, Ed. Didn't you like it?"

"It just seemed a bit artificial, changing the time period to a contemporary setting and using modern slang. I can't imagine what Chekhov would make of it . . ."

"Oh, come on! It wasn't that bizarre!" Liz scoffed. "Besides, Chekhov used the slang of his own period—what's the difference?"

Ed started to make an analogy to the King James Bible, but Liz interrupted. "Come on, I think you're rationalizing. It was an interesting production, and the acting was good. I think you just weren't paying attention. Why not?"

"Hey, I thought I was supposed to be the psychologist!" he protested, but then stopped. *I should know by now. Liz always reads me.* "Well, you may be right," he conceded. "Why don't we talk about it over some food?"

"Sounds good. How about that Thai place on Thayer Street?"

Shortly after, they were seated at a table in a small room, its colorful tablecloths and Thai artwork making it seem cosy rather than cramped. Even better, the air was filled with tantalizing aromas. Although it was almost eleven p.m., the restaurant was still nearly half full. In part, this reflected its proximity to Brown University and RISD, and in part, that the place was simply very small.

After they ordered—*tom yum* soup with shrimp, *pad thai* noodles, and a coconut curry chicken dish—Liz continued their interrupted conversation.

"So what is it, Ed? It's not like you to be so distracted."

"I know, Liz. I'm sorry. I hope it didn't spoil the play for you."

"Don't be silly." She smiled and reached across the table for his hand. "But I know you well enough to know that it must be something important. You don't usually let little things bother you. It's one reason you're usually good company!" She smiled again. "So, tell me—what's going on?"

"That's the funny thing, it's not that big a deal," Ed replied, frowning. "In fact, it's not even my problem!" He went on to relate the conversation he'd had with Henry Cohen, concluding with his advice to do nothing.

Liz listened without interrupting, and when he finished, she took several moments to reply. She had only met Cohen once, at a company party, so most of her knowledge of the man came from Ed.

"Well," she began, "it certainly is bizarre. I mean, you hear about crank letters to movie stars and things like that, but is Cohen really a public figure? The kind to attract the kooks?"

"No, I wouldn't say so. Sure, he does charity work, but that's hardly front-page material."

"Do you think he could be lying about the possibility of blackmail?"

Ed shook his head. "No. . . . If he really thought it was that, why—" His words were interrupted by the arrival of the soup, a large steaming tureen containing a clear broth with shrimp and various other tidbits in it. He waited while the waitress ladled portions into individual bowls for each of them. When she departed, they both sampled the soup, their conversation momentarily forgotten.

"Mmm . . . That's good!" Ginger, lemongrass, chili peppers, and other flavors created a dance on his tongue. Ed proceeded to wolf down his bowl, and then refilled it from the still half-full tureen. Only after making a start on the second serving did he continue. "Anyway, I've thought of that—that Henry might be hiding something—but it doesn't make sense. After all, if there's something embarrassing, why would he consult me in the first place?" He sipped his soup and shook his head once more. "No, it must be something else, but I'm not sure what."

Liz had finished her bowl while he was talking but made no motion to refill it.

"Could it be some crazy person?" She shuddered. "Even the idea of it is pretty creepy."

"It's hard to say. I mean, the letters really don't give much away. Other than the fact that somebody spent considerable effort to prepare them, there's nothing to support the idea that it's more than a prank."

"Well, then, why are you so absorbed by it? I mean, even if it is more than a prank, Henry received them, not you. It's really his problem to deal with."

"I know that." Ed paused, reflecting on his own response. "I guess the difficulty is, it sounds like a prank, and that's what I advised Henry . . . but something in the back of my mind keeps saying it's for real."

"What do you mean?"

"I can't explain it." He hesitated, searching for words. "It's kind of like haragei in *karate*: You sense an attacker you can't see or hear, like someone behind you. You can't explain how—you just know they're there."

Liz nodded. "I've heard you talk about that before, but honestly, I don't know what to make of it." She absently twirled her soup spoon. "So you think the letters represent a real threat?"

"Yes, the more I think about it, the more sure I am. But I told Henry the opposite—in part, because I wasn't focusing on what my instincts said." He shook his head. "That's what intellect does to you."

"You know, Ed, for a hard-nosed psychologist, you don't sound like one!" She laughed lightly. "I mean, I'm supposed to be the airy-fairy, artsy one!" They both started laughing, and almost on cue, the main courses arrived.

For the present, the mystery of the anonymous notes was put aside.

That morning, a small parcel arrived at a mail-drop service. Addressed to an "Arnold Benedict, Box 38," it was picked up in the early afternoon by the box holder. He'd rented the box a few weeks earlier, but the parcel was the first mail he'd received. The rather bored clerk who handed him the package mentioned that box rents were due in a few days. The box holder gave a noncommittal nod, knowing he would not be renewing. The clerk, having been through such situations many times, did not push the point. The mail-drop company had many similar customers over the course of a year and, given the large profit in its operation, was not inclined to ask too many questions of those who rented and paid cash.

Like other customers, "Mr. Benedict" had not been required to produce an ID at the time of rental. He remembered the scene—filling out the form before the same dull clerk. When he'd handed it over, the clerk had read "Benedict, Arnold" without any hint of humor or irony. The renter had smiled at the clerk as he handed him the money for the box rent. *Idiot*, he'd thought, smug in his superiority.

The package, when he opened it, was just what he'd ordered: a Ruger .22 caliber pistol. It was a fairly cheap, American-made model, but it would be more than sufficient for his needs. As expected, the mail-order company had asked no questions, nor had the bank where he'd gotten the money order. For someone as smart as him, it was easy to get a gun without anyone knowing who you were.

After ordering the pistol, he'd checked some barrel measurements, then gone to a small machine shop in Cranston. Like the mail-order company and the bank, he'd known they wouldn't ask questions about why he wanted something. They'd done the threads and holes on a piece of steel tubing to his specifications, and he'd done some of the other work on his own, using hand tools. By the time the pistol arrived in the mail, he'd finished making a silencer using the plans from the *Soldier of Fortune* magazine.

Once he'd picked up the parcel, he went into a discount store in Cumberland and bought a package of .22 caliber longs. The store was not far from an abandoned quarry, and as he headed there, it was already late in the afternoon. There was no one around, but he parked down the road from the actual quarry anyway, just to be safe. He took out a paper bag containing some empty beer cans, as well as his recent acquisitions.

At the quarry, he set up the cans on a stump and walked back about twenty feet. Glancing around once more, he took the pistol and silencer from the paper bag. The homemade device fit neatly on the barrel. He loaded the ten-bullet clip and aimed, arm outstretched, squinting as he sighted down the short barrel. He only hit four of the cans on his ten shots, and the clatter of the flying cans made a few birds take wing. Rather than being displeased, he grinned broadly. After all, he didn't intend to use it from twenty feet away. And he was pleased to know that when he did use it, the gun would make almost no noise at all.

FIVE

Wednesday, April 29, 1987

DANNY L'HEUREUX GLANCED at his watch yet again: ten past two. He sighed and threw the cloth he'd been using to clean the counter into the sink. Two a.m. was always the slow time—the bars had already closed and there were several hours to go before shift change. The only ones out now were either cabbies or those up to no good. In this business, he saw plenty of both.

Good Time Donuts was the only all-night food place in the area. Located on Branch Avenue, right near the ramps for Routes 146 and 95, it was a brightly lit beacon on a darkened street of strip malls, mill buildings, and tenements. Business was usually pretty good till about one-thirty, but staying open all night was driven by practicality, not demand: in order to have fresh donuts for the morning crowd, they had to start preparations at about four-thirty. Since Danny doubled as the night baker, it was just as easy to stay open and pick up the odd bit of business. If nothing else, the cops liked coming by for a coffee—the owner, Frank Palucci, always made it on the house for the boys in blue.

Generally, Danny recognized the late people who came in. Some he was happy to see, like Eddy Sanchez, a cabbie who, like Danny, preferred working nights. Others, like "Deuce," a pimp and small-time pusher, he could do without. Everybody—Danny, Frank, even the cops—knew that dealers like Deuce sometimes did their transactions in the parking lot. As long as it didn't get out of hand, no one was going to do much about it. Besides, Danny suspected that Frank was running a sideline in the numbers racket and wasn't eager for the police to pay too much attention to activity around the donut shop.

Now, as he sat behind the counter, a man cut across the parking lot, heading towards the entrance on foot. Pedestrians were rare in this neighbourhood, especially at this time of night. The man, wearing a worn blue wind-breaker, leather gloves, and chino trousers, strode in.

"Say, you got a phone?" he asked.

"Uh, yeah. Over by the washrooms." Danny gestured to the far corner. He watched the man search through the yellow pages and then make a brief call, still wearing his gloves. Danny wished the radio playing out back weren't so loud, so he could hear better; instead, he just moved along the counter, pretending to wipe as he went. From what he could tell, the guy had phoned for car service. Danny felt the butterflies in his stomach settle down. The man came and sat at the counter.

"Car trouble?"

He nodded. “Tire.”

“Can I get you something?”

“Is the coffee fresh?”

Danny glanced at his watch. “About twenty minutes ago.”

“OK. Give me a cup with double cream, and a honey donut.”

Danny brought the order. The coffee, as always, was in a real cup, with a saucer; the donut, though, was on waxed paper. The man reached for the sugar dispenser on the counter, still wearing his gloves, while Danny retreated to the register at the end of the counter, by the kitchen door. He pretended to listen to the radio, but continued to examine the man as he drank his coffee in silence. A few minutes went by, and then the radio played “Light My Fire” by the Doors. Danny loved the Doors, even though Jim Morrison had died before Danny was out of diapers. As he began humming with the music, he noticed the customer head toward the washroom.

“Light My Fire”—the seven-minute, extended version—was still playing when the man returned. He finished his coffee, leaving the donut untouched, and moved toward the register. Danny, singing along with the Doors, only half noticed as he approached, reaching into his jacket. Just as he came up to Danny, the song finished, and Danny turned. With a chill, he saw the pistol. In what seemed like slow motion, he watched it rise until it was pointed at his head. Even worse, he recognized the ugly extension of the barrel as a silencer.

“H-h-hey, it’s OK, man. Take the money. No sweat!” Danny jerkily opened the drawer of the register.

“Into the back room,” the man ordered, gesturing with the barrel of the gun.

“Wh-what for? We don’t have a safe, if that’s what you’re after. It’s all in the register. Take it. I don’t care!” Danny felt suddenly cold and had a terrible urge to piss.

“Just move. Now.” The man stared at Danny, his eyes narrow slits. The hardness in his expression spoke more than his words.

Without further protest, Danny shuffled into the back, where the radio still blared.The gunman glanced around and motioned Danny to the far corner, near the dough mixer and sacks of flour. The only windows in this part of the building were up near the ceiling, for ventilation more than lighting.

Now completely terrified, Danny couldn’t bring himself to look at the man. “Jesus, please don’t kill me, mister. Please don’t kill me. I don’t know you. I don’t know nothing. Please don’t—”

“Turn around,” the stranger said.

“Sure, anything, just don’t hurt me, please!”

Ignoring the pleas, the stranger brought the gun to Danny’s head, right at the base of his skull, and fired. There was a muffled sound, more like a thud than a sharp report, and Danny slumped. As he fell, his arm tipped the empty metal bucket of the dough mixer, which tumbled off its pedestal with a loud clang. The stranger took a quick glance toward the doorway to the front, but then, hearing nothing, relaxed. He looked down at Danny, who was likely already dead. Danny’s watch, like the clock on the wall, said two thirty. The man smiled, slipped the gun back into his coat, and exited by the back door of the kitchen.

Some time later, Deuce came in, having done a deal nearby. *Shit*, he thought, *sometimes this business is a real pain—assholes calling any old time 'cause they're hurtin'. Shee-it.* He was still cursing to himself as he entered the donut shop. It took him a moment to realize nobody was behind the counter, but he heard the radio playing, so he figured Danny must be out back. While they weren't exactly friends, Deuce had no grudge against him, either. Danny was OK.

"Yo, Danny!" He paused. Not getting a reply, he moved towards the doorway to the back. As he got to the corner of the counter, he saw the open register. He stopped and reached for the 9 mm pistol he carried in the back of his belt. Then, moving slowly, he went through the doorway.

Danny's body had fallen facedown against the sacks of flour. At first glance, seeing the overturned mixing bowl, Deuce thought maybe he'd passed out. But then he saw the small dark stain at the base of the skull, and the dribble of red on the bag beneath Danny's head, and knew.

"Shee-it!" Deuce looked around in a half panic. It wasn't that the sight of blood bothered him—he'd seen his share—but getting nailed for somebody else's shit was a whole other thing. He considered grabbing the cash he'd seen in the register, but thought better of it. Instead, he looked around, spotted the back door, and—like the killer had—pushed the release bar to make a quick exit. Still rattled, he gunned his Corvette, squealing out of the lot onto Branch Avenue, without turning on his headlights till he got to the Route 146 ramp, heading south towards Route 95.

It was after four a.m. when Mike Langan got the call. After years on homicide, he was no longer surprised when the phone rang in the middle of the night, though waking up never got any easier. Clare stirred, turning to him with half-closed eyes as he answered the phone, but he patted her forehead, urging her back to sleep. By the time he was dressed and bent to kiss her, she had already returned to a deep slumber.

The streets were quiet as he drove from his home in Cumberland to the scene. Taking Route 295 to 146, he exited at Branch Avenue, not far from Good Time Donuts. In the mid-distance, the illuminated dome of the state house gleamed on its hilltop. Langan recalled a geography teacher who had once compared Providence to ancient Rome—both were built on seven hills, with a river flowing through. Even the city's name had a classical ring to it, with echoes of divine intervention. At four thirty in the morning, Langan found nothing classical or divine about the purpose of his trip.

As he pulled into the parking lot at Good Time Donuts, he saw a patrol car, an ambulance, and an older sedan that he recognized as belonging to Joe Goodering from the medical examiner's office. Not surprisingly, given the time and location, there was no crowd of rubberneckers, though as he got out of his car, a car with a "Press" sign jammed in the visor pulled up. He ignored it and stepped over the yellow tape that cordoned off the building.

The patrolman by the entrance was a young guy—they always pulled the late shifts. Langan pulled out his badge and asked his name.

"Tom Petrusic, Sergeant."

"What've we got here, Tom?"

"A male. Shot in the head."

"Any idea who it is?"

"Yeah—yes, sir. His name's Danny L'Heureux. He did the night shift here."

"Oh. Any witnesses?"

"No witnesses that we know of."

"Who called it in?"

"Er, me and my partner. We—we were stopping for coffee—you know, we usually—"

"It's OK, kid, I know. Look, I'll talk to you more after I look around. Meanwhile, keep the press out, OK?"

"Sure—I mean, yes, sir, Sergeant."

Wearily, Langan nodded and headed inside. The ambulance driver and attendant were standing by the front counter. One was eating a donut. *Ambulance drivers and cops*, he thought, *nothing puts them off donuts*. He nodded to them and went into the back room. The other patrolman was there, standing just inside the door, while the assistant medical examiner, Joe Goodering, was kneeling near the body. Goodering looked up at the sound of footsteps on the tile floor.

"Hi, Mike. Take a look."

Langan had already been scanning the room, noting the pool of blood on the flour sack, but no obvious blood spots on the wall. Now he knelt down beside Goodering, who gestured with a rubber-gloved hand.

"See? One shot, just at the base of the skull. Small caliber—my guess would be .22. There's no exit hole. The bullet would go in and just bounce around, shredding the brain. And close range—see the powder burns?" Goodering paused, letting it register for Langan.

"What a minute, Joe—are you saying he was whacked?" Langan asked. It made no sense that this kid would be the target of a contract killing.

"You tell me," Goodering replied. "My job is telling cause of death; yours is figuring out who and why." He turned to look directly at Langan. "But if you're asking me if it looks like a pro job, I think maybe yes."

"Christ, he's a kid in a donut shop. Why would anybody want him hit?" Goodering gave no response, just shrugged and shook his head. "Well," Langan said finally, "get what you can, Joe. We'll have the lab boys do a full work-up in the morning." He stood up again and went over to the patrolman by the kitchen door, who was looking very edgy.

"Jesus, Sergeant, what's going on? Are you saying somebody was deliberately out to kill Danny? That makes no sense!"

"It never does, kid. What's your name?"

"Jim Makowski, Sarge."

"Well, Jim, tell me what you know." Langan took out his notebook and jotted down what little information Makowski could tell him—like his partner, he'd only been on the force two years, and homicides weren't a regular occurrence for patrolmen. They'd come in at about three, saw no one at the counter, then found Danny's body. Looking around from the doorway to the back room, Langan noted two things: the cash register was open and the back door of the building stood ajar.

"Did you or your partner touch anything?"

"No! I mean, no, sir—we know enough not to—"

"Uh-huh," Langan cut him off, nodding. "So, the register was open when you came in?"

"The register?" Makowski turned. Even from where they stood, it was clear there was cash in the open drawer. "Oh! I didn't see—"

"Right," Langan interrupted. "Were there any cars when you pulled in? Could you and your partner have surprised somebody, who maybe beat it out the back?"

"Cars?" He pondered a moment. "No, I didn't see any cars . . ."

"Did you hear anything? Could a car have been out back?"

Makowski shook his head, looking more and more crestfallen. "No, I don't think so—I mean, I didn't notice anything. I'm sure we would've . . ." He dropped his head, then looked directly at Langan. "Danny was an OK guy. Who'd wanna do this, Sarge?"

"I don't know, Makowski. But I hope we'll find out." Langan made a note in his book to make sure the back door was dusted for prints. He went to the front to talk to Petrusic again.

Like Makowski, Petrusic had little to offer, though, unlike his partner, he said he'd noted the register. He also insisted it was unlikely a car had slipped away as they arrived. A faster thinker than his partner, Petrusic said to Langan, "But if we didn't scare them off, then robbery probably wasn't the motive—which means it was a hit? But why? Why Danny?"

Stan Osiewicz, the reporter from the *Journal*, was standing just outside the yellow tape, about five feet away. At the word "hit," his ears perked up. "Hit? This was a hit? Who's the victim?"

Langan inwardly groaned. He didn't know Osiewicz very well, but in his view, journalists were ranked with politicians, about three steps from the bottom of the social scale. (Wise guys and other scum were at the very bottom, with lawyers just above.) Now he had to deal with this guy, if only to try to reduce the sensationalizing in tomorrow's paper.

"Take it easy, pal. Nobody's saying it was a hit. All we got right now is a dead guy."

In exchange for giving him the bare details—name of the victim, approximate time of death, etc.—Langan got Osiewicz to agree to keep a lid on it until they'd finished processing the crime scene and had the basic paperwork. In reality, the detective knew that if they had nothing different to say after the guys from the crime lab checked the place over, it would appear in the evening paper as a hit, citing "sources in the police department." And then this case could quickly become a hot potato.

Rather than deal with more questions from the reporter, Langan went to the back room again. Goodering said the time of death was probably between two and three a.m. That meant the patrol car probably hadn't interrupted the killer, though it didn't rule out someone else having done so. It took another half hour before Goodering finished his work and cleared the ambulance attendants to take the body to the police morgue. Langan phoned dispatch and a relief team came to watch the scene until the lab team arrived. Petrusic and Makowski headed to the station to make their own reports. Langan glanced at his watch: ten to six. The sky was turning from black to grey. By the time he got home, Clare and Jamie would just about be waking up. *So comes another day*, he thought. *Should be an interesting one.*

Stan Osiewicz stuck around for a while after talking with Langan; the morning edition had already gone to press, so there was no immediate rush to turn the story in. While Langan obviously disliked reporters, Osiewicz thought he might get something more from the others at the scene. In the end, very little was added, though the ambulance driver dropped a few remarks as they wheeled out the stretcher with the body bag. Even so, combining what he'd learned and a large dose of gut instinct, he concluded this story was going to be a big one. The adrenaline started flowing at the very prospect.

Osiewicz was a veteran reporter, having been with the *Providence Journal* for over ten years. He mostly covered the police beat but preferred doing features—what his editor grandly called "investigative reporting." In practice, this often meant little more than doing some sort of topical piece, but occasionally, it led to real stories. He had even been nominated for a Pulitzer for a series on corruption in the state pension system. He had the talent and instincts of a great reporter and was always hoping to find "the big story" that would lead to the majors, like the *New York Times* or *Washington Post.* It wasn't that he hated working for the *Journal.* He was just tired of Providence.

Once the medical examiner and ambulance had left and the replacement patrol crew came to await the forensics team, Osiewicz figured it was time to go. He briefly debated waiting for the crime lab crew, but decided the wait, likely two or three more hours, would not be worth the results. In any case, he knew a couple of people in the police department who could probably help out. Later, he could contact the owner of Good Time Donuts to get some background on the victim. If need be, he could even try contacting Langan again. Right now, it was time for a shower and breakfast. After that, it would be soon enough to go to the office and tell Joe Houle, his editor, what was happening.

Joe Houle was at his desk when Stan Osiewicz came in. The clock on the wall of the newsroom showed nine-thirty.

"Hey, Stan!" Houle bellowed through his open door. "What kept you? Hot date last night?"

"Right, Joe," Osiewicz deadpanned. "You should have seen her!" His love life—or rather, the lack of it—was well-known in the newsroom, and the jokes were a standard part of Houle's repertoire of jibes. At the moment, he was just expressing his displeasure at Osiewicz's late arrival.

Knowing that, Osiewicz saw no reason to take offense. He stopped in the doorway of Houle's office.

"Actually, Joe, I think I've got an interesting one."

"Oh?" Houle's face was immediately serious. In the years they had worked together, he had come to recognize that Osiewicz had good instincts. More than once, he'd parlayed his knack for finding a good story into major pieces, the kind that make both a reporter and his newspaper look good. If he thought he had a story, Houle was ready to listen. "Have a seat, Stan. What's the scoop?"

"Have you heard about the shooting last night on Branch Avenue?"

"Yeah, the radio had it this morning. I've assigned Taylor to get the background—just a kid in a donut shop, wasn't it? What's the big deal about a botched robbery?"

"Uh-uh," said Osiewicz, shaking his head vigorously. "It was no robbery. It was a hit."

"What the hell are you talking about, Stan? The radio said—"

"The radio was wrong, Joe. I know. I was there."

"You were there? You mean you saw it? Jesus, Stan—"

"No, no," replied Osiewicz, interrupting again—when he was excited, he tended to do that. "I couldn't sleep—you know how I am sometimes—anyway, I was listening to my scanner for lack of anything better to do and I picked up the call. I got there at the same time as the homicide cop, a guy named Langan. I did some eavesdropping and asked a few questions, and pieced it together. It looks like a pro did it—one shot to the back of the head, small caliber, and boom . . ." He gestured with his hand, pantomiming a gun and dropping the thumb like a falling hammer.

"Christ . . ." Houle paused, thinking it through in his own head. "Are you sure you got this thing right, Stan? Maybe it was just an addict with a small piece. You know, a botched robbery, like the radio said. I mean, it doesn't make any sense for somebody to put a contract on a kid who works in a donut shop. . . ."

"Exactly," agreed Osiewicz. "That's why I figure there's something in it. Maybe the hit was meant for the owner, or maybe this kid was into something besides donuts. Anyway, I want to do some digging. And to begin with, I'd suggest we do a piece tonight, hinting at the real stuff—you know, describe it as 'gangland-style', maybe mention 'sources in the police department'. That way, we scoop the other media on the real story without going out on a limb. I could patch it together right now, and then do some more digging. That is, if you don't mind pulling Susan off it . . ." Against his will, a smirk briefly crossed his face. While he didn't exactly hate Susan Taylor, it was also no secret that there was a bit of rivalry between them. Five years his junior, she was sharp, and a hustler—fully capable of pushing others aside if it meant she might gain from it.

"Huh!" snorted Houle. "You know how she is about having stories taken away—especially good ones." He rolled his eyes.

"But she doesn't know it's a good one!" Osiewicz exclaimed.

"But she will." Houle frowned. "Once your piece breaks, she will. That is, unless all your speculating turns into hot air."

"Speculation!" Osiewicz threw up his hands. "I already told you, I got it right on the scene. Come on, Joe, let me go with it. When have I ever been wrong about a story?"

"Where have I heard that before?" Houle replied, rolling his eyes again. He remained silent for several moments, thinking, until the phone rang. He picked it up, and without finding out who was on the other end, barked into the receiver, "Yeah, Houle here. Hang on a minute." He covered the mouthpiece and turned to Osiewicz. "OK, Ozzie, you write it up. If I like how it reads, we'll go with it." Osiewicz jumped up, elated—then froze as he started for the door, looking back with a question on his face. "And I'll call off Taylor. Now get out of here and let me get some work done!" Before Osiewicz could answer, Houle had turned his attention to the phone.

Osiewicz headed for his desk, his fingers itching to get at the keys. He was sitting down when it registered that Houle had called him "Ozzie." It was a nickname that had stuck with him since childhood. Old friends often called him Ozzie instead of Stan, but most people at the paper, including Houle, used his given name. In fact, the last time he could recall Houle using the nickname was when he'd offered congratulations on the corruption piece that had earned the reporter a Pulitzer nomination.

Maybe this would be the big one Stan had been hoping for.

Mike Langan was at his desk, thinking about the case from his own perspective, which had nothing to do with Pulitzer Prizes. For him, it was one more murder in a long line of cases. He had no interest in the dramatics of the press, and very little patience with most of their sensationalizing, but in one respect, he did agree with them:

every case led into the dark side of the human heart. Solving a murder was often a matter of connecting hard physical evidence to the intangibles of human emotions. It was seldom easy, but it was never boring.

Danny L'Heureux's death, though, had the signs of becoming a major headache. Langan gave a weary sigh. *As if sorting out the Sanelli case weren't enough right now, somebody had to pull a hit.* Like Stan Osiewicz, he was virtually certain it was a contract job, though figuring out who and why was likely to be difficult. On the surface, it made no sense. The L'Heureux kid was clean—Langan had already checked his record—and seemed an unlikely target. Still, there was no mistaking the telltale signs of a professional. Although the lab boys would be going over the scene, Langan instinctively doubted they'd find much. The best he could hope for was that it wouldn't get much publicity, so at least he could go about things in his own methodical way. If it turned into politics—meaning the mayor and the chief started breathing down his neck—well, Langan didn't like the pressure or the distractions that politics brought.

He sipped at his coffee, the third since he'd arrived at the station. *For this, I miss a night's sleep.* He gave a reflexive shrug. *No point in worrying about it. What's the old saying? Plenty of time for sleep when we're in the grave.* He looked at the new binder in front of him, bearing Danny L'Heureux's name on the cover. Danny wasn't yet buried, but rest was no longer a concern for him. Putting the binder in the top drawer of his desk, Langan stood, picked up his coffee, and headed for his car. Good Time Donuts awaited.

At the donut shop, it was a different scene than the one Langan had left a few hours earlier. There was still the yellow barrier, with a uniform standing by it, but other details had changed. There was an unmarked car, which Langan knew belonged to the crime lab, but there was another car that was unfamiliar. In addition, there was a small cluster of people pressing up to the yellow tape. *Rubberneckers*, he thought. *People love crime scenes.* He wasted no energy pondering why—in his job, the downside of human nature was all too clear.

Langan flashed his badge at the uniformed officer and went inside. At the counter a glum-faced man sat nursing a coffee. His face—fiftyish, with dark eyes and a hawk-like nose—was unfamiliar; given the circumstances, Mike figured he must be the owner of the donut shop. The detective stopped and introduced himself.

"Hi, Sergeant," the man replied. "I'm Frank Palucci. This is my place."

"I thought so." Langan paused, and then continued. "Sorry about the kid."

"Yeah, me too . . ." Palucci looked away briefly and sipped at his coffee. "Danny was a good boy. He was always reliable—I let him have the keys, and he did nights alone. Jeez, who'd wanna do this? Some druggie?"

"Maybe," Langan said noncommittally. "Actually, I wanted to see what you might know. Can you tell me anything about Danny that might help?"

"You mean, like was he in with the wrong kind of guys or something?" Palucci asked warily. To Mike's ear, he didn't exactly sound guilty, but he certainly sounded defensive.

“Was he?” Langan asked. “Mixed up with the wrong people?”

“Nah. . . .” Palucci countered. “He was a good kid. Quiet. Still lived at home. His mother’s a real gem—regular churchgoer and all . . .”

Langan didn’t see the relevance of the last point, but made no comment. In his view, although a practicing Catholic himself, churchgoing was no guarantee of model behavior. And regardless, it was Danny L’Heureux, not his mother, who was the focus.

“So,” Langan continued, “you don’t know of anyone that might have had it in for Danny?”

“Wish I did know someone—whoever did it deserves the worst.” Palucci’s eyes wandered over to stare at the wall.

“And what about the register? Have you checked the count yet?”

“Yeah, a little while ago,” Palucci replied. “At first, your people wouldn’t let me near it, but then I checked the tape against the till—it’s all there.” He looked at Langan. “So I guess it wasn’t a robbery?”

“Maybe, maybe not. It’s possible the killer got interrupted before he could take the cash.”

Palucci’s brows arched. “Huh? Who?”

“That’s part of what we need to find out . . .” Langan made some jottings in his notebook and looked back at Palucci. “Anyway, what about you? Is there anyone who would want to get back at you? Any business or personal problems?”

“Me?” Palucci’s eyes darted back to look at Langan. “Nothing I can think of.” His eyes dropped to his coffee cup, and he paused to take a swig. "Besides, it don't make sense—why kill Danny if somebody hates me?"

Langan let the remark hang unanswered. It seemed an unlikely possibility—after all, even if a contract killer were involved, who could possibly mistake the kid for this guy? Still, the detective knew that murder often involved circles within circles, and decided to do some checking into Palucci. For now, he let it drop.

"Well, if you do think of anything else, let me know. You can reach me at this number." He handed Palucci his card and headed into the rear of the shop, where the lab team was just finishing up.

"Hi, Mike. How ya doing?" Hank Trubic, the head forensics technician, was always upbeat. This cheerful temperament often came across as highly incongruous, given the nature of many of the settings he worked in. However, Langan had known him long enough to know there was nothing ghoulish about Hank. Far from being a gallows humor cynic, he simply took pride in doing his job well and knowing his efforts could help bring the guilty to justice.

"It's been a long night, Hank. How about you?"

"I'm OK. But I can't say a lot for this place." He frowned slightly.

"What've you got?"

"The victim was standing about here, by the flour sacks, facing the wall." He walked over to the mixing machine. "The killer stood close behind him. We might be able to estimate the killer's height, depending on the initial path of the bullet into the brain, but I'll have to see the autopsy. It looks like the kid just collapsed when he was shot and ended up falling against the flour sacks."

"Yeah, that's what I was thinking." Langan nodded. "Nothing to indicate a struggle?"

"Not really. We figure the mixing bowl got knocked off as the kid fell after being shot. Nothing else seems disturbed." The technician looked around, as if confirming his conclusion. "We'll run the blood work, but it's likely just the victim's." Trubic paused for a moment, then continued. "We've dusted the register, but there's only about two decent prints. We'll have to see. They may just be the victim's. We also dusted the back door. There are a few palm prints, as you'd expect with a crash bar. We got a partial thumb and forefinger set, but again, we don't know, they might just be the victim's or the owner's. Same with the frame of the doorway to the back room—there are a few prints, but they may not tell us much. The only item that may help is a coffee cup we found on the counter. It might or might not be related, but we'll take it to the lab. If it's connected, we might get saliva, even if there are no prints."

"Any other physical evidence?"

"Not so far. We'll seal up the place, though. We may get some ideas after we get to the lab and Yoshida is through with the autopsy."

"So what's your thinking, Hank?"

Trubic gazed away for a moment, and then looked back. "Well, you know me, Mike. I don't like to jump the gun." He glanced down, shifted his feet, and then looked directly at Langan. "Let me put it this way: It looks very neat, much neater than your average impulse killing. I think we're going to have our hands full with this one, Mike."

Langan nodded. "Me too, Hank. Me too."

Mike Langan's feelings of frustration were sure to be enhanced when he saw the evening paper. Stan Osiewicz had used his contacts at police headquarters, and by early afternoon, was able to put together a story. As he'd promised Houle, it didn't go so far as to leave the newspaper out on a limb, but it was enough to generate sales. The headline, "MYSTERY SHOOTING LEAVES MAN DEAD," covered two columns in the middle of the front page, and was followed by the reporter's byline.

The feature was a little light on details, but Osiewicz was a good storyteller, and the piece would leave the reader with the strong sense that this was more than just random violence. While it never used the phrase "hit man," the story referred to "organized crime overtones" and "concerns that robbery was not the motive," closely followed by references to "reliable sources in the police department." Osiewicz had even phoned the mayor's office for comment. Since no one in the mayor's office had yet been informed of the incident, the reaction was, of course, "No comment." With slight dramatic license, he was able to make that seem significant.

By the end of the day, the story was big news all over the state. To Joe Houle's immense satisfaction, the newspaper was being quoted on the late news on TV. In a world where television had become the dominant news influence, both the editor and the reporter relished a chance to scoop the broadcast guys.

Not everyone was happy with the media coverage. The man sat with the *Evening Bulletin* on his lap, the story about the killing face up, as he scanned the local late news shows on TV. It was clear to him that the television reporters were just rehashing the paper's story, despite the charade of on-the-scene reports showing the outside of Good Time Donuts and the police barrier. It was also obvious that none of them had any real idea what was going on.

Dammit, he thought, *three attacks and still nothing. These cops are more stupid than I thought!*

When he'd first made his plan, after Sanelli's death, his memory of the cyanide-laced painkillers had made it seem like it would be simple to destroy Barton. He thought about it and concluded, *Maybe I'm gonna have to make it clearer.* He turned off the TV and his gaze fell on the table across the room, on which sat a small cloth bundle.

But first I'll get rid of the gun.

SIX

Thursday, April 30, 1987

THE HOMES ON Holden Street were generally large, classic structures that, in most cases, were over a hundred years old. The neighborhood was not as old or elite as the East Side, but its two- and three-story homes, done in a mix of Italianate and Federalist styles, were still impressive residences, the kind one associates with doctors, lawyers, and successful businessmen. Most of the houses had clapboard or wood shingle siding, painted either white or occasionally ochre or blue, but there was also a scattering of brick buildings. Holden Street was technically part of the Smith Hill neighborhood, but its location was also close to downtown, the State House, and Federal Hill (site of Little Italy). Both the location and the large, elegant residences were appropriate for the home of Lou DiNova. DiNova was not a doctor or lawyer, and his business was unconventional, but there was no doubt that he was both successful and powerful. To his associates, he was the *capo dei capi*—the "boss of bosses." To the police, he was the head of the New England branch of the Mafia.

At the moment, DiNova was sitting at the head of the dining room table, reading the morning *Providence Journal* as he finished breakfast. The room, like the entire house, was large and ornate, filled with antique furniture, including a sideboard with sculptures reminiscent of ancient Roman figures. His lieutenant, as always, sat on the side, waiting for the day's instructions.

"Johnny, what the fuck is going on?" DiNova was clearly unhappy, and his words reflected it. Most of the time, he consciously used a more genteel, almost patrician, form of speech—an affectation that, like most of the furnishings in the house, conveyed a cultured image that was really only window dressing.

"What's that, Lou?"

"You didn't hear the news? It was on the front page of last night's *Bulletin* and on TV, and now in the morning *Journal*. Some kid in a donut shop was killed and they're calling it a hit!" He threw the paper across the table to Giovanni Palmieri, aka Johnny Palms.

In turn, Palmieri read the story on the bottom of the page. Written by Stan Osiewicz, it was a follow-on to the larger story in the previous evening's paper.

"This is crap, boss! This reporter's blowing smoke. There was no hit!"

"Yeah? I know *I* didn't order it, but shit like this is bad for business. Find out who the kid was and who did this. I want this dealt with before some politician decides they need to use us as a fuckin' scapegoat."

"Right, boss. I'll have Marv Siegel look into it right away."

Siegel was a lawyer who, as unofficial *consigliere* (adviser), received an annual retainer from DiNova. Though he occasionally was called upon to provide legal representation for someone from the *famiglia*, his more important role was as a well-connected information source, with a wide range of contacts on both sides of the law. He was a paper-handler, not a street guy; if circumstances eventually required it, both DiNova and Palmieri knew there were others who could be called upon to take action. Right now, information was what they needed.

Marv Siegel was not surprised when he got the phone call from Palmieri; unlike Palmieri, he'd read the evening paper and seen the TV news. To him, it seemed very unlikely that a twenty-two-year-old working in a donut shop would have run afoul of DiNova's organization—especially to the extent that killing him was the chosen solution. Still, he knew the world was not always the way it appeared; if it were, he would probably have much less business.

"Morning, Johnny. How are you?" Siegel always believed in the social graces; in his line of work, being seen as affable and even gracious was a virtue. Money could lubricate some situations but being well-liked was more useful in many of the circles he moved in. Even better was the ability to exchange favors. Having struggled for years to reach his current position, Siegel still had the outsider's innate drive to cultivate both social connections and favors.

"I'm good, Marv. But this donut shop thing is giving Lou high blood pressure. We need to find out what happened and put a lid on it."

"Right now, I don't know anything, Johnny. But I'll make a few calls and get back to you later today."

"Do that. Lou's really pissed."

"I understand. Let me get back to you, Johnny. And by the way, how are Danielle and the kids?"

"Great, Marv. They're all great. Call me later." With that, he hung up. Unlike Siegel, Palmieri had little use for graciousness.

Siegel thought about the news reports, and whom he should call. Given that the police investigation was in its early stages, getting a copy of the homicide file was not likely to be very helpful, but he nonetheless made a mental note to contact a desk sergeant who had access to the paperwork. A better lead, he thought, would be the lab work, so he called Harry Smith, a technician in the forensics lab, and offered to buy him lunch. They agreed to meet at Leona's, a diner close to Smith's lab, just after twelve.

Harry Smith was in his forties, thin, with a narrow nose and face that made him look slightly pinched. He had worked in the forensics lab for almost twenty years. It was steady work—as a civil servant, his position was unionized, so the pay and benefits were decent. Some people might be bothered by the subject matter, but he was a lab guy, not a medical examiner. This meant he ran the tests and seldom had contact with bodies, dead or alive. Getting out for lunch with Marv Siegel was a break from the repetitive nature of his job, and he knew Siegel was good for more than a sandwich.

"Harry! Nice to see you!" said Siegel, sliding into the booth. The family-style diner was casual, but as usual, Siegel wore an expensive suit, with a red silk tie to offset the dark wool. His hair was thinning and grey, and his face showing the wrinkles of aging, but his demeanor and style of dress still managed to convey a kind of Old World gentility.

"Nice to see you, too, Marv. It's been a while."

"Yes. Yes, it has." Siegel nodded solemnly. "No offense, Harry, but I'm happier when work takes me in other directions, if you know what I mean. Of course, that's nothing to do with you personally—I'm always happy to see *you*. How's your diabetes, by the way? Did you see that specialist at Roger Williams that I mentioned?"

"Oh, you know. I still hate passing up desserts, but the doc was good. He's managed to keep me off injections, at least." Smith looked away from the table; whether he was thinking about a favorite dessert or something else was not clear. Siegel waited, not wanting to push Smith.

Finally, Smith looked at him, saying, "So, what's up, Marv? To what do I owe the honor?"

"Harry, you always were direct!" Siegel gave a chuckle that sounded almost genuine. Then his face quickly sobered. "It's this thing in the donut shop. Just between you and me, it had nothing to do with the people the news media are blaming." Siegel, as always, tried to be both circumspect and clear. "The fact is, they are very upset that this happened. A young man—such a terrible thing." Siegel slowly moved his head from side to side, the sadness of all the world's injustices seemingly mirrored in his face. "In fact, they would like to assist in seeing that justice is done for this terrible crime." Unspoken was the fact that the form of justice DiNova sought had no real connection to the courts; it was about eliminating an irritant that was bad for business, by any means necessary. "A speedy resolution would make people feel better, I think." Siegel kept his eyes on Smith, but his hand withdrew an envelope from a folded newspaper he was carrying and slid it across the table. "Is there anything you can tell me that might help?"

Smith looked at the envelope, then looked out the window, and then back at Siegel. He'd been in this situation before, and normally had no discomfort with sharing information. At the same time, this particular case was looking like a political hot potato, and he did not want to be caught in the mess, whatever was going on. He palmed the envelope into his lap and took a quick look. He saw the portrait of Ben Franklin, and that there were several bills. Clearly Siegel, and whoever he represented, was very interested in this case, to be paying in hundred-dollar bills.

"Well, Marv, forensics didn't get a lot. Most of the scene was pretty clean, and from what I hear, there were no witnesses. I can tell you that the bullet was a .22 long; they actually got the shell casing, which doesn't fit with a pro job. Not many fingerprints at the scene, but they did get a couple of partials from the crash bar on the back door. Right now, there's not much to say they belong to the shooter, but we did get a match to our database."

"Oh? So quickly?" Siegel was surprised by what Smith had shared. Leaving the shell casing behind was clearly not the mark of a professional hitman, which of course reflected what Palmieri had told him in the phone call. But getting a match on fingerprints, especially partials, in barely one day was unusual. Usually fingerprint data had to go to the FBI for processing and that could take weeks or even months.

"Well, as you can imagine, there's a lot of heat on this case, so we had somebody look at the local records and found a match. It's a small-time dealer named Maurice Washington, aka 'Deuce.' They're looking for him right now. Nobody really knows if he's involved or not. Maybe he'd been there recently to sell the kid some weed and left by the back." Smith again looked away, thinking about what it all meant—or didn't mean. In the end, his job was just processing lab tests; deciding innocence or guilt was for somebody else to deal with. He looked back at Siegel. "Anyway, Marv, that's all there is. If you want, I can call you if something else comes up."

"Thank you, Harry. That would be very kind of you." Siegel started to slide out of the booth, but extended his hand, grasping Smith's hand firmly. "Very good to see you. And watch your sugar!" With that, he was gone, leaving Harry to gratefully pocket the envelope—but not before a quick count. *Five hundred. Not bad for fingering a small-time dealer.*

While Harry Smith finished his lunch, Mike Langan was sitting down at his desk, reviewing the status of the cases on his plate. The Sanelli case was at a standstill. He and his partner, Frank Dunn, had reviewed the statements taken from everyone who'd been present when the investigators arrived at Sal's Bar after the 911 call. Predictably, no one had seen anything.

They'd also talked to Sanelli's widow—never the easiest part of working homicide. After the appropriate condolences, they'd asked her about possible enemies. As expected, there weren't any obvious suspects. Sanelli had spent the last twelve years as a sales manager for D'Agostino's, a wholesale grocer. Nothing in his work situation suggested problems, though at some point, they would have to check it out.

Hoping to pick up a lead, Langan and Dunn had gone back to the bar earlier in the day to talk to the bartender, an ex-vet named Salvador Quinone, aka Sal.

Sal's was quiet when they entered—not a big surprise at ten-thirty a.m. Like a lot of bars, Sal's also served food, including lunch specials to draw people in, but that traffic was absent in mid-morning. The TV over the bar blared loudly, while a couple of old-timers sat in a booth, nursing beers.

Having found Quinone's name on the original interview report, Langan had checked him out beforehand and didn't find much. He was a vet who'd apparently served in Vietnam; like a lot of returning vets, his life since seemed to have drifted. He'd never married and had started the bar about six years ago. In spite of—or because of—being a bartender, Quinone seemed to have issues with alcohol, including a DUI that somehow ended up dropped, but otherwise he seemed clean.

"So, can I get you something, detectives, or you just here to chat?" Quinone had spotted Langan and Dunn as cops as soon as they entered.

Not surprisingly, Quinone knew most of the regulars, including Rico Sanelli, but when asked if anyone unfamiliar had been present the day of Sanelli's death, he was unsure. The murder had happened during happy hour and the bar was busy. Quinone thought there might have been one or two non-regulars in the bar, but nobody who seemed out of place. Langan asked if he'd noticed anyone follow Sanelli out of the bar, but again, Quinone's memory seemed vague. Langan pondered whether he might be holding back, but the circumstances of the death did not suggest any reason for that, and it was not unusual that details could go unnoticed in a busy bar. Still, the upshot was that the trip back to Sal's to talk to Quinone had been unproductive.

With no new leads from interviewing Quinone, Langan had turned to the forensics. The crime lab had confirmed that the brick found at the scene was the weapon. Flakes of it were found in Sanelli's scalp, and blood that matched his type was found on the brick itself. Beyond that, there wasn't much: no fingerprints were found on the brick, though a small fiber of leather was found. This might mean the killer had worn gloves, but given the debris in the alley, there was no way to determine whether the leather was from a glove or something else. In either case, it provided little in the way of leads. The angle of the blow suggested Sanelli had been hit from behind by someone right-handed, who was probably a couple of inches taller than the victim. Overall, the limited information from the crime lab didn't do much to point to a possible killer.

With no witnesses and nothing significant from the forensics, the case was heading nowhere. Langan was frustrated by that—he never liked to see a case going cold, because that meant the chances of solving it would plummet drastically. But with no leads, it was likely headed to O-U—the limbo world of open-unsolved cases. Technically, such cases remained open, but the reality was that they were not revisited unless something happened to force a review. Since that seldom happened, a case sent to O-U was typically never solved. Langan lived to close cases by catching the killers; once assigned a case, he hated to let it go, especially to O-U.

As much as he hated O-U cases, a greater frustration for Langan at the moment was the political attention the L'Heureux case was drawing. As soon as he'd seen the newspaper headline the previous evening, he'd braced himself for heat from upstairs. Sure enough, this morning Lieutenant Briggs, head of homicide, had called him into his office.

"Morning, Mike. How's it going?"

"Morning, Lieutenant." Without knowing the purpose of this little conference, Langan was unwilling to say things were good or bad.

"I got a call from the chief, Mike. The mayor is upset about the attention the L'Heureux case is drawing, so he's wants us to give this one our best effort and try to wrap it up quickly."

It's amazing, Langan thought, *how shit obeys gravity—it always drops down from the highest point.*

"So, you and Frank Dunn are working this one, right?" Lieutenant Briggs looked directly at Langan. "You're both experienced guys, and I've got no worries on that front. But this needs to be a priority. You still have the Sanelli case? What's the situation?"

Langan could see where this was going, and he didn't like it. With only half-concealed frustration, he outlined the results of the interviews and lab work.

Briggs, whatever his limitations as unit head, had enough experience in homicide to assess the case realistically. He paused for a moment, his lips forming a thin, tight line.

"Well, I'm not saying we should O-U this one yet, but it doesn't sound like there are any active leads. So unless something changes, I want you focusing on the L'Heureux case. I don't really think this is mob stuff—sounds more like a drug deal gone sour—but as long as it's on the front page, it's gonna cause me heartburn." Langan glanced at the bottle of Tums that Lieutenant Briggs kept on his desk. "So do me a favor, Mike. Wrap this one up."

And soon went unsaid.

Now, back at his desk, Langan put aside the Sanelli file and opened the file for the L'Heureux case. Frank Dunn had picked up the forensics report earlier and Langan reviewed it now. As they'd expected, the murder weapon was a small-caliber gun, fired at close range to the base of the skull. Being small caliber, the bullet had not had enough energy to penetrate the skull opposite the entrance wound. Instead, it had caromed around the brain as it bounced off the skull, causing extensive damage—and also ending up deformed into a lump of lead, which would not be useful for any ballistics matching. Finding the shell casing was fortunate. It confirmed that the bullet was a .22 caliber. The fact that the casing had been ejected indicated the gun was a pistol, not a revolver, and the firing-pin mark suggested it came from a Ruger—a relatively cheap make whose pricing meant it was also common. There was gunshot residue on the area around the entrance wound, confirming that the shot had been at close range. The weapon and wound was reminiscent of a mob-style hit, as the newspaper had speculated, but Langan was not ready to say this really was a hit. At the moment, the victim and circumstances didn't seem to fit, and he couldn't see a professional leaving the shell casing. More importantly, there was nothing to indicate *why* L'Heureux would be targeted for a hit.

Looking for something more, Langan reviewed the other information gathered from the crime scene. All the blood samples matched L'Heureux's blood type, and there was nothing under the victim's fingernails to suggest there had been a struggle. The forensics team had looked for fingerprints on the cash register and at various points in the back room where the shooting occurred. It had been decided that there was little point (at least initially) in trying to collect prints from anywhere else in the front area of the shop, given the volume of people who went through in a day. Most of the prints found were from the victim or the two employees who worked the day shift. The only promising lead had been a few partials found on the crash bar of the rear service door. Given the pressure that was already being placed on the case, the forensics lab had looked for a match in their records. Sure enough, the prints belonged to a small-time drug dealer named Maurice Washington, aka Deuce. This suggested that a drug deal gone sour might have been the motive for the murder.

Still, the hit-style shooting and the small caliber gun didn't really fit—most small-time perps like Deuce would carry at least a .38, if not something more. Still, finding the prints at the scene meant he was a person of interest, and Langan decided the next step was to track him down. He left a message for Tom Scofield, a detective in the drug squad, to see if he could provide a lead on where to find Maurice Washington. Hopefully, Scofield would get back to him later in the day.

Henry Cohen sat at his desk, with the sunshine streaming in through the large windows across the room. The view faced toward the Providence River in the middle distance, but was otherwise unexceptional—largely industrialized, this part of Cranston wasn't noted for its scenic qualities. At least the sky was clear, and the sun's intensity suggested that spring had fully arrived. On his desk were the latest figures from accounting. Both the costume jewelry and the watchband lines were selling well, and profits for the current quarter were showing signs of healthy year-over-year growth. Normally, he would be in a very good mood on a day like this. And so he was—until the morning mail had brought yet another brown envelope. Inside had been another anonymous note. Like the first two, it was made of letters cut out and pasted onto newspaper. However, this time there was a distinctly more menacing tone to the note: "It's time to pay for your crimes." *What crimes? Who was sending these notes, and what were they upset about?*

Taking a cue from Ed Underwood, he looked at the postmark on the latest envelope. It had come from Pawtucket. *So Ed was right*, he thought. *Whoever is sending these is making an effort to hide their location.* It still wasn't clear what they wanted, but it seemed increasingly obvious that this was no petty prank. *Maybe it's time to involve the police.*

While contacting the police seemed appropriate given the situation, Cohen did not relish the turmoil it could create in the company, or at home. As a prominent member of the business community in Providence, he had built relationships with various political leaders and city officials, but he knew that calling in favors always came with a price. Sometimes, the price was small—like some jewelry for a wife or girlfriend at Christmas—but Cohen always worried that such debts could be called in more awkward ways, like a financial contribution or public endorsement at election time. Still, with these messages continuing and becoming more threatening, what choice did he have? Making a decision, he picked up the phone and connected to his secretary.

"Joan, can you get me Chief Parker of the Providence Police?"

Henry Cohen wasn't the only one to receive unexpected mail that day. At about the same time Cohen was calling

Chief Parker, Stan Osiewicz was going through his mail at work. There were a couple of letters from readers, commenting on recent stories he'd done. One complained that his coverage of the L'Heureux case was maligning Italian-Americans by implying that serious crimes were always the fault of supposed Italian organized-crime groups. (The writer avoided terms like "Mafia" and "Cosa Nostra," presumably to reinforce the view that not all criminals were Italian.) Osiewicz felt strongly that the criticism was misplaced; having grown up as a member of an immigrant group (Poles) that had attracted its own share of ethnic slurs, it was not in his nature to cast stones at others. Even so, as a reporter, he felt obliged to go where the stories led, even at the risk of offending some readers.

He next came to an envelope that had been addressed with a black marker, in crudely printed letters. There was no stamp or postmark, indicating it had been dropped off at the paper's offices, not mailed. Opening it, he found a sheet of typing paper, with letters that had evidently been cut from a newspaper. Pasted onto the blank sheet, they spelled a short message: "If you think it's a hit, you're missing the point. Look for connections to Barton Jewelry."

Osiewicz reread the message several times, trying to sort out its meaning. The crude printing and clownish use of pasted letters made it seem like a prank, or the work of somebody who was short a few marbles. Or maybe it meant that the killing actually was a mob hit, and this was a creative attempt to deflect attention. He thought about it for several moments, considering the possibilities, but realized he had too little information to do anything with the cryptic message. What's more, he knew it could be just a prank—it was not the first time he'd gotten off-the-wall correspondence. So, he put the note back in the envelope, and put the envelope in the center drawer of his desk. He made a mental note to talk to a couple of people in the Providence police (including Detective Langan, if he would cooperate) to see how the investigation was going.

He also considered showing the message to a psychiatrist he knew over at Rhode Island Hospital, Dr. Heinrich Brandt. Brandt had been helpful to him when he had been covering a case several years before that involved a series of rape-murders. It was a big story, sensational and scary—and the first one to get the young reporter's byline on the front page. Three women, ranging in age from eighteen to thirty-five, had been raped and then stabbed repeatedly—sometimes with multiple knives and dozens of stab wounds. Because the murders occurred in different towns, investigators had not initially seen any connection. In addition, one victim's body had been dumped in a pond in early winter, and because the pond froze over, the body had not been found for several months. Instead, it was treated as simply a missing-persons case. In the end, the crimes turned out to be the work of a mentally-disturbed high school football star, a seemingly model student with straight-A grades who, beneath his scholar-athlete veneer, was a cold-blooded psychopath. Ultimately, the state's case was made easier when the assailant was spotted leaving the third crime scene; unexpectedly, when he was apprehended for questioning, he calmly confessed to all three killings.

Osiewicz had started covering the third case as a solo crime, until the confession morphed the story into a headline-grabber about a serial killer. Covering the case had given his career an early boost, but his stomach still churned when he thought about the crimes and the victims. The question he had asked Dr. Brandt, and which still made him queasy, was *why*? At the time, Brandt had said that psychopaths often seem cold and emotionless, but can also be extremely impulsive. Actions that would imply a state of blind rage in most individuals may occur with little overt emotion, almost as if on a whim. After they act, they seldom feel remorse, as normal individuals do. As one of the police investigators had put it, the killer "simply had an urge to kill."

Thinking back to that case, Osiewicz found his mood darkening. He looked out the newsroom window, his eyes unfocused. The crime beat seldom showcased humanity's finer moments, and in cases like the student-killer, it suggested there was no level of depravity that was impossible. When he got into such reflections, he had to force himself to move on—while also wondering when the day might come that he would feel a need to leave the crime beat completely.

Ed Underwood left work, following his usual routine of heading to the *dojo* for a workout before joining Liz for a late dinner. Because it was a Thursday, they had no special plans—dinner would be at her place, with a focus on catching up on daily events and maybe cuddling on the couch to watch a bit of TV. Since Cohen had not spoken to him that day, Ed did not know about the third note; given his ambivalence about the advice he'd given Cohen after the first two notes, this was probably a good thing. In any case, his mind felt reasonably clear when he entered the *dojo*—a refreshing change from recent sessions.

On good days or bad, Ed always found that he left a workout in the *dojo* feeling more energized than when he entered. As a psychologist, he knew that research had shown that aerobic exercise has positive effects on mood, but his experiences in *karate* left him convinced that this was not the only factor. *Karate* in Japan had a long association with Zen Buddhist practice, as did a range of other activities, from swordsmanship and archery to calligraphy and flower-arranging. In each case, the focus was on using the specific activity to foster mental discipline and and to create a sense of serenity derived from living in the moment. These qualities led to Zen being readily embraced in feudal Japan by many of the *samurai* warrior class, who saw maintaining focus and calm as a critical skill, especially since their job sometimes meant facing death. Ed recognized that, thankfully, his job did not involve such risks. Regardless, he believed that *karate* training both helped him cope with stress and made his life generally better, and the time spent on workouts almost always felt worthwhile.

Now, as he was packing up his gym bag, Yoshikawa-*sensei* came into the dressing room. It was nearing the end of the evening schedule, and the dressing room was empty apart from one other student, who quickly packed his things and exited, bowing to Yoshikawa as he did so.

"Good evening, *sensei*." Ed stopped packing his bag and bowed.

"Good evening." Yoshikawa sat down on the bench and indicated for Ed to sit as well. Physically small, only five foot six and with a wiry frame, Yoshikawa nonetheless exuded an aura of intense energy. More than twenty years older than Ed, his bearing conveyed a sense of authority—and his students recognized it, without exception. He looked intently at Ed for a long moment, then finally spoke in a quiet voice. "Ed, how are you doing?"

Ed was startled. He and Yoshikawa had become good friends over the years, despite the differences of age and role. Ed knew the basics of his mentor's regular life—running the *dojo* was an avocation, not a way to make money, and Yoshikawa also had a successful landscaping business. They had often shared meals, and even special occasions with Yoshikawa's family, but as *sensei*, the older man seldom dropped his formal role within the *dojo*. Now, it almost seemed as if the teacher had been replaced by a small man with thinning grey hair, speaking to a younger friend.

"I—I'm okay," Ed stammered, inwardly cursing his loss of equilibrium. He could not bring himself to refer to Yoshikawa by his first name, Hisao, as he would have outside the dojo.

"You've been unusually distracted lately," Yoshikawa continued, but his voice held no trace of criticism. "I'm concerned, my friend. What is happening? Are things okay between you and Liz?"

"Liz? Yes, she's great—I mean, we're great." Ed took a deep breath, trying to re-center. "I know I've been off lately. Work has been a little intense, but I'm trying to sort things out." He considered mentioning his concerns about the notes to Cohen, and the advice he had given Cohen, but decided against it.

Again, there was a long pause while Yoshikawa simply sat, seemingly not focusing on anything, but fully aware of Ed's demeanor. Finally, he spoke, "Well, if there's anything I can do, please let me know, Ed. You know I will always help however I can."

"I know. I do, and I appreciate it." He managed to smile. "Thank you."

Yoshikawa stood, and instead of bowing, extended his hand. "Take care of yourself, Ed." He turned and left the dressing room, leaving Ed alone with his thoughts.

Early evening is often a good time for fishing, and the day's weather had been mild, making it a pleasant option for those given to recreational angling. Many of the ponds and reservoirs in Rhode Island still had decent fishing, so it was not unusual to see people trying their luck. Thus it was that someone was standing by the side of the road, tossing a line into the Wenscott Reservoir in North Providence. Douglas Avenue crossed the reservoir, and at the south end, there was a large parking area adjacent to the beach and recreational facilities in Governor Notte Park. It was too early in the season, and too late in the day, for anyone to be on the beach, and finding a space in the nearly empty lot was not a problem. From there, it was an easy walk up the road to get to the midpoint of the reservoir, where one could easily cast a line.

The fish in the reservoir were mostly bass, both large-mouth and smallmouth, though an experienced angler would probably say the fish were more likely to be in the weeds along the edge than in the middle. Still, this particular fisherman didn't care, because he wasn't really interested in fishing. He'd come to drop something in the water, and the fishing was just a cover. That morning, he'd taken the homemade silencer off the pistol he'd used at the donut shop; he intended to dismantle it and dispose of the parts in various garbage bins. Since the gun was more traceable, he had filed the serial numbers from the Ruger. Then he'd wiped the gun with a cloth soaked in Varsol to remove any fingerprints, even though he knew it was unlikely the gun would ever be found—and it if was, little residue would remain after soaking in the water. Still, he prided himself on attention to detail, and disposing of the gun was important enough to warrant such attention.

As he stood by the edge of the road, the gun sat in a paper bag in his tackle box. He did a few casts into the water; as he slowly reeled the line back in, his eyes scanned the area warily, checking for anyone who might observe his actions. It was dusk, and the sun was low in the sky behind him, meaning that anyone at the park would see only a silhouetted figure. An occasional car went by, but the engine sounds gave him ample warning when a vehicle was approaching.

Finally, when the moment was clear, he bent down and picked up the bag from the open tackle box. The road at this point was actually a viaduct, allowing the water on the two sides to circulate freely; he estimated it was probably twelve to fifteen feet deep at this point. Keeping the package close to his body, and holding the rod in his free hand, he did an underhand toss into the water. The package landed with a small splash about fifteen feet out and immediately sank. He smiled briefly and went back to casting the line into the water. After another fifteen minutes, with no indication that anyone had even been near enough to notice, he packed up his gear and walked back to his car.

As he walked, he was already thinking about the logistics of the next attack. He also decided it was time to increase the attention on Barton Jewelry.

SEVEN

Friday, May 1, 1987

STAN OSIEWICZ ENTERED the *Journal-Bulletin* building just before nine a.m. He nodded to Paul, the retired cop who sat at a high desk in the lobby. Paul, who mostly served to greet visitors, preferred not to be called a security guard—like most cops, retired or not, he regarded private security staff as well below him. Instead, Paul preferred to be considered a sort of "concierge" (even if he wasn't entirely sure what the word meant). On this morning, as Osiewicz walked by, Paul called out to him.

"Hey, wait a minute, Ozzie!"

Osiewicz paused. "What's up, Paulie?" He used the name deliberately. There was a limited circle of people whom he accepted calling him "Ozzie," and Paul wasn't among them.

Paul, overweight and over the hill, grimaced at the usage, but otherwise ignored it. Instead, he beckoned

Osiewicz to come closer and reached down from his high perch to hand him an envelope. "Here, somebody dropped this off for you."

As Osiewicz reached out to take it, he momentarily froze. He had no idea about the contents, but the eight and a half by eleven manila envelope seemed like a flash of *déjà vu*: crudely addressed with a black marker, and no return address or postage. He turned it over, then turned it back to look again at the lettering: "Stan Osiewicz, the Journal" was written in block letters.

"Thanks, Paul." He paused, then continued, "Say, do you happen to recall who dropped it off? And when?"

"It was about eight o'clock this morning. I remember, 'cause I was still finishing the coffee I brought in when my shift started."

"Uh-huh. And do you remember *who*?"

"Gee, let me think." Paul's gaze shifted up and to the side. Over the years of doing interviews, Osiewicz had often seen this behavior when he asked people questions. He'd come to recognize it as an indicator that they were checking their memory, almost as if it was a box sitting on the upper shelf of an imaginary closet. By contrast, when he asked people questions that should have required recall and their gaze didn't shift, he'd come to interpret it as an indicator they were lying.

In this case, after checking his memory, Paul said, "It was a kid—a teenager. He had a backpack, looked like he was on his way to school."

"Do you know who he was? Ever see him before?"

"Nah, not really. If you're wondering who sent it, the kid probably wouldn't be much help. He said some guy gave him five bucks to drop it off." Paul seemed incredulous at the sum for such a simple task. "Hell, I wish the guy had given it to me!"

Osiewicz nodded. "I know what you mean, Paul. Anyway, thanks." He headed for the elevator, wondering what message the envelope carried.

Once seated at his desk, Osiewicz stared at the envelope. Before opening it, he carefully felt its surface, trying to determine whether there was anything beyond a piece of paper inside. His examination revealed little, so he then reached into his center drawer, where he had placed the envelope that arrived the previous week. The previous envelope had been a standard number ten white envelope, like the kind used for most mail, not a full-page manila one. Despite this difference, both had been addressed with black marker in crude block letters, by what seemed to be the same hand. In both cases, the slant of the letters suggested the writer was left-handed.

At length, his curiosity getting the better of him, Osiewicz opened the envelope, doing his best to unseal the flap rather than rip it. Inside was another sheet of typing paper, with individual letters once again cut from a newspaper and pasted to form new words. Noting this, Osiewicz wondered if there was some message in the medium, ironic or otherwise—using newspaper letters to send a message to a newspaper. Clearly, there was no way to determine that, but the words the letters formed seemed all too clear:

"People have been dying and more will die. Barton is to blame."

The signature, if one could call pasted letters a signature, was "The hand of justice."

Osiewicz read it several times, trying to make sense of it. When taken with the first note ("If you think it's a hit, you're missing the point. Look for connections to Barton Jewelry"), it suggested that somehow Barton Jewelry was responsible for not only Danny L'Heureux's death, but unspecified others. Though Osiewicz knew relatively little about Barton Jewelry, he knew it was a large and profitable company, and had been around for something like fifty years. On the surface, he could not see how the company, or someone in the company, would benefit from a killing, mob-style or otherwise. After mulling it over, he decided it was time to talk to Joe Houle about the situation. If nothing else, it seemed likely to justify spending more time on the L'Heureux story.

A few minutes later, Stan Osiewicz was sitting in the editor's office. Houle had the two notes laid out in front of him, and had said nothing for over a minute. Finally, he looked up.

"So, what the hell is this, Ozzie?" (Stan noted his use of the nickname, suggesting that however skeptical his words, Houle was on his side.)

"I'm not sure. If I had only received the second note, I'd have figured it was somebody with a grudge against the company, maybe just a crackpot. Or it could be some kind of whistleblower. From what little I know, a lot of the materials used in costume jewelry production can be toxic—heavy metals, acids, a real witch's brew."

Some ten years earlier, there had been a high-profile case of industrial pollution near Niagara Falls—the so-called Love Canal disaster. While the federal government had stepped in and the case made big headlines, his impression was that despite the passage of a decade, there had not yet been a full cleanup. He couldn't recall details, but then, pollution wasn't his area—the *Journal* had a couple of reporters who handled science, the environment, and similar matters. Houle, of course, was well aware who covered various beats, and if this was really about industrial pollution, he would reassign the story.

Reading Houle's mind, Stan quickly added, "But the problem is, how does this relate to the first note and the shooting of Danny L'Heureux?"

"Maybe it doesn't, Stan." Houle reached for his bottle of antacid tablets—never a good sign.

"But look, Joe," Stan pressed, "both notes arrived in the same way, addressed in the same type of black marker and block letters." He reached across Houle's desk to pick up the envelopes, which Houle had put aside after a brief initial glance. Houle nodded, but didn't answer.

"And don't forget, Joe, they both use the same type of paste-up letters for their message. There must be a connection."

Houle looked at the envelopes, then back at the letters. Again, he nodded, but this time replied, "Yeah, I see. But where's the logical connection? I mean, even if we say somebody at Barton arranged a hit, what's it got to do with the second note?" Houle drank from a glass of water on his desk, washing down the antacid tablet. "This all sounds too off the wall. I'm thinking we're dealing with a nutcase, and none of this really means anything."

"Maybe you're right, Joe. Maybe it's all bullshit. But keep in mind, at this point, no one's come up with a reason for L'Heureux's death—and somebody killed him. What if he saw or knew something he shouldn't? Maybe while he was working, he overheard a conversation about illegal dumping of chemicals? That could provide a link between the letters. Even if Barton Jewelry isn't directly involved in L'Heureux's murder, maybe these notes are trying to raise the alarm on something. And maybe the notes are so weird because the writer is worried about ending up like Danny L'Heureux."

"That's a lot of maybes, Stan." Houle leaned back, clasping his hands behind his head. His gaze defocused, and for a long moment, he said nothing. Finally, he sat upright and looked at the waiting reporter. "OK, do some quiet digging on Barton. Find out who the main people are, and find out more about the way their business works. Tell Chu and Jenkins I said to help out."

Gene Chu covered the science beat and Larry Jenkins was the lead business reporter. Stan knew they had knowledge he didn't—and equally important, neither was likely to poach his story. Pleased at Houle's response, Stan started to rise, but Houle continued. "While you're at it, see if you can get anything from the cops about the shooting—maybe talk to the lead detective." Houle paused again. "And go softly on this, Ozzie. I don't want to get heat because your questions have upset somebody. Keep me informed, and let's see where it leads. If there's nothing by the middle of next week, I may have to pull the plug. By then, nobody's gonna care about the L'Heureux story, even if the killer hasn't been found."

Houle handed back the notes and envelopes and returned to the work underneath. Stan knew the conversation was over. He exited, but not before saying, "Thanks, Joe. And don't worry, I know how to handle it."

"I always worry," grunted Houle, without looking up.

Johnny Palmieri sat in his car, nursing a coffee from Dunkin' Donuts. He'd been sitting for almost half an hour now, and the coffee had grown cold. Still, cold coffee was better than nothing while he waited. Patience was not his strong suit, and as the minutes ticked by, he was growing frustrated. He had been told by a punk named Scoots—a crackhead—that he knew a dealer named Deuce. Scoots had said Deuce drove a yellow Corvette, and that he could usually be found working out at Barney's Gym on Douglas Avenue on Friday afternoons—at least, that was where Scoots usually looked if he was trying to score from Deuce. The location made sense. It was less than a mile from the scene of the shooting, so the area was probably Deuce's home turf.

Barney's was located in a former textile mill building that had been repurposed for stores and offices, and though the building had a number of tenants, the large parking lot was less than half full in mid-afternoon, which made it easy to spot the yellow Corvette in the parking lot. So far, there was no sign of Deuce. Johnny had considered going into the gym, but he preferred to talk on the street, so here he was, waiting.

Finally, after about forty-five minutes, a tall black guy sporting an Afro and carrying a gym bag exited the gym and headed in the direction of the Corvette. Johnny got out of his car, and came up behind Deuce as the latter reached his vehicle. Deuce was wearing headphones, apparently playing a Walkman, so he didn't notice Johnny's approach until he felt a hard object poke in his ribs as he reached into his pocket for his car keys. He froze, immediately thinking it was a gun.

"Don't move, and don't do anything stupid, asshole. I just want to talk."

"Uh, yeah, man. No problem." Deuce craned his neck, trying to see who it was.

"I said, don't move. Keep your eyes in front, and put your hands on the roof of the car." Deuce felt a jab against his ribs as Johnny spoke, emphasizing the words.

"Yeah, sure. Easy, man." Deuce dropped the gym bag and placed the palms of his hands flat on the roof over the driver's door. With the low profile of the Corvette, it meant he was leaning forward. He knew it was not a position favoring a quick reaction—and besides, he still felt the hard pressure in his ribs. "What you need, man? I got weed and crack. No need for guns, we can deal."

"I don't want no fuckin' drugs, shithead. I want you to answer some questions. So listen up." Johnny paused to make sure his words had registered.

"Uh, OK, man. Ask away." Deuce's mind was racing. The intruder's approach—coming up with a piece in his hand, and having Deuce lean on the car, smelled like a narc. After all, who else would risk pulling a gun in broad daylight like that? Deuce couldn't see him and didn't recognize the voice, so he wasn't sure. But whoever it was, they hadn't blown him away—at least, not yet.

"I hear you like donuts. Is that right, asshole?"

"Donuts? What the fuck?"

"You like eating at Good Time Donuts? Or is it just a spot to deal?"

"Good Time . . .?" Deuce's mind went into overdrive. The death of the kid had been all over the news since the morning after Deuce had come across the body. But who was this guy, and how did he know Deuce had been there? "Hey, man, what you sayin'? You think *I* did that kid? No way, man!"

"Yeah? No way?" Johnny jabbed at Deuce's ribs again. "So how come you were going out the back door of Good Time last Wednesday night?"

"Who, me? No way!" In his mind, Deuce recalled bolting out the service door after he spotted Danny's body. He had no idea how this guy knew, and denial was the best defense he could think of. He knew if the cops placed him at the scene, it would not be good.

"Yes, you, asshole." Johnny gave him another poke. "I know you were there, so stop the bullshit. If you didn't kill him, what were you doin' there, and what else did you see?"

"OK, OK." Deuce still couldn't figure how his interrogator knew. *Maybe somebody saw my 'Vette as I left?* "Yeah, I was there. I sometimes meet customers in the parking lot, and sometimes I get a coffee. You know, they're open all night. But I had nothin' to do with that kid. He was dead when I got there, I swear."

"Right, like I should believe your word, you piece of shit."

"I'm tellin' you, man. It wasn't me. What would I kill that kid for? He only bought nickel bags and gave me free coffee."

"Yeah, *that* I might buy." Johnny smiled thinly. "But if you weren't involved, what do you know about it? You see somebody?" Again, he poked at Deuce's ribs.

"No, man. I didn't see nobody. I went in to get a coffee, and the front was empty, so I went to the doorway to the back. I saw the kid sprawled out, and I knew it was trouble. I never even looked close—just saw the blood around his head and beat it out the back."

There was a lengthy silence while Johnny paused to consider. Deuce's story was plausible, even if he was a low-life crack dealer. Still, Johnny wasn't entirely convinced. He debated what to do, and decided that rather than take further action, he'd better report back to Lou. Finally, he spoke.

"OK, asshole. That's enough for now. But if I need more, remember, I know how to find you."

"Yeah, sure, man. I ain't going nowhere—it's bad for busi—" Before Deuce could finish, Johnny blindsided him with a punch from his left fist—the one that wasn't pressed into Deuce's ribs. Deuce collapsed, his body sliding down the side of the car to the pavement.

Johnny calmly walked back to his car, barely glancing to see if anyone had observed. When he got in the car, he tossed the shorty screwdriver he'd been poking into

Deuce's ribs onto the passenger seat. After all, he knew enough to not openly carry a gun when it wasn't necessary.

Within fifteen minutes, Johnny Palmieri was relating his conversation with Deuce to Lou DiNova, who was sitting in the library of his home. It was on the main floor, just off the entrance hall of the large house. When necessary, it served as an informal office for receiving business guests. His real office, not surprisingly, was not in his home, but sometimes business matters spilled over into family life. Now, as he listened to Palmieri, he frowned.

"What do you think, Johnny? Do you believe the guy?"

"I don't know, Lou." Palmieri had known it would come to this, and he was reluctant to come to a conclusion. "The story squares with what we know, but he's a punk who sells crack—what's there to trust?"

"So he is." Lou paused, thinking about options. "My main concern is that we get this story off the front page. And if we found this guy, so will the cops. If he were to mention your visiting him, they might think we are involved. It's messy." He paused again. "Since he admits he was there, maybe that's good enough. I think you should have Mickey O'Donoghue pay him a visit tonight—for a more intensive interview. And tell Mickey that whatever answers he gets, he should ensure that this Deuce doesn't give any more interviews thereafter. But he should handle it discreetly. No body to be found. It should look like the guy skipped out of town. . . ." Having finished with the topic, Lou returned to the pile of mail on the table beside his chair.

Mike Langan was preparing to head home. It had been a frustrating day at the end of a frustrating week. With not much else to work with, he and Frank Dunn had gone to D'Agostino's, the wholesale grocery firm where Sanelli had worked. Though their earlier conversation with Sanelli's wife had not suggested any problems, there could still be a workplace link—a disgruntled co-worker, a bad debt that the wife didn't know about, or whatever. Sanelli had been a sales rep; his job was to visit grocery stores, taking orders and pushing various new products. His boss, Joe Almeida, had provided nothing surprising: Sanelli was easygoing and friendly, in the way that many salesmen are. There were no problems with anyone at work, and no complaints from customers. The only interesting bit of information was that Sanelli liked to gamble, and had been known to take an occasional afternoon off—unofficially, but nonetheless known by his boss—to go to the track. Langan remembered witnesses saying Sanelli had been celebrating some kind of big win and had bought rounds for the whole bar; the absence of cash in his wallet at the crime scene had suggested robbery as the motive. However, gamblers lose as well as win, and Almeida's comments raised the possibility of gambling debts to a loan shark. Whatever the truth, at least it was another lead to pursue.

Beyond the question of bad debts, nothing new had surfaced in the case. And even assuming that Sanelli had owed money to some bookie, the prospects were not promising. The actual killing would almost certainly have been done by hired muscle, and finding that person would not be easy, even if Langan figured out who held the debt.

The situation—limited crime scene evidence, and limited time for further investigation—meant the chances of closing the case were poor at best. With the pressure from above to focus on the L'Heureux case, time was running out. The reality was, the Sanelli murder was looking more and more like it was headed to open-unsolved, and Mike Langan hated the very thought of that happening.

Langan's mood might not have been so bad had he at least made progress on Danny L'Heureux's death. When the crime lab had turned up a partial fingerprint at the scene for Maurice Washington, Langan had been encouraged. While the weapon used didn't fit with your typical drug dealer, he was at the very least someone worth talking to—and that was posing a problem. Langan had talked to his contact in the drug squad, Tom Scofield, late yesterday afternoon, and Scofield had phoned him back just after lunch today.

"Hey, Tom, how you doing?"

"Usual, Mike. Too many of them, and too few of us to deal with it. Some days I think the whole fuckin' state is gonna zone out on drugs. . . ." Scofield's mini-rant faded to silence. "Anyway, that perp, Washington, you were asking about—his street name is Deuce. He usually works a few spots around Douglas Avenue, including the donut shop where that kid got knocked off. The killing doesn't sound like his style, but I thought it was worth grabbing him, in case he saw or heard something. Anyway, I've been asking my contacts, and he seems to be making scarce. At least, nobody admits to seeing him."

"So what do you figure, Tom? You think he's involved? Or was he at the donut shop at the wrong time, and now he's lying low?" As he spoke, Langan realized there was a third possibility. "Or is his making scarce nothing unusual?"

"I dunno, Mike. You know me—I got enough to handle with the obvious stuff, without worrying about what I don't know." Scofield paused. "I leave that stuff to you guys in homicide." Mike ignored the barb, and Tom added, "Anyway, I'll keep asking my snitches. Maybe he'll turn up in a couple of days."

"Thanks, Tom. I'd appreciate it. I'm getting real heat on this one." To Langan, it all represented another delay, another homicide case that was rapidly losing momentum—even as word from above told him to speed things up.

"No sweat, Mike. Enjoy the weekend!"

Langan hung up. Two cases, both going nowhere fast. A real shitstorm of a week. His frustration was starting to get the better of him, and he recognized it. *Fuck it—time to call it a day.*

On the way home, Langan drove by the Stop and Shop grocery store on Mineral Spring Avenue. Clare had phoned him mid-afternoon, asking him to pick up a few things. As bleak as his mood was, he knew it would only get worse if he failed to arrive with the items she had requested.

At just after five o'clock, the store was crowded with people who, like him, were stopping to pick up a few items on their way home after work. Standing just inside the entrance, he reached for his wallet to find the list he'd scribbled earlier. Among other items, he noticed Ragu spaghetti sauce and hot Italian sausages from the meat counter. Always thinking like a detective, Langan concluded they would be having spaghetti and sausages for dinner. This in turn made him realize that if he'd thought about it earlier, he might have been able to get a loaf of Italian bread from a bakery on Federal Hill during his day's travels. As he paused to review the list, he heard someone call his name.

"Hey, Mike!"

Langan looked in the direction of the voice, and spotted Charlie Bickert from the Pawtucket force just picking up two bags of groceries from a cashier's counter. Bickert was several years younger than Langan, but had been promoted to homicide a few years ago. In a large city force, he would have had to wait to make the transition, but Pawtucket was not a large city force.

"Hey, Charlie! Still eating regular?"

Bickert approached, juggling his bags in order to shake hands.

"Good to see you, Mike. It's kind of a coincidence, given our conversation the other day."

"Oh, yeah." Langan hesitated for just a beat, and then remembered their phone conversation, which had actually been more than a week ago. "You got that hit-and-run case, right? The one with the kid on the bike?" He paused again. "So, how's it going? Any leads?"

Bickert grimaced before answering. "I wish I could say we got the SOB. I mean, a nine-year-old kid . . ." Bickert looked away briefly, then turned his eyes on Langan again. "But hey, that's our job, right?"

"Yeah, Charlie. We go after the killers. And most of the time, we get them."

Bickert nodded. Truth was, he wasn't eager to dwell on the case. He left unsaid that they had no real leads. The only witness was a nearsighted old lady, and the paint chips found on the bike had just been matched to a 1986 Ford Tempo. A check with the manufacturer revealed that the color was the most popular choice for their best-selling model, and a cursory check of inventory records showed that about four hundred had been sold in southern New England. In short, the case was running into a dead end.

Rather than share all this with Mike, Bickert shifted the conversation. "What about you, Mike? Are you working that shooting that the press are calling a hit?"

"Yeah, I got that one." It was Langan's turn to grimace. "Lucky me." He thought for a moment. "Between you and me, it doesn't look like a hit, but the press is having a field day with it, and the mayor and the chief are both posturing like crazy. . . ."

"I hear you. It's about the same for my case." Bickert made a noise like a half-snort. The hostility both men felt about politics intruding on their work did not need to be voiced.

"Well, look, I've gotta run, Charlie. If I don't get home with the stuff Clare wants, I'm gonna be in worse trouble at home than anything at work!"

"Good to see you, Mike, and give my best to Clare."

"Will do, Charlie. You take care."

The evening TV news, like the day's newspapers, had little to offer. The donut shop death had dropped off the top stories, and so far there had been no response to his notes to either the reporter or Barton Jewelry. Sitting in his overstuffed armchair in front of the TV, he crumpled the not-quite-empty beer can in his hand.

What the fuck, he thought. *Is everybody in this friggin' state clueless?*

By now, he had expected more reaction. After all, there had already been three kills, including lots of media attention on the last one. Still, it seemed the cops weren't making the connection.

And what about Barton? He'd sent that bastard Cohen three notes, yet there was no sign he'd gone to the police or newspapers, or was even at all alarmed. *Not yet, anyway.* His lips set in a tight line, neither a grin nor a frown.

He was getting impatient, and that wasn't good. He believed in careful planning, not impulsive action, and impatience was not conducive to calm deliberation. He realized that it was impatience that had pushed him to send the first note to that reporter at the *Journal-Bulletin*. After he'd sent it, he'd had a couple of bad days, wondering if it had been a mistake. Eventually, though, he'd realized that it was probably a good thing—after all, that Son of Sam guy in New York had left notes, and the attention from the press had really created an uproar. Of course, he'd been nuts—a schizophrenic, they said—and that meant he was careless. The notes had ended up contributing to his capture. *That's not me*, he thought. *As long as I plan properly, it'll all go well. The cops are pretty clueless.*

In the end, he'd sent the second note to the newspaper, and would send more when the time was right—but always, always, carefully planned. The notes were a tool to be used, along with the killings, to achieve his goal of revenge.

Still, as he evaluated where things stood, he realized that he needed to keep the pressure on. So far, it had been easy. Almost too easy. What he wanted now was something more challenging. Remembering the kid's expression in the donut shop gave him an idea: The next one should be up close.

He went to the fridge and grabbed another beer, then sat down heavily in the armchair. Popping the tab on the can, he took a deep swig. *Yeah. Now I got it.* A self-satisfied smile formed. *This will get people worked up—and scared. Real scared.* His sense of frustration gone, he drank his beer while Johnny Carson finished his monologue.

When Carson finished, he turned off the TV, and went to bed, dreaming of the next kill.

EIGHT

Tuesday, May 5, 1987

THE WEATHER WAS perfect for May—sunny and mild, warm enough that some people were walking around in short sleeves. The pedestrian mall on Westminster Street was fairly busy, packed with a mix of midday shoppers and office workers who were going either to or from lunch.

Sam McIntyre made his way down the mall towards Mathewson Street, heading for the parking garage on Weybosset Street. In his early forties, he wore a dark sport coat and a blue Oxford shirt, but no tie. Physically, he might be called either average, or maybe nondescript—average height and a medium build, with dark brown hair. His one distinguishing characteristic was that he walked with a slight limp, the result of a childhood injury to his left leg that had never properly healed. Until the accident, McIntyre had nurtured dreams of playing pro basketball—he'd grown up in the era when relatively short white guys, like Bob Cousy of the Celtics or Vinny Ernst at Providence College, could make it in hoops. Still, he harbored no resentment or regrets. Real estate sales might not have the glamor of pro basketball, but he made a more than decent living.

McIntyre glanced at his watch: twenty to twelve, plenty of time to drive over to Thayer Street village for noon. As a real estate agent, he had the luxury of a flexible work schedule, and he didn't want to be late for his lunch with Sam Jr. It had taken too much work to repair their relationship after the divorce to want to jeopardize it by being late.

As he walked along, McIntyre was focused on the meeting with his son. Although Sam Jr., a sophomore at Brown, was living nearby, the reality was that father and son did not see each other regularly. The divorce between Sam and Barbara had been messy, and Sam Jr. had been thirteen when they first separated—not a great age for it to happen. Now, six years later, the relationship with his son was getting better, though that might be due simply to Sam Jr. maturing rather than McIntyre's attempts to reconnect. In any case, it still wasn't easy, and Sam hoped the lunch would go smoothly. Their mutual interest in basketball always made for a safe topic; asking Sam Jr. about school could be tricky, depending on how things were going at that particular moment.

Preoccupied with these thoughts, McIntyre did not notice the figure following him as he turned from Westminster onto Mathewson, heading towards the parking garage. The fact that he'd been followed since the pedestrian mall, moving slowly because of his limp, hadn't registered at all. Even if he had noticed the other's presence, it likely would not have been cause for concern—after all, it was midday, and Providence was not Detroit or the South Bronx. He entered the garage, walking up to the second floor.

Like McIntyre, the figure behind him knew that most people in Providence felt safe going about their business in broad daylight. That attitude of casual obliviousness made it easy for him to close the gap as McIntyre approached his car and paused, groping in his jacket pocket for the keys to his Oldsmobile. Just as he was pulling out the keys, McIntyre became aware of someone coming up behind him. He started to turn, but the person was a few inches taller, making it easy to reach around McIntyre's left shoulder, clamp a gloved hand over his mouth, and pull him backwards, off-balance.

At almost the same instant, the other hand came across from the right, bearing a large hunting knife. The razor-sharp blade sliced across in one long motion, severing McIntyre's left jugular vein and carotid artery, his vocal cords, and the corresponding blood vessels on the right side of his throat. Blood gushed outward, spraying the side of the Oldsmobile, and McIntyre felt himself dragged to the ground beside the car. He lay there, bleeding out, his severed vocal cords rendering him unable to scream or call for help. As the attacker walked away, McIntyre was already losing consciousness.

The assailant moved about five cars away from where McIntyre lay and slowly looked around in a full circle. Most cars on this level belonged to all-day parkers working in nearby stores and offices, so the odds of someone coming along at this time of day were low. Still, the risk existed—and it added to his pleasure in the up-close kill. He had been monitoring the scene as he and his victim entered the garage. If anyone else had been in sight, he would have walked away—there were plenty of other potential victims in the area. He'd observed McIntyre checking his watch on the pedestrian mall, and noted his small stature and his limp—both good indicators for a vulnerable target. Now, satisfied that he had not been observed, he pulled off his windbreaker, which had blood from the victim on the sleeves, and stuffed it in a bag along with the knife. He then walked out of the parking garage, suppressing a satisfied smile. He headed down Mathewson toward the *Journal*'s office on Fountain Street. Time to drop off another note.

Hopefully this one will get that reporter's attention.

As Sam McIntyre's life ebbed away, Stan Osiewicz was in the *Journal*'s morgue, researching Barton Jewelry. He had always thought it odd to call a newspaper's archives a morgue, as if stories died after publication. During his years of writing, he had encountered many usages that reminded him of Shakespeare's old phrase, "What's in a name . . .?" In some cases, he didn't agree that the alternatives smelled as sweet—and "morgue" was definitely one such case. Regardless, whether called a morgue, archive, or whatever, the files were the first option when a reporter was looking for background information.

Stan had already talked to the *Journal*'s business reporter, Larry Jenkins, earlier that morning. In contrast to Stan, who usually wore a sport shirt, and occasionally a blazer, Larry Jenkins typically dressed in a suit and tie. While not elegant, he looked well-groomed, especially by journalistic standards. When approached at his desk, Jenkins had responded to Stan's query about Barton Jewelry in a perfunctory way, giving the basics off the top of his head.

"Well, Stan, there's not much to say. Barton's a private company, family-owned, so nobody really knows their numbers. By all appearances, they make a good profit. Costume jewelry in general has a good markup, and their Twisty watchbands are huge sellers, available in every jewelry and department store in the country, as well as internationally." Larry paused, searching his mental filing system for more. "The family are socially prominent but not splashy. They're big givers to several charities, but pretty conservative and buttoned-down. Typical old money types."

Larry paused again, but this time he was thinking, not remembering. "But what's up, Stan? Why's Barton got your interest? You got an angle on something?" The word "criminal" went unstated.

Stan waved off the queries. "Oh, nothing, really. I got a note bad-mouthing the company, so I'm just curious. Figured I'd check them out, and asking you was the easiest way."

The two men eyed each other for a long moment, not speaking. Finally, Jenkins said, "Well, hope that helps. If you get anything for my beat, let me know." He turned back to his computer and his WordPerfect document.

Inwardly, Stan felt both relief and anxiety. Based on what Joe Houle had said, he figured he could probably keep the story, regardless of Larry's possible interest, but misleading colleagues was not a great career move. If the notes he'd been getting did lead to a big story, he was going to have to give something to Jenkins.

Now, in the paper's archives, he first checked for material on Barton Jewelry. There was a file folder with clippings from old stories; none of it provided much more detail than Larry had given him. One story did mention an issue related to toxic waste: There had been a brief shut-down of production at Barton a few years earlier when the company that handled their waste had gone on strike. Nothing suggested that Barton had acted at all improperly; no fines were levied and, in fact, the company seemed to have handled it in a way that was beyond reproach. Overall, nothing in the clipping file suggested a source of trouble.

With no obvious leads, he thought about the possible motives behind the notes he'd received. The main options were revenge and altruism—for example, a disgruntled employee (present or former), business partner, or competitor might be seeking payback. Alternatively, maybe someone either inside or outside the company wanted to raise an alarm about unethical or unsafe practices. Based on the clippings and the comments by Larry Jenkins, neither the company nor the family seemed a likely target for revenge. So, what about a whistleblower? Could there be a safety issue, like mishandling of toxic chemicals? The story about the work stoppage suggested that chemical wastes were significant in costume jewelry production, but Stan realized he knew very little about the topic. Given the limited leads to pursue, he decided he should at least find out more about the processes and chemicals involved. Stan decided it was time to talk to Gene Chu, the paper's science reporter. Even if Chu didn't know much about the details, he might be able to give Stan the name of a suitable contact.

Back up in the newsroom, Stan sought out Gene Chu before heading to his own desk. Since it was early afternoon, his timing was good. He found Chu at his desk, which was situated by a south-facing window—a perk he had earned because of his long years at the *Journal*. (In contrast, Stan's desk was still in the middle of the large open area of the newsroom shared by most reporters.) At the moment, Chu was staring out the window.

"Hey, Gene, got a moment?"

Chu looked away from the window, focusing on Stan through his owlish glasses. His straight hair, which had tinges of gray, was cut long—not exactly hippie-style, but longer than was typical. He had a slight build and looked a bit disheveled--pretty much what you might expect of a science guy.

"Oh, hey, Stan." Chu looked up to focus on him. "Um, yeah, I can spare a minute. What's up?

"Can you tell me anything about costume jewelry production? You know, like the chemicals involved and any pollution issues?"

"Costume jewelry?" Chu stared out the window, as if the answer might be written on a billboard across the street from the *Journal* building. “Um, I don’t know a lot, but it’s basically a combination of metal fabricating and electroplating. Generally, they use cheap metals for the base. Stainless steel would be pretty common. Then they plate it with something else—maybe chrome, or silver or gold for the fancier stuff. In general, you need acid to clean the surface before you plate the metal, to get a good bond, and then various solutions depending on what the base metal is and what finish you want to apply. The basic concepts are pretty standard chemistry, but the details can vary—again, depending on what you’re using.” These comments came out in an unbroken stream. Chu was a true science nerd.

“Oh. Interesting.” Stan said the word without much feeling, as a sort of socially expected response. He paused to absorb the information. “So, if you’re using acids and whatnot, is the stuff toxic?”

“Well, sure. I mean, it could be. Lots of stuff could be. Even household cleaners can be toxic if you mishandle them. Mix bleach and ammonia, and you end up with cyanide vapors that can kill you.” Chu paused to consider. “So, what’s with all the questions? You think some jewelry company is poisoning people?” Like Larry Jenkins, Chu knew Stan’s area was crime, so asking about the technical details of making costume jewelry seemed odd.

“Actually, I don’t know. I got an anonymous note saying a jewelry company was killing people, and Joe said I should check into it a bit. My guess is it’s just a crank, but I figured you could give me a bit of context on how things work.”

"Christ. You're looking at a Mafia hit, and he tells you to check out a crank letter?" Chu rolled his eyes, then looked sharply at Stan. "But you never heard me say that, right?"

"Right, Gene." Stan moved off towards his own desk, glad to end the conversation without more questions from Chu. He liked the guy, but like most reporters, Stan wanted to keep control of his stories.

As he sat down at his desk, Stan let out a heavy sigh. He was frustrated that between talking to Jenkins and Chu and the time digging in the paper's morgue, he'd spent nearly half a day, but had no tangible progress on the Barton story. What little information he'd gathered hadn't shed any real light, so he was no closer to understanding either what the notes meant or the motivation of the sender. His gut told him that everything was connected, but he wasn't clear how. *There's something going on*, he thought. *I really don't think the notes are from a loony tune. I'd better go over to Barton and see if I can find a link. Otherwise, the way things are going, Joe's gonna shut it down before I figure out what's happening.*

He was about to get up and leave when he noticed an envelope on his desk. As soon as he saw it, his mind went to full alert. It was a generic letter-size white envelope, and the block letters in black marker were the same as the two previous notes he'd received. He stared at it for several seconds, then turned it over. As expected, the flap on the back of the envelope was sealed, but there were no markings.

Stan used his pocketknife to cut open the flap. Unlike the previous notes, this one was not on a sheet of typing paper. Instead, someone had printed on a paper towel with a cheap ballpoint pen. Like the writing on the envelope, the slant suggested it was done by someone left-handed. In addition to the change in format, this message was more specific than the others: "Another person is dead because you've been too slow to make the connections. Barton Jewelry's been making a killing. Now it's my turn."

Like the previous note, it was signed, "The hand of justice."

Stan's mind started racing. *Another killing? Why hadn't he heard about it?* In addition to having a scanner to listen to police calls, Stan regularly paid a small sum to someone in dispatch at the police department to give him a heads-up on interesting calls. Doing so wasn't technically illegal, and it sometimes helped him get a jump on stories. He thought about this for a minute, and then it struck him: "Now it's my turn."

Was the note writer claiming he'd killed someone? And did that mean he was behind the L'Heureux shooting too? Suddenly, this felt like much more than crank messages.

Stan Osiewicz was not the only one getting more concerned about cryptic notes. Later that afternoon, Henry Cohen was sitting at his desk, staring at the fourth note he'd received. Like the others, it had come addressed to him personally, with no return address. Like the earlier notes, his secretary, Joan Davis, had passed along the envelope unopened. If she was curious, she kept it to herself. Having worked for Henry Cohen for over fifteen years, she understood his boundaries and preferences.

The latest note, like the earlier ones, had been created with newspaper letters arranged and pasted on a partial sheet of newspaper. However, where the earlier notes had been cryptic, albeit progressively more threatening, this one seemed very explicit: "Your time is up. The next casualty will be your company."

Cohen thought about the wording and what it meant. It seemed evident that the writer's intention was to destroy Barton Jewelry. But how? Create a scandal? Or something even more destructive, like a toxic spill? And equally important, why? Frustratingly, none of the four notes he'd received gave any indication of motive.

The previous week, after the prior note, he had contacted Sean Parker, the chief of the Providence Police. Sean was a decent cop, but like many people in such positions, he'd risen to chief more on his political instincts than his job record—in his case, it was his Irish-born social skills. After listening to Cohen, he'd tried to reassure him that it was all probably the work of a crank, someone who disliked Cohen or the company, or maybe both. Henry Cohen was not reassured, and made it clear he wanted something done about the situation. Parker, not one to ignore the expectations that went with Cohen's social standing, then offered to take action.

"Look, Henry, how about I have someone pick up the notes, and I'll have the crime lab take a look? They might turn up something like fingerprints. And if not, we can discuss what more to do, if you're still concerned. And Henry—don't worry. We'll do whatever's necessary."

Cohen agreed, and the next day, a patrol officer had picked up the notes, sealed in an envelope addressed to Chief Parker. To be prudent, he had photocopied the notes before handing them over.

Now, faced with the new note, his first impulse was to phone the chief again. However, he sensed that the chief's response to the previous call had just been window dressing. He suspected that even if the notes made it to the crime lab, they were unlikely to be a high priority, especially with all the news about a Mafia hit. Instead, he decided to talk to Ed Underwood again.

"Joan, can you ask Ed Underwood to come see me? Thanks." He hung up the phone and sat down, staring into space. *I hope Ed has some ideas. This is getting me worried.*

Ten minutes later, Ed Underwood was seated in Henry Cohen's office, looking at the new note, along with the photocopies of the previous three notes. His first reaction, like Henry's, was that the latest note expressed a more direct threat, though it was still somewhat cryptic.

Underwood shook his head slowly. "I don't know, Henry. This is certainly disturbing, but I don't much insight to offer." He paused to reflect. "Maybe if I were a clinician, I could tell you more, but my background is more organizational than clinical. Have you considered looking outside the company for guidance?"

Cohen nodded. "I already have. After the third note, I contacted Sean Parker, the Providence police chief. We know each other socially, so I thought he would be helpful."

"And what did he say?"

"I got the sense that he thought it was a crank, and basically harmless. However, for the sake of our relationship, he said he'd have the crime lab look at the notes." Cohen frowned slightly. "I don't expect much from it."

"Well, I have a friend at Rhode Island Hospital who's a clinician. I could show him the notes."

Cohen shook his head. "No, I don't want more people involved at this point." He paused. "If somebody is serious, who could it be? Do you think it's a current or former employee? Maybe somebody we fired?"

Underwood thought about it. Being in charge of personnel, he was certainly in the loop in terms of employee issues. "I guess it's possible. Let me look at the files and see if I find any concerns." He looked out the window, thinking. "But it might not *be* somebody connected to the company." He looked back at Cohen. "What about someone outside? A supplier or customer?"

"We try to do business on the fair and square. I'd be surprised if it were one of them." Cohen paused. "Besides, if somebody were upset enough to start making threats, I think I'd hear about the problem more directly. You know how things work in the company, Ed. Do you think it could happen without me knowing?" He looked directly at Underwood, a questioning expression on his face.

"No, I agree, it doesn't seem likely. I'm just trying to consider the possibilities." He looked again at the latest note, and was startled to realize he'd overlooked something. "Um, Henry, did you notice this? It says the company will be 'the next casualty.' Doesn't that mean there have been others?"

Cohen grabbed the note and read it again. He'd missed the significance of the word "next." "Oh, God, Ed. What the hell is going on?"

Equally puzzled, Underwood replied, "Could it mean other companies? Is this some kind of serial blackmailer?" He searched his memory for something similar. "It's not quite the same, but do you remember the Tylenol incidents about five years ago?"

"Wasn't there something about cyanide being put in bottles of painkillers?" Cohen's memory was vague on the details, but he remembered it causing a lot of public alarm. "But what's that got to do with us? Nobody's ever died from our jewelry."

"No, that's true. But as I recall, the authorities decided it was an attempt to destroy the company, though they never caught the person responsible." Underwood thought further. "It probably doesn't mean anything. But just in case, do you want to hire more security people for the plants?" He hesitated, and then added, "And do you think you should look into some kind of arrangement at home?"

Once more, Cohen shook his head. "No, not right now. Since we're really not sure about anything, I don't want this alarming our employees." More emphatically, he added, "And I certainly don't want to alarm Emily or the girls." Barton had two daughters, both in college, but nearby enough that they were frequently around. Free food and laundry are hard for most college students to resist. "For now, we'll just see what develops."

Underwood started to rise. "I'll look into the employee angle and let you know as soon as I can, Henry."

"Thanks, Ed. I know I can count on you."

It was about three-thirty p.m. when Mike Langan saw Francie Weber walk into the homicide area. Francine, known as Francie by nearly everyone, was the only female homicide detective in the department's history. A few years younger than Langan, she was stocky, almost butch, and not given to feminine niceties. In his view, she was smart and mentally tough. This was not surprising, given she'd made it to her current position in a department not known for treating women kindly. Weber gave as good as she got, and he knew she was a good detective, able to sort through the often-conflicting leads in a case. On his bad days, he wondered if she was actually better than him.

"Hey, Francie, what's up?"

"Hey, Mike." She nodded towards him as she sat down, dropping her notepad on her desk and reaching for a new binder. "Got a dead guy in the Weybosset parking garage." She paused, thinking about it. "Looks like maybe a mugging that went wrong—really wrong. The killer slashed the guy's throat almost from ear to ear. The ME says the guy bled out in moments. He was probably dead before he hit the ground."

"Christ." There were days when even Langan found the human capacity for violence hard to comprehend. "Who was the victim?"

"A real estate agent named Sam McIntyre." She looked at her notepad. "Age forty-three. According to his driver's license, he lived on the East Side. I still have to find out about family and work."

"So it happened in the parking garage?"

"Yeah, on the second level. We found him next to his car. The keys were on the ground beside him and we ran the plate number."

"Anybody see anything?"

"Not that we know. I put a couple of patrolmen to work canvassing the area, but at noon, it wouldn't be surprising if no one else was on that level of the garage. It's mostly all-day parkers. I'm betting the perp came and went on foot. Funny thing, though—there was lots of blood, including spray on the side of the car, but no bloody footprints going from the scene. I have to talk to the lab guys to see if they have any ideas, but it looks like the attacker handled it to not get sprayed." Weber grimaced. "Anyway, it's too early to sort the puzzle. Too many pieces still missing. Right now, I've gotta track down the guy's family, if he had any."

Langan nodded without saying anything further. He'd been through the beginnings of more new cases than he could count. It was always exciting, with the possibility of putting a killer away and, in the process, providing some sense of justice. He knew that any homicide had more than one victim; family, friends, even people who simply lived near the scene were always impacted. And unlike the deceased, they still had to go on, and try to make sense of what had happened.

At the moment, Langan had his own cases to deal with, and he wasn't making headway on either of them. He'd run out of leads on the Sanelli case, and it was looking more like a crime of opportunity than anything premeditated. The guy had no known enemies, and he had been bragging about his winnings at the track. Contrary to what Langan had speculated, he didn't seem to have gambling debts, either to the mob or to acquaintances. So, it could well have been a robbery. Given the lack of physical evidence and the absence of witnesses after two attempts to canvass the bar, the odds of solving the case were decreasing. Langan knew it would soon be classed as open-unsolved. It wouldn't be his call, and he hated when it happened, but it wouldn't be the first time. *Or the last*, he thought, scowling without even realizing it.

The L'Heureux case, it seemed, was headed the same way. Langan had called Tom Scofield a couple of times, but no one seemed to have seen Maurice Washington since the day after the donut shop shooting. Langan had tracked down his address in the University Heights project, but no one answered. At this stage, with his fingerprints the only evidence, there wasn't sufficient probable cause to get a warrant to search his place. In any case, even if he were the shooter, Langan doubted they'd find the gun on the premises—drugs, probably, but not the gun. No dealer with a rap sheet like Washington's was going to be stupid enough to take the gun home. The question now was, why had he gone missing? If he was the shooter, he might be on the lam. While possible, it didn't fit with his priors. Had he seen something and gotten scared, or had somebody gotten to him? Of course, if the shooter or someone connected to the shooter had gone after him, who should Langan be looking for? Despite the newspaper headlines, he doubted the killing had been a mob hit. Even so, given the lack of other leads, maybe it was time to pursue that angle. Tomorrow, he'd pay a visit to Lou DiNova, who ran the Mafia in Rhode Island.

At five o'clock, Ed Underwood left his office at Barton and headed for the *dojo*. Following habit, he took Route 95 up to Smith Street, and then cut across to get to the *dojo*'s location on Mineral Spring Avenue. Somewhat surprisingly, rush-hour traffic through town was not too bad, and he made the trip in just under a half hour.

The evening class would not start for another fifteen minutes, but as he entered the changeroom, Ed could hear Yoshikawa-*sensei* talking to a student in the main training area. As always, his voice was calm, but nonetheless conveyed intensity. "Johnson-*san*! You are doing the *kata* with your head! Let go and allow your body to do the movements!"

It was a familiar refrain. Too many students tended to intellectualize their actions, trying to use their mind to direct, and control, what they were doing. The difficulty was that the mind was always too slow; instead, training required doing movements repeatedly, until they could be executed as a reflexive process. To Ed, it was like a piano performance: In some pieces, the sequence of notes was too fast to be executed by thinking of each one separately; instead, they had to be practiced until they could be done smoothly without direct control. This concept was familiar to Ed from his study of psychology. Still, like Johnson, he sometimes struggled to put it into practice in his training.

As he put on his *gi*, he recognized that he was still thinking about the conversation with Henry Cohen. The latest note was both puzzling and disturbing, and Ed realized that he was concerned about the risks to Henry's family. Though the writer's threats were directed at the company, not Henry personally, the impulses that drove such threats could not always be assumed to follow a clear path. He decided he should speak to Henry the next morning and again urge him to consider some form of security.

Now, as he stowed the last of his clothes in his gym bag, his mind shifted to the class ahead. He bowed as he entered the training area, and any further thoughts of the outside world were dismissed—at least for the moment.

Approximately an hour and a half later, Ed was putting on his shoes by the door of the *dojo*. As he tied the laces, he glanced at his watch, which indicated twenty past seven. *I should be able to get to Liz's place by quarter to eight. I'm glad I told her not to expect me till eight.* With a start, he realized that his mind was already shifting back into mundane mode before he had even left the building. He smiled ruefully, chagrined at how quickly the everyday set of mind returned, but he was also grateful for the respite he had experienced during the training session. He recognized that, lately, his focus had been pretty inconsistent—a problem Yoshikawa had noticed. After the previous workout, and again in an aside during today's session, Yoshikawa had tried to explore the issue, but Ed gave only an awkward denial. Yet, despite his response to Yoshikawa, Ed was struggling. "Detachment" was a fundamental Zen concept, involving both acceptance and letting go—but for Ed, living that way outside the *dojo* still tended to elude him, even after years of training. That realization triggered a further worry. *If I don't get on top of this, what will Yoshikawa do?* Unsure of the answer, he called out his ritual goodbye and left the dojo.

The drive across town to Liz's house on the East Side was uneventful, and the trip actually took a few minutes less than Ed had estimated. When he rang the doorbell, he was greeted by Karen.

"Hi, Ed! How are you?" As she opened the door, she leaned toward him to kiss his cheek. As always, Karen was in high-energy mode. Although in her late twenties, she sometimes seemed like an exuberant teenager.

"Hi, Karen. I'm pretty good. How are things for you?" Inwardly, he recognized that his words were more superficial than honest—another reflection of his mental state.

"Great, thanks. I'm just on my way out to meet some friends. We're going to VanAllen's—they're supposed to have a good band tonight." She grinned broadly. "Oh, that reminds me—I need to ask Liz about borrowing some jewelry." She turned away and headed up the stairs, but paused halfway to call down, "Make yourself at home. Liz will be down in a sec!"

Ed smiled and answered, "Not to worry, Karen. I know my way around. And tell Liz she doesn't need to rush!"

He made his way to the kitchen, where the cooking aromas put his tastebuds on alert. Liz had a busy teaching career and did not routinely cook, but when she did, the results were usually well beyond ordinary. Tonight, Ed picked up the scent of Middle Eastern spices—cumin and cinnamon, and others he couldn't immediately pick out. Just as he was about to open the oven to investigate further, he heard footsteps behind him.

"No peeking! You're just going to have to wait to find out, Ed!" He felt Liz's arms wrap loosely around his waist, and her mouth nuzzled the back of his neck. He turned around and their lips met in a lingering kiss. "Mmm, nice to see you too!" Liz laughed throatily and broke the embrace. "Now, make yourself useful. There's a bottle of red on the counter. You know where the corkscrew and glasses are, so hop to it, and I'll get the food out!"

Not long after, they were seated at the table in the dining room, a classic early-century design with dark oak wainscoting and large windows on two sides. Liz had sometimes talked about painting the wood to brighten up the room, but thus far, she hadn't been able to bring herself to cover up the beautiful oak grain.

Once the food and wine were placed at the table, they touched glasses and sipped the wine, which was a full-bodied Australian shiraz. The aromatic main course turned out to be leg of lamb roasted in a Middle Eastern style; it tasted as good as it had smelled when Ed first entered the kitchen. They ate the first bites with little conversation, a tradition they'd developed in the first year of their relationship. It reflected the awareness that both worked, and often one or both needed a bit of time to decompress at the end of the day. There would be time enough for conversation later.

As the meal progressed, they began chatting about the events of the day. Liz had been teaching a studio course in the afternoon, and commented on how various students were either progressing or struggling. The names meant little to Ed, but he understood the importance of sharing. In turn, Liz recognized that Ed's *karate* training was often a more significant part of his day than the routine work of human resources. Consequently, he seldom had much to say about work. Today was different.

"Liz, do you remember my mentioning some notes Henry Cohen got?"

"Of course, Ed. Is there something new?" Liz's expression showed a combination of curiosity and mild concern. In her experience, it was not like Ed to hold on to work issues once he left the office. Instead, he seemed to embrace the Zen story about a monk and his pupil who meet a woman at a river crossing. Hours later, the novice is still thinking about her—but the master tells him he should have dropped his thoughts of her when they left her at the river.

"Well, Henry Cohen called me in again. He's gotten two more notes." He paused and ate a couple of bites of lamb, uncertain how much he wanted to say. It wasn't because he didn't trust Liz—she was the bedrock of his life—but because he didn't want to worry her.

"He's gotten two more notes, and while they're still vague, they've become increasingly threatening. The latest one, which came today, actually says the writer is going to destroy the company." He took a long sip of wine, letting Liz process his words.

"What do you mean?" Liz was stunned. "Like bankrupt it? Ruin their reputation? Or what?"

"That's the thing, Liz. The notes don't say exactly what, or why." Ed took another drink of his wine and reached for the bottle to top up the glasses. They had more or less finished their plates, and Ed didn't really have the appetite for seconds.

"Well, surely you have some idea? I mean, you said there are several notes. Don't they give some clue?"

Ed shook his head. "That's just what Henry was asking me. Somehow, as a psychologist, I'm supposed to know what it all means." He sipped at his wine and looked away, caught up in memories. "You know me, I gave up on the clinical stuff while I was still an undergrad. Trying to assess people's mental states and emotions always seemed too vague and ambiguous."

"Come on, Ed, don't be so intellectual! What does your intuition tell you?"

Ed shook his head, frowning. "I'm trained to focus on evidence, not opinions. And I don't see much to go on in this situation." He looked at her, half smiling. "You're the creative one. What do you think?"

"I think you're living too much in that big, smart brain of yours and trying to avoid admitting that you have intuition too." She smiled back at him. "But OK, I'll bite." She sipped at her wine, and her eyes dropped as she thought, trying to come up with possibilities. "Well, clearly somebody has a grudge. Maybe someone who got fired?"

"Yes, Henry and I talked about that, and I'm going to look into it. So what else?"

"Maybe a customer? Somebody who felt cheated somehow."

"I think that's a stretch, Liz. I mean, we make costume jewelry. Can you imagine someone getting this upset over a ten-dollar piece of jewelry?"

Liz nodded. "No, probably not. I certainly wouldn't. But what if it's a crazy person? You know, somebody who's paranoid and thinks the company is ruining their life?"

It was Ed's turn to nod in agreement. "Interesting idea. But if it is somebody who's paranoid, maybe someone with schizophrenia, I don't think we've got any simple way to look for them. I mean, their actions are going to be unpredictable, almost by definition."

"So? That doesn't mean it's impossible, right? What's the old line? 'Just because you're paranoid doesn't mean somebody isn't out to get you'?"

"Sure, I know. But I don't think Henry would find it helpful if I suggested there's some random psycho out there who's writing these notes. I know *I* sure as hell wouldn't want to be in that position." He looked away, thinking about the implications. "OK, let's leave that one aside. What other possibilities can you think of?"

Liz sipped her wine and was silent for several moments. "Well, what about somebody who sees themselves as morally justified in hating the company?"

"Huh? I don't follow you. . . ."

"You know, somebody who's decided the company is evil and that destroying it would be a good thing. Maybe an environmental crusader who thinks the company is dumping toxic chemicals into the Providence River. Or someone who thinks costume jewelry is all vanity and the work of the devil. I mean, like you said, this kind of anger isn't rational, so why should you assume the reasons make sense?"

Ed smiled. "That's why I admire you—you think of things I can't even imagine!" He reached across the table to take her hand and gave it a gentle squeeze.

"OK, Ed," Liz answered, smiling. "Flattery will get you nowhere, at least until we get the dishes cleared. . . ." With that, the topic of notes and psychos was closed for the night.

The late-night news carried a story about the death of a real estate agent in the Weybosset parking garage. As was typical, they cut to a reporter standing outside the garage entrance, which was cordoned off with yellow crime scene tape. TV demanded visuals, even if they added no information.

As he watched the report, the killer shook his head. He didn't know whether to be happy that the cops obviously had no leads, or angry that the killings weren't drawing the right attention. Even with the note he'd dropped at the *Journal* after the attack, there was still no mention of Barton. *What's wrong with that fuckin' reporter? Why isn't he talking about the notes?* While enjoyable, the attacks were really intended to get people afraid, and then convert that fear into anger against the jewelry company. He wanted everyone to be as angry as he was. Then he could get the revenge he deserved.

Well, it'll happen. I'll make sure it happens.

NINE

Wednesday, May 6, 1987

STAN OSIEWICZ ARRIVED at Barton Jewelry at ten a.m. He had called first to set up a meeting about "the history of the company and the costume jewelry industry in Rhode Island." When he arrived, he was directed to the office of the company's advertising manager. Apparently, the company thought he would be the best equipped to deal with the press.

Horst Kleinburg appeared to be only a few years older than Stan but had a pronounced paunch. His blond hair was thinning, and he had a habit of running his fingers across the top of his head when he was ill at ease, as if having his hair in order would also put the world in order. His desk was covered with various piles of paper, as well as what appeared to be layouts for future magazine ads. He stood to shake hands as Stan was ushered into his office by a secretary.

"Nice to meet you, Mister—er, how do you say your name again?"

"It's OK, just call me Stan." He tried to put on an ingratiating smile. The truth was, he alternated between resenting people's mispronunciations and wishing his parents had simplified the family name.

"You know, I've seen your stories in the *Journal.* You seem to be good at getting the facts." Now it was Kleinburg's turn to be ingratiating. "But what can I do for you? Your request for a meeting got passed to me, but frankly, I don't know how I can help you."

"Oh, it's pretty straightforward. I'm doing a piece on the costume jewelry industry in Rhode Island—how it developed, how it's important to the economy, things like that."

"Well, yes, costume jewelry is a big industry here and, of course, Barton is one of the bigger players. We're a second-generation, family-owned business and proud of it. Proud of our growth. You know, our products are advertised in several national magazines, and we've even started a campaign to promote our Twisty watchbands on TV. Maybe you've seen the ads?"

"Um, yeah, I think I have." Stan wasn't interested in their advertising. He just needed a smoke screen to try to cover his real interest. Unfortunately, he sensed that Kleinburg was not likely to have the kind of information he was looking for. "The company seems to be on a roll. But tell me, Horst—you mind if I call you that?—tell me a bit about yourself. I like the human side of things." He paused just long enough to make eye contact. "Have you been here long, for example?"

Kleinburg nodded several times. "Actually, you came to the right person if you want human interest. I started in the shipping room, working part-time while I was in high school, and gradually worked my way up to advertising manager." He nodded again and smiled. "The company believes in developing its employees. Most senior people have worked their way up, including the president, Henry Cohen."

"Oh, really?" Stan gave an ironic smile. "I thought he became president by marrying the boss's daughter."

"Oh, sure, he married Emily Barton." Kleinburg was now frowning and his hand involuntarily combed through his hair. "But it's not like you're suggesting. I don't know the whole story about how they met—it was before I started working here—but believe me, you won't find anybody in the company who doesn't think Henry deserved to become president!"

This remark prompted another line of thought for Stan: maybe somebody *didn't* think Cohen deserved to be president. Being passed over could breed a lot of resentment. He made a note to check this angle. For the moment, though, he moved on to other topics.

"Well, it sounds like you can be proud of your achievements, Horst. That's quite a story."

The advertising manager nodded silently, relieved to move away from the topic of nepotism.

"Tell me, Horst, do you know much about the production process? Like, is everything designed in house? And what about how the jewelry is manufactured? Does it take a lot of silver and gold, for example?"

Horst frowned again. "Um, I don't really know much about those things. I know the designs are done here.

It's a very competitive business, costume jewelry. If one company comes out with something that's a big hit, others rush to produce something similar. So design stuff is very hush-hush. In terms of production, all I can say is that when I worked in the receiving department, I used to have to sign for materials—you know, sometimes we'd get whole truckloads of things! But as for gold and silver, you have to remember, costume jewelry is meant to sell at a low price. Often there's no gold or silver at all, or at most it's plated. Chrome is more common."

"I see," Stan said, pretending that this was highly informative. "Wow, I didn't realize. So, how does this plating work? What's involved? Is it dangerous or anything?"

"Gee, Stan, you got the wrong guy!" Kleinburg laughed. "I know there are a bunch of chemicals involved and we use a lot of electricity, but if you really want to know about that, I'd have to get somebody from the production plant!"

"Oh, that's OK. But maybe I could do that later, if the story needs some further background." Stan pretended to make some notes on his pad, but realized he wasn't going to get much from Kleinburg. After a few more dead-end queries, he moved to close the conversation. "I think I've got enough for now." He shook hands with Kleinburg. "Thanks for your help."

He exited the office, mulling over the nepotism angle and how he might dig deeper on it.

Shortly after Stan Osiewicz left, Horst Kleinburg was in Henry Cohen's office, describing the meeting with the reporter. He knew Cohen well enough to realize that word would quickly reach him about the visit, and he felt he should be proactive in providing the information. As he expected, Cohen's secretary was not surprised to see him and ushered him in with little hesitation.

Cohen rose from his desk as Horst entered. "Hello, Horst. Good to see you." In the normal order of things, the two men did not regularly meet. For routine matters, Cohen was not particularly hands-on in overseeing operations. Instead, he preferred to employ people he trusted and let them do their jobs.

"Hello, Henry. Thanks for seeing me." Kleinburg shook his hand and, taking a cue from Cohen, sat down in a large wing chair in front of the desk.

"I hear you had a visitor from the *Journal* today?" Cohen expressed it as a question, but Kleinburg realized Cohen already knew.

"Yeah. He said he was doing a story about the costume jewelry industry in Rhode Island and knew we were a big player, so he wanted some background." His brow furrowed as he thought about it. "The thing is, I don't buy it. I think he was after something else."

"Oh? What makes you say that?"

"Nothing direct . . . I mean, he asked about the history of the company and that kind of thing, even wanted to know about my background, how I started in the stock room and all." In relating the interview, however, he carefully chose to omit the discussion of Cohen's ascent to the presidency and the reporter's comment about marrying the boss's daughter. *No point in stirring up mud*, he thought.

"Then what makes you think he was after something else?" Cohen's instincts suggested the reporter's explanation was bogus, but he was curious about what had led Kleinburg to be suspicious.

"Well, for one thing, the guy's not a business reporter. I've read some of his stuff and he mostly does stories about crime. In fact, I saw a piece he did last week about some Mafia hit." His brow creased again. "What's a guy like that doing writing a fluff piece about the jewelry business?"

"Good thinking, Horst." Cohen was pleased that Kleinburg had not simply taken the interview at face value, given who was asking the questions. "So, what do you think he really wanted?"

Klienburg ran his hand through his hair, reflecting his discomfort with the query. "I dunno." He frowned, his brow furrowing deeply. "I mean, this is a good company, we both know that. So I don't really see what kind of dirt he could be after." While a loyal employee, Horst was not a deep thinker. "Maybe he's got us mixed up with somebody else, like that outfit in Warwick that got fined last year for dumping stuff in the sewers."

Cohen understood the reference: another costume jewelry company, a smaller outfit known to sometimes cut corners, had been the subject of scrutiny after they were found to be spilling waste into a river, including a witch's brew of heavy metals, acids, and other toxic by-products. While they hadn't been put out of business, the charges laid against them had led to a temporary production halt and the largest pollution fines in the state's history. Barton Jewelry had always operated well within the regulations, but Cohen knew pollution was becoming a hot-button issue for both the public and politicians.

"You may be right, Horst." Cohen rose to end the conversation. "In any case, I appreciate you filling me in. If you think of anything else that might be significant, please let me know."

After Horst Kleinburg left, Cohen reviewed the situation, thinking about whether the reporter's visit was somehow related to the notes he'd received. He remained frustrated that the notes were so vague, but pollution fears could be a reason for someone to target a leading company in the industry. If so, he wondered if the reporter's visit had been triggered by notes sent to the *Journal* as a way to apply more pressure to Barton. The reporter had given no indication of this, but as Horst had commented, Osiewicz's justification for the visit seemed implausible. *Are the threats becoming more public, as well as more intense? And what's the motive?*

Cohen sensed that an already worrisome situation was about to get worse.

Stan Osiewicz arrived back at the *Journal* offices and sat down heavily at his desk. He was becoming frustrated: so far, he had made no real progress on either the notes or Barton Jewelry, and Joe Houle would soon pull the plug on his inquiries. Stan admitted to himself that he had nothing solid, but his gut told him there was something big going on, and he had always trusted his instincts.

The problem was, the situation didn't make sense—why make vague claims and threats to a newspaper if you had a grudge you wanted addressed? Why not say what the problem was? Stan took out the file folder holding the notes he'd received and reread them, looking for something he may have missed.

"If you think it's a hit, you're missing the point. Look for connections to Barton Jewelry." Clearly, the first note was referring to Stan's coverage of the Danny L'Heureux killing, suggesting his theory of a mob hit was wrong.

The second note made no reference to the L'Heureux killing, but instead suggested a link between Barton Jewelry and other deaths. "People have been dying and more will die. Barton is to blame." What other deaths? Even if Barton was somehow responsible for L'Heureux's death, who were the others?

The third note again talked about Barton and made no reference to L'Heureux's death. "Another person is dead because you've been too slow to make the connections. Barton Jewelry's been making a killing. Now it's my turn."

After getting the third note the previous afternoon, Stan had wondered about the reference to "another death," and also the last sentence: "Now it's my turn." When he'd received the note, he'd had trouble connecting it to anything—but then he'd gotten word of the death of Sam McIntyre in the Weybosset parking garage. At first glance, it looked like a robbery gone wrong. But what if it wasn't? Was the writer claiming responsibility for McIntyre's death?

Stan thought about recent events—both the notes and the two unsolved deaths in Providence in the past week. Though the details of each case seemed very different, it was unusual to have two deaths in the city in that period of time. If one excluded auto accidents and domestic violence, it was even less likely.

Could the two deaths be related? And did the person sending the notes know something, or were they involved? Could the notes be from the killer?

As he followed this train of thought, Stan suddenly found himself sitting bolt upright. *Son of Sam!* Though he'd never worked on the case, Stan remembered it vividly: Roughly ten years ago, New York City had been hit with a rash of murders by a killer who left notes at each scene. Eventually, he was identified and caught, but not before killing six people and wounding seven more. The nickname "Son of Sam," used by both the police and the news media, came from the signature used on the very first note. The notes taunted the police, with the first note saying, "Please inform all the detectives working the case that I wish them the best of luck."

Arguably, the publicity around the notes had terrorized people nearly as much as the killings. The killing spree had gone on for nearly a year, mostly targeting young women with long brown hair tied in a ponytail. When the killer, David Berkowitz, was eventually caught, it was because of a fluke, not direct evidence. While looking for leads, the police had traced a parking ticket for a car spotted near a crime scene, leading them to Berkowitz's home address—and to their shock, he confessed. Berkowitz had suffered from paranoid schizophrenia, and in his confession, said that his neighbor's dog, whom he called Son of Sam, had told him to commit the crimes.

The bizarre rationale for the deaths, and the associated notes, made Stan wonder about the notes he was looking at. The ranting against Barton Jewelry and the repeated references to killing seemed, for want of a better word, crazy. *Was the sender another Son of Sam?* As he thought about the two cases, he suddenly remembered that, in addition to leaving notes at the crime scenes, Berkowitz had written to New York crime reporter Jimmy Breslin.

If someone was now writing to him at the *Journal*, did that suggest there were other notes the Providence police hadn't revealed publicly? He knew he had too little information to be certain, but he thought the parallels needed to be explored. If it was a similar case, it meant the stakes were high for both the public and the police—and the paper could be right in the center of it. But checking it out would require more time.

And that would require convincing Joe Houle.

Ten minutes later, Stan Osiewicz was sitting in Joe Houle's office. As always, the editor's desk was covered with various piles of paper, and Houle himself wore an expression suggesting his patience was strained. His brow furrowed and he looked away, pondering what Stan had been saying.

"So, you're saying there's some kind of nutjob loose in Providence who's killing people, and that he thinks Barton Jewelry is forcing him to do it?" The way he spoke suggested Houle was more than a little skeptical.

"Well, that's oversimplifying, but yeah, Joe, I think the notes and the two recent deaths are connected, and that it's probably somebody who's crazy, likely someone who's got paranoid schizophrenia. They hear voices and things—hallucinations—the same way David Berkowitz was driven by his delusions."

Houle frowned and reached for his bottle of antacid tablets—never a good sign—but Stan pressed forward with his argument.

"I mean, the notes don't make sense, and neither do the two recent killings. I admit, I thought the L'Heureux thing looked like a hit, but there's nothing to back it up other than the method of killing. If it wasn't a hit, there's no indication of motive." Stan hurried on before Houle could cut him off. "And the guy who was killed yesterday—the cops are speculating it was a robbery gone bad, but think about it: The guy's throat was slit from ear to ear, there was no sign of a struggle, and the wallet wasn't taken. I mean, does that sound like a screwed-up robbery to you?" Stan hadn't done the story on McIntyre's death, which was a bit of a sore point for him, but he didn't want that to become the focus in talking to Houle, so he resisted commenting on it. "And the timing of the notes—this last one talks about killing and 'my turn,' and it came at almost the same time McIntyre was killed. He either had it planned when he sent the note or it's the weirdest coincidence in this whole situation." Stan paused to gauge Joe's reaction.

"OK, I follow you. But coincidence doesn't make proof. If we run a story about anonymous notes and a possible crazy killer, and you're wrong, we're gonna get hammered. Never mind the possibility of Barton suing." Houle fingered the antacid bottle, which was still in his hand. "The cops will freak out, the publisher will get a call from the mayor complaining about creating a panic, and you and I will both be out of work."

"But Joe, what if I'm right? Don't we need to do something? I mean, this guy's reaching out to us, and if we just ignore it, aren't we partly to blame?" His eyes looked away, absorbed in an unwelcome memory. "I can't help remembering that high school kid in Pawtucket. Nobody knew what was going on until he got caught for the third murder. It wasn't till he confessed that anybody even realized the three cases were connected." Having covered the case, the memory was still both vivid and unpleasant for Stan. While it had given his career a boost, the details continued to leave him unsettled.

Houle was silent for a long moment. He hadn't been editor at the time, but remembered the story clearly. It was unlikely that anybody living in Rhode Island back then had forgotten the case.

"We're not the cops, Ozzie, and we're not psychiatrists." Despite his objections, Houle had switched to using Stan's nickname—a good sign. "I'll tell you what. You've got a contact who's a psychiatrist, right? Show him the notes, see what he thinks. And at the same time, you talk to the homicide guy who's running the L'Heureux case, and you let him in on your theory and the notes." He paused, looked out the window, and then looked directly at Stan. "You do that, and if they don't blow you off, then you give me a draft of a story. Say something about 'possible links between two recent deaths in Providence' without mentioning the notes directly, and definitely don't say 'serial killer.' If I like it, we'll go with it and see what happens after that." Houle gestured with his hand, as if shooing away a fly. "Now get out of here and let me do some real work."

Stan nodded and uttered a quick, "Thanks, Joe," and dashed out the door. He had a lot to do.

Mike Langan was at his desk going through the binder on Rico Sanelli's death once more, trying to see what he might have missed. After three weeks, he was no closer to finding the killer and had no leads. It was beginning to look like the case would become one more open-unsolved file, which meant neither Langan nor anyone else would actively work it—and Rico Sanelli's family would never receive justice or closure. For Langan, every unsolved case meant some perp was still out there, free, and maybe killing again. It pissed him off, and he hoped he never got to the point that it didn't piss him off.

It was in this dark mood that the front desk sergeant rang him, saying there was a reporter from the *Journal-Bulletin* asking for him. He gave the name, and Langan gave a grunt. Stan Osiewicz. He'd been following the L'Heureux case, and that was almost certainly why he was here now. Langan briefly considered saying he was on his way out and didn't have time. Still, with the political heat the case was drawing, he knew there would be blowback if he tried to dodge the meeting. Grudgingly, he told the sergeant, "OK, tell him I'll be down in a minute."

The encounter in the lobby of the department was uneasy for both men. Stan knew Langan both by sight and reputation and thought he was a pretty good cop, but also knew that under most circumstances, Langan had little use for the press. However, these were not ordinary circumstances: Stan had information to share that could put a very different light on the L'Heureux case. At the same time, he needed support from Langan to convince Houle his theory was right.

"Detective, thanks for taking time to see me." Stan extended his hand and received a firm but cursory handshake in return.

"Yeah, well, you got lucky with your timing." Langan inclined his head to the right, indicating that the reporter should follow him upstairs to the homicide department. As they walked, both men refrained from making small talk. Once upstairs, Langan sat down and gestured to the wooden chair beside his desk.

"So, I'm guessing you're here about the L'Heureux case." It was a statement, not a question.

"As you may know, I've been covering it for the paper. Awful thing—just a kid."

"Yeah, I know. Your stories have got everybody from the mayor on down in an uproar." Langan frowned. "But from where I sit, every homicide is awful. I just do my best to get the assholes responsible."

Stan winced. He understood the pressure that Langan must be feeling, and the resentment it caused. He also agreed that all murders were terrible and all killers deserved to be caught.

"I hear you. And I'm sorry my stories are bringing political heat. I know that doesn't solve cases."

"You got that right." Langan looked briefly away, uncertain where this was going.

"Look, I'm not here to waste your time. And I won't bother asking if there are any new developments. I assume if you have anything to share, you will." Stan paused, knowing the next few sentences he spoke could be critical. "I think I've got some information that might help you." He let that hang in the air for a moment.

Langan stared at him for a long moment, wondering what the angle was. "Oh, and what would that be?"

"We both know the MO looked like a Mafia hit—the small caliber pistol, the single shot to the back of the head—and that's what I said in my stories." He paused again. "But I think I got it wrong, and I have information that might lead in a different direction." Langan's eyes momentarily widened but he said nothing, just looked intently at the reporter.

"From what I know, there's nothing to connect the kid to the Mafia and no obvious motive for them to kill him. In fact, it's the opposite—I can't see the mob wanting the attention or the political heat that something like this draws. I think we both know that whatever else he may be, Lou DiNova isn't stupid, and he keeps tight control of his operations."

"Maybe so." Langan nodded briefly and fixed his gaze on Stan. "But tell me something I don't already know."

Here goes, thought Stan, and involuntarily took a deep breath. "I think it may be something else entirely. This killing may actually be connected to one or more others—including the parking garage murder yesterday."

Langan stared at him, his mental wheels spinning in high gear. Finally, he spoke. "You got something, or you just blowing smoke 'cause your last pet theory was a bust?"

"No, hear me out, please." Stan's tone and expression suggested he was serious, that he really believed what he was saying. "Suppose that there's somebody out there killing people, but it looks random. How would we even know, if the MO keeps changing?" He hesitated. "Remember that case in Pawtucket? Everyone thought the first two women were just missing until the kid confessed when he was questioned about the third murder."

Langan grimaced and his head dropped as he remembered. It had happened when he was first starting in homicide, and it was in Pawtucket, not Providence, but every cop in the state knew about the case and the failures to connect the dots. "Yeah, nobody picked up on it, but even so, his MO was always multiple stab wounds and always female victims. You trying to say the L'Heureux and McIntyre cases look the same? 'Cause I ain't buying it. A hit and a robbery don't sing the same song."

"I know, I know, it sounds hard to believe." Once again, Stan paused. "But I've recently received some notes that have me thinking differently."

"Notes? What kind of notes?" Langan stared hard at him. "What the fuck are you talking about? You withholding evidence of some kind?"

"To be honest, I don't know if it's evidence or not." Stan had copies of the notes with him, but he wanted to lead Langan through his theory rather than just turn them over to the detective. "You see, in the past week, I've gotten two anonymous notes. Are you familiar with Barton Jewelry?"

Langan nodded. "So?"

"These notes made vague allegations of wrongdoing by Barton, along with claims that people were dying because of something Barton did or was doing."

"You trying to tell me you think somebody at Barton killed these two guys?" Langan rolled his eyes.

"No, no. At first, I thought it was some kind of disgruntled customer or anti-pollution activist." Stan looked directly at the detective. "I tried to check it out, but it didn't make any sense—that is, until I got a third note yesterday. That one talked about being a killer, and it was delivered at roughly the same time McIntyre's body was found."

Langan stared at the reporter for several moments. Finally, he said, "Lemme see these notes. I'm not saying I'm buying it, but if I decide there's something in it, you better make sure you're giving me everything."

Stan opened his briefcase. "These are copies. The originals are safe, and of course we'll turn them over if they're subpoenaed. Right now, I'm just trying to shed any light I can on these deaths." He looked at Langan. "You may think I like murders, because they sell papers. But the truth is, I like to see cases solved. Knowing there are killers walking our streets brings me no satisfaction, personally or professionally."

"Uh-huh." Langan's attention was on the notes. He shuffled through the Xeroxed pages, with their assemblies of pasted letters. "Well, I can see why you didn't rush down here after the first two notes. They certainly look like the work of a nutjob, somebody who's pissed at Barton." He reread the third note. "You say this one arrived yesterday, around the time McIntyre was killed?" He shook his head. "Even if I believe he was talking about killing McIntyre, that still doesn't tie it to L'Heureux."

"I realize that, but why send these notes? And who did kill Danny L'Heureux? We know that the Son of Sam killer in the nineteen-seventies wrote messages that initially didn't make sense. How do we know that's not what this is?"

Langan was still dubious. "You probably know more about those cases than I do. And we both know there are sickos who have committed multiple murders. I'm no science major, but I still believe that old notion that the simplest explanations are likely true. From what I can see, we're dealing with a misguided Mafia hit and a would-be robber with a really sharp knife." He waved the notes and looked at Stan. "You leave these and I'll look into it, but right now, I'm not buying your theory." He paused and stared at the reporter. "And if you're thinking of drumming up newspaper sales by talking about some kind of serial killer, you better think twice, or you could be the one in the slammer for inciting public panic."

Stan nodded in what he hoped was a conciliatory way. "I understand, Detective. And please believe me, I'm more concerned with getting at the truth of these cases than I am with selling papers." He looked back at Langan, matching his gaze. "I hope I'm wrong. But answer me this: If there is a serial killer out there whose MO is random, how would we know?" He left the question hanging as he got up and left.

Stan was thinking about his own last question as he drove to Rhode Island Hospital to meet his psychiatry contact. While meant as a challenge to Langan, the question resonated in Stan's mind. A random killing could be seen as an intellectual puzzle, but someone commiting a series of such killings posed a worrisome threat to the whole community. As a reporter, he wanted to be the one to break the story, and as a person, he wanted to escape the fear that the concept of a lurking killer evoked. Shaking his head, he forced these dark thoughts away from his mind and turned on the radio as a distraction. *Can't let it get to me, or I'll be the one needing a psychiatrist!*

Dr. Heinrich Brandt had an office on Blackstone Boulevard, where he met with mostly wealthy private clients, and an office at Rhode Island Hospital, where he was chief of psychiatry. He was also an adjunct professor at Brown University. As Stan waited in the doctor's outer office in the outpatient wing of the hospital, he glanced around at the decor. There were a couple of framed documents—whether diplomas or awards was unclear from this distance—and a couple of cheap landscape paintings, done in a style that suggested they were likely chosen to be soothing, not as high art. There was a receptionist's desk, but now, at five-fifteen p.m, it was vacant. Stan had called in advance to set up the meeting, and soon Brandt emerged from the inner office.

The psychiatrist was about sixty, tall, a bit heavyset, with graying hair and a well-groomed salt and pepper beard. He looked exactly like what most people imagined when they heard the word "psychiatrist." Brandt came forward, smiled, and extended his hand. "Hello, Stan. Nice to see you again."

"Good to see you too." Stan avoided using a name, never certain whether to use "Heinrich" or "Dr. Brandt." Over the past ten or so years, he had contacted the doctor as a consultant on three or four occasions. In each case, he had come away with useful information. "I appreciate that you agreed to meet me on such short notice."

"Well, it's the end of the day, and my wife will understand if I push back dinner by twenty minutes!" He smiled, pleased at his own remark—the kind of light jest he made frequently, mostly to put patients at ease. "You said you needed some advice for a story?" As he spoke, he ushered Stan into the inner office, where they sat in well-upholstered leather armchairs. There was a couch and desk as well, but this was not a therapy session.

"I do. You see, in the past week, I've received three anonymous notes at work and I'm not sure how to interpret them."

"Someone is threatening you?" Brandt furrowed his brow in an expression of concern.

"No, no. Nothing like that, though the notes do make threats against a prominent company. It's like they think the company is criminal."

"I see." Brandt paused. "May I see them?"

"I've made copies," Stan replied. "But of course this is all confidential. I don't want the newspaper to be sued or anything." In his mind, "anything" included "my story idea being leaked."

"Of course, Stan. I'm a psychiatrist, I understand confidentiality." He looked at Stan directly. "Or do you feel I've failed you in the past?"

"Oh, no, not at all. You've always been really helpful!" Something about the older man's demeanor always made Stan feel slightly defensive, as though all his inner thoughts were on display. "I just need to say that, to protect myself." *Shit—not the way I wanted to say that!*

"That's fine, Stan. No offense taken." Brandt briefly smiled again. "So, can I see these mysterious notes?" The reporter handed over the copies, and the psychiatrist looked carefully at each one, then went through them again. He looked at Stan quizzically. "I assume you gave them to me in the order you received them?"

"Yes, that's right."

"And how did they reach you?"

"They were dropped off at the paper's offices. I tried tracing their arrival, but didn't get anywhere. The second one seems to have been given to a kid to drop off, but I don't have any leads on the kid or the sender."

"I see. Did you happen to keep the envelopes?"

Stan was briefly surprised by Brandt's question. Langan hadn't asked about either the delivery or the envelopes, and Stan wondered whether that reflected a lack of insight, or maybe a lack of interest.

"Uh, yeah, I still have the envelopes, but I didn't think to bring them. Just the copies of the letters."

"Mm-hmm. Well, maybe later they would be useful in telling us more." Brandt read the three notes again and looked up. "So, what are you thinking? Why have you come to me?"

"Well, my first reaction, when I got the first two notes, was that it was just some crazy—you know, somebody with paranoid ideas or just letting off steam. But the third note, when it says, 'Now it's my turn,' has me worried that there's something more serious going on." He paused to think about how to phrase it, aware that the conversation with Langan had not been exactly smooth. "I think this person is threatening to kill—and maybe already has, at least twice."

"A scary thought." The phrase was spoken in the tone Brandt used when encouraging a patient to face their fears. This wasn't therapy, but the mannerism was a professional habit. "Do you want to know what I think?"

"Please."

"Well, I don't think you're dealing with someone with schizophrenia or other form of psychosis. The sender is not incoherent, just somewhat elliptical in the meaning." He again read through the three notes. "In addition, the first two notes were assembled from newspaper letters. That takes deliberate planning and a fair amount of effort. Someone with poor impulse control would not do such a thing."

Stan nodded. "I hadn't thought about that."

"Sometimes, the meaning is in the medium, as Marshall McLuhan said!" Brandt smiled at his own wordplay.

Stan nodded again. He'd heard the name before but wasn't sure who McLuhan was. "So, if it's not somebody psychotic, what do you think is going on?"

"It's clear this is someone with a lot of anger—rage, even. The person has clearly fixated on Barton Jewelry as a focus of their anger, but it's not clear why. It's even possible that Barton has very little to do with the real source of their anger—what we call displacement."

"So, does that mean it's all hot air, that there's no real danger?" Stan was half hoping that was true.

"No, I didn't say that. I said that it's not clear what the origin of the anger is, not that the anger isn't real." Brandt paused, thinking about how to explain it. "You mentioned you thought the sender was a potential killer, and you mentioned schizophrenia. I immediately thought you saw this situation as being like the Son of Sam case in New York."

"Yeah, I admit that came to mind."

"Well, David Berkowitz was caught and it became clear that he was suffering from paranoid schizophrenia." Brandt looked upward, as if reading a report on the ceiling. "But there are several crucial differences. First, Berkowitz left his notes at the scene of each killing. They were handwritten, scrawled in the moment, and it was clear that they were as much a plea for help as a form of intimidation."

"So you're saying this is different?"

"Berkowitz was driven by impulses he could not control. These notes were clearly premeditated."

"What tells you that?"

"Consider the first two notes. The sender went to considerable effort to compose, produce, and deliver them. There is a clear intention to drag Barton into the situation, which seems preplanned. The first note links Barton to the first killing, and the second says the company is linked to other deaths."

"But what about the third note? The handwritten one?"

"That concerns me. The anger is becoming more intense, and also more focused. The change to handwritten suggests a greater sense of urgency. What is unclear is whether that is driven by a concern about Barton or by some other source of emotion."

"So, does that mean the person is suffering some kind of breakdown? Could they be on the verge of going psycho?"

"Well, first, 'going psycho' isn't a useful clinical term." Brandt smiled, pleased once again at his own turn of phrase. "The real question is what sort of mental dynamic is driving the behavior. It's clear that all three notes convey a sense of confidence, of superiority. In terms of content, they make assertions without any attempt to justify them. The third note directs a put-down to you, complaining that you're not smart enough to understand what is happening."

"Yeah, I noticed that," Stan said, without offering further comment.

"The degree of planning and detailed execution, the strong desire for control that is manifested, the attitude of superiority—none of this is consistent with paranoid schizophrenia." Brandt nodded almost unconsciously, about to deliver the key point of his lecture. "I think you're looking at a person who is highly intelligent and self-centered, and who feels unfettered by the normal standards of society—in short, a sociopath."

"Is that like a psychopath?"

"Well, yes. 'Psychopath' is regarded as an outmoded term today—too much baggage in its past usage—but the core characteristics are basically the same."

"So, not a Son of Sam type?" Stan was almost relieved. Better two unrelated murders than a random killer on a rampage.

"No, not a David Berkowitz. But if you want my gut feeling about what's going on, I'd say it's more like the Zodiac Killer in California back in the sixties."

"The Zodiac Killer? I've heard of him, but I was too young to really know about it when it happened."

"Well, I haven't reviewed the case details in some time, but basically there was a series of killings in northern California, mostly around San Francisco. The killer sent notes to area newspapers, taunting police to catch him. It's not clear how many people he killed. The police confirmed at least five deaths and believed two more were connected, but the notes claimed there were actually thirty-seven."

"Thirty-seven? That's unbelievable."

"Yes, the police thought so. There was no obvious pattern to the choice of victims—they were men and women, of various ages—so it was hard to be certain whether other deaths were the work of the same killer or not. But the notes were clearly both carefully planned and arrogant. Each note contained a portion written in code, along with the claim that if all the codes could be decrypted, it would tell the police who the killer was."

"And what happened? Did they solve it to catch the killer?"

"The coded message, as it was eventually interpreted, had a number of misspelled words—whether actual errors or defects in the code decryption is unclear—and talked about 'harvesting slaves for the afterlife.'"

"Well, that sounds pretty psychotic. And was the killer schizophrenic?"

"Nobody knows." Brandt frowned. "The notes stopped and so did deaths that were presumed to be related, but the killer was never caught." He paused to let that sink in. "As a psychiatrist, I've studied a number of cases of sociopaths, and even encountered a couple in my practice. More than once I've tried to interpret the Zodiac case. In my mind, either the killer was himself killed, maybe during an attack, or else he tired of taunting the California police and moved on to something else, somewhere else."

Stan tried to absorb it all. "So, this guy sent letters to newspapers, killed multiple people without any obvious pattern, taunted the police, and then just disappeared?"

"In essence, yes."

"Shit." Stan felt like he had just fallen off a boat mid-ocean, drifting in a storm-tossed sea of questions. "You know, the same day I got the third note, a guy was killed in a parking garage downtown. When I read the phrase 'now it's my turn,' I started wondering whether that wasn't just a coincidence. You see, I've also been working another story, a killing that looked like a Mafia hit, but it didn't make sense as a hit."

"Yes, I saw something in the paper last week."

"So, is it possible that the note writer killed both victims, but isn't directly saying so?"

"In this world, I've come to think almost anything is possible, Stan." Brandt rubbed the bridge of his nose with his thumb and forefinger, suddenly tired. "But if it is a sociopath who has started killing, and the victims don't follow an obvious pattern, then it's very possible that there have already been more than two, and that there will be more. If that is the case, potentially no one is safe." He continued to massage his nose, then looked up. "And I'm not sure I would even know how you might identify them. My only thought would be, try to encourage more communication and hope it reveals something."

"Yeah . . ." Stan thought back to his earlier conversation with Langan. Brandt had been helpful, but Stan was now more worried than when he arrived. Doing a story wasn't a concern, as he thought he'd be able to convince Joe Houle to run something. But if a sociopath was behind the recent deaths, who or what was going to stop the killer?

The shadowy figure who was now the center of Stan Osiewicz's concerns had his own worries. He'd expected more reaction to the previous day's killing, After all, it had taken place in the heart of downtown Providence in the middle of the day—could it be any more public? True, there'd been coverage on last night's news and a story in the evening paper. But they were just calling it a random robbery gone wrong, and by this morning's paper, it was buried in the back pages. Even the latest note to that reporter hadn't drawn any reaction, despite saying he was going to kill somebody. *Does the guy need a billboard to get the message?* Sitting in his chair, he crumpled a not-quite-empty beer can, causing a few drops to splash out. Cursing, he got up, threw it in the trash, and sat down again.

OK, calm down now. Getting pissed isn't going to do the job. Planning, that's the key. He mentally reviewed the steps ahead that would lead to the big event. Some details still needed work—he was not about to wing it on that one. In the meantime, he needed to get more public reaction, to stimulate fear. Right now, people didn't know what was happening, and without that, there would be no blowback on Barton. For that, he needed publicity from the newspaper, so he had to do another note to that reporter, dense as he was.

For this note, he would go back to the pasted-letters format. In thinking about it, he'd decided the handwritten note was too risky and impulsive, even though he'd used his left hand. *Risk and impulsiveness are my enemies.* At the same time, the attack on that guy downtown had felt good—being so close, right up against him, as his throat opened up and his blood—his life—flowed out. The adrenaline rush had felt great, and the risky location, if anything, had made it even more exciting. *I gotta be careful of that. The rush is fantastic, but if it makes me careless, it's not worth it. . . .*

He thought about what to do next. It would have to be public enough to get media attention and scare people, but not as risky as the last one. As he reviewed the previous attacks in his mind, it suddenly hit him—he hadn't picked a woman yet. So, where would he find a woman target in a place that was public but not really crowded? He sat thinking for several minutes, and an idea slowly formed. *Yeah, that's it; that should be perfect.* He smiled to himself, satisfied that he was thinking clearly again, and went to the refrigerator for another beer.

TEN

Friday, May 8, 1987

ON THURSDAY, AFTER recapping his meetings with the police detective and the psychiatrist, Stan Osiewicz had gotten approval from Joe Houle to run a story suggesting a new angle on the recent murders. Consistent with his prior comments, Houle had placed constraints on what could or couldn't appear in the piece. In the end, the headline in *The Evening Bulletin* read, "Are recent violent deaths in Providence connected?" Stan reported that the newspaper had received information suggesting that the deaths of Danny L'Heureux and Sam McIntyre were connected. The story went on to state that the details had already been shared with the Providence police. There was no mention of what type of information was involved, nor any mention of a serial killer being responsible. The short piece was really a trial balloon, to pique the interest of the public while waiting to see what the official reaction would be.

Now, the day after the story ran, he was meeting with Joe Houle once again.

"Well, I'll give you this, Ozzie, your story has really raised a shitstorm." Houle absentmindedly reached for an antacid tablet. "I've had the publisher, the mayor, and the chief of police all burning my ear."

It was obvious that Houle did not like getting political pressure, but the use of "Ozzie" suggested that, at some level, he was pleased with the story. Controversy could sell papers, and the publisher was only concerned that they had the goods to back up the story. Houle had assured him that there was indeed additional information in hand. He also noted that an outside expert who had reviewed the information had suggested that connecting the two deaths was plausible—a reference to Stan's conversation with Dr. Brandt. Now the question was, what to do next?

"I know, Joe. Even though we didn't come straight out with it, people can read between the lines, and I'll bet most people are thinking that if there's two murders, maybe there's more." Left unsaid was the fact that this was precisely Stan's intention when he did the piece.

"So, when you saw that detective on Wednesday, he didn't seem to buy it, but said he'd look into the idea, right?"

"Yeah, that's what he said, anyway."

"So maybe it's time to follow up with him." Houle looked toward the window beside his desk, though his mind was not focusing on the view. After a long moment, he turned back to face Stan. "See if you can get a read on his thinking." They both knew Langan was still likely to hold back most information, given that the two killings were under active investigation, but he might be open to a bit of quid pro quo. "I spoke with the legal department and they've said we can run the notes, so maybe tell him we're planning to do that in tonight's paper and see how he reacts." Releasing the notes would draw more public interest and likely increase speculation about what was happening—and put more pressure on the police department.

"And what if he won't cooperate?"

"Well, there's a public interest angle to all this. We'll run another story tonight—with or without his help."

Mike Langan was at his desk, trying to deal with both the cases themselves and the political heat Thursday's story had generated. In his gut, he still thought the two murders were unconnected, but he also realized that the L'Heureux case was going nowhere from the angle of a Mafia hit. The only person of interest they'd identified—suspect was too strong a word at this stage—was the drug dealer, Maurice Washington. Despite several efforts, they'd been unable to track him down. At the moment, Langan wasn't sure if this meant he knew something and was lying low, or if he had seen something and had now been removed from the picture by the actual killer.

He'd also checked with Francie Weber about the McIntyre case. She'd told him the autopsy revealed that McIntyre's throat was cut with a large, non-serrated knife—something with a razor-sharp edge, given the depth of the wound and the lack of tearing at the edges. The killer had come from behind, and the cut was from left to right, indicating a right-handed person. The attacker was probably someone a couple of inches taller than the victim, and strong enough to control the victim's head with one hand while he sliced with the other hand. The slight upward angle of the cut suggested that McIntyre had been pulled backwards against the killer's body. The slash had likely come before the victim could realize what was happening, let alone recover his balance or defend himself against the attack. Once the blood vessels were cut, death from blood loss would have been swift, and the slashing of the vocal cords would have made crying out impossible. A quick, if nasty, way to die.

"So, apart from how McIntyre was killed, what do you think, Francie? What about motive?"

"Right now, it's hard to say, Mike." Francie Weber was a good detective, and she seldom jumped to conclusions. "McIntyre's wallet was still in his coat, and his car keys were on the ground beside the body. It looks like he was about to get in when the killer attacked him." She paused, as if mentally reviewing the file. "If it was a robbery, something or somebody spooked the killer, because the money and all was still there. But if I had to guess, I don't think it was a robbery. A robbery would have meant some interaction, and the victim wouldn't have been facing away like he was. You'd also likely see some signs of struggle, maybe defensive wounds on the hands. The scene looked like the killer just came up from behind and attacked without warning."

Langan thought about this. Both detectives had handled enough homicides to be familiar with a range of scenarios. "So, if not a robbery, then somebody who was out to kill? Any leads?"

"We're doing the drill, trying to talk to family, friends, and so on to see who might have had motive. But we've only had a day to work on the leads, and so far there's nobody that looks good for it. He was divorced, but the ex-wife and son both say it was pretty amicable. I don't think she's part of anything."

Langan hesitated, and then decided to ask the question that was likely on both their minds after seeing Thursday's paper. "Do you think it's connected to the L'Heureux case?" Langan hadn't yet told her about the notes sent to the paper but had shared that information with Lieutenant Briggs, the head of the homicide unit.

"I don't know, Mike. Other than the fact that both murders seem like they were unprovoked, I don't see much connection. You tell me."

"Right now, Francie, I don't know. I wish to hell I did. It would maybe make both our jobs easier."

Weber nodded. She headed back to her desk, adding, "Let's share what we find; maybe something will point to a link."

Mike Langan was definitely feeling pressured on the L'Heureux case. The word had come down from the mayor, the chief, and Lieutenant Briggs: Solve this thing and get it out of the news. He didn't really care about what the news media said, but solving this case—or any case—was what drove him. At the moment, he didn't have to handle the McIntyre case, but if that reporter, Stan Osiewicz, was correct, he might soon be dealing with both. Lacking any clear link, he decided to check with the state police, to see what their crime reporting section had to offer.

Calling state police headquarters in Scituate, Langan was connected to Constable First Class Andy Chow. Chow was assigned to administrative duties, tracking crime statistics and related matters. A computer geek by background, he was an oddity in the state police—physically small, introverted, and, most significantly, non-white in an organization that was not known for diversity. It wasn't clear why he'd applied to join the department, or how he'd passed the physical, but his race and computer skills had, apparently, contributed to his hiring. The current chief was trying to bring the department into the modern era in terms of both personnel and procedures. In the chief's mind, a geek could help with introducing computerization to the department's recordkeeping and being Asian would help with the department's white-bread image.

Langan had never met Andy Chow and knew nothing of how he'd arrived at his position. All he really cared about was what information Chow could offer.

"Constable Chow, this is Detective Mike Langan of Providence PD."

"Hello, Detective. Uh, you can call me Andy."

"OK, Andy. Call me Mike." Pleasantries aside, Langan cut to the issue. "Look, Andy, we've got a couple of homicide cases that don't add up, and we're trying to figure out if there's some pattern we're missing. I thought you might be able to help."

"Um, sure, if I can. But what do you mean, pattern?"

"That's the thing, we don't see one. But we've had a source suggest they're connected." Langan preferred to reveal as little as possible; it wasn't a matter of not trusting

Chow as much as an old habit. He never liked other jurisdictions poking into his cases.

"Gee, that's a weird one." Chow paused, evidently thinking. "Usually you connect cases because of suspect descriptions, or location, or the MO. Do any of those match?"

"Actually, no. We don't have a suspect in either case. They happened in different parts of the city, and there was a different cause of death in each. So what else could we look for to indicate a pattern?"

"Huh. You sure there is a connection?"

"If I was sure, I wouldn't be calling." Langan was starting to think the call was a waste of time. "Look, let's say there's some kind of psycho loose and he's randomly killing people. How could we tell?"

Chow paused again. "Well, sometimes there are common factors that get overlooked. What you need to do is track everything so the pattern stands out from the noise."

"Can you explain that?"

"Well, to give you an example, there are people starting to record all the details of violent crimes in a database, which can then be searched for commonalities and patterns. I was at a conference recently where a Mountie from Canada talked about a system they're developing. It lets them track, for example, areas where armed robberies are occurring in order to increase patrols and identify suspects. He called it the Violent Crime Linkage Analysis System, or ViCLAS. Apparently it's helped spot patterns nobody noticed."

"Interesting." It was—but Langan wasn't sure how it could help him right now. "Does your department have a system like that?"

Chow laughed ruefully. "I wish. We don't even have our current files on computer yet. I told the chief about it, but I'm not holding my breath on when we might move on it."

"Got it. So, what can we do right now?"

"Well, if you're looking for somebody doing random killings, some type of serial killer, then I guess the first thing is to figure out how many cases you're looking at. I mean, you're the homicide guy, but I'm guessing some random killer would boost the number of murders occurring."

"Yeah, that makes sense." Langan was thinking. "We've had two recently—and maybe a third—in Providence." He was starting to wonder if the Sanelli case was linked. "Is that unusual?"

"Well, if we look at the whole state, in the last few years there've been about thirty-five homicides a year. So that works out to about three per month. If you're saying there have been three in Providence . . . What's the time period?"

"About three weeks."

"Well, that might be a little high. Of course, we're ignoring what's been happening in the rest of the state."

"Right. I only know what happens in Providence. Do you have information on the rest of the state? Like homicides in nearby locations? Maybe just over the city line?"

"Mike, I wish I could help." Chow sighed. "The reality is, I don't even know what's been happening in your department, let alone elsewhere."

"How come? I thought your job is collecting crime data."

"It is, but the current processes are a mess. Every department collects their own stats and they don't always share them with us on a timely basis. And even if they did, with the paperwork involved, it could be months before we get the information and put it together. I mean, even the FBI's crime reporting, which is supposed to be standard across the country, is not always consistent, and it can take a year to get released."

"Shit." Langan knew how screwed up paperwork could be in his department, but he'd never thought about how such things could affect getting the bigger picture. In many ways, he didn't care—for him, homicide was always particular, and the generalities didn't matter. But in this situation, he could see how it could hamper his investigation, and he didn't like it. "OK, Andy. So you're telling me I should be looking to see if there's an abnormal number of murders, but you don't have any information to help me."

"That's about the size of it, Mike. Wish I did."

"Well, let's say it looks like there are more cases than normal, but we don't see a pattern. You're saying I should list all the details in every case and see if there's anything that matches?"

"Yeah, that's what I'd want to do." Chow thought about it. "Look, I don't have the numbers you're looking for, but maybe I can help in another way."

"What's that?"

"Well, finding the pattern in details is easier for a computer. If you make lists of the details in all the cases, I can create a database and see what we can find."

"Huh." Langan thought about the idea—and then, almost by reflex, added, "You realize these are *my* cases?"

"Sure, no problem. It wouldn't take me a lot of time to do. I could probably do it off the books, at least at first."

Chow hesitated. “Of course, if it ends up being helpful to you, I'd want to use it to sell the chief on funding this kind of thing in our department.”

Langan smiled to himself. “I hear you, Andy. Truth is, you help me solve these, I'll go to your chief myself to make the pitch.”

“You got a deal, Mike. Get in touch when you have the information you want me to process.”

“Will do, Andy.” Almost as an afterthought, he added, “And Andy, you mind keeping all this to yourself for now?”

Chow gave a short laugh. “No problem, Mike. Talk soon.”

Langan hung up, his mind racing. For the past while, he'd felt stymied by a series of dead ends. Now, Osiewicz's notes and Chow's comments suggested a new direction, even if it seemed bizarre. And if there was a serial killer at work, then Sanelli's case needed to be considered in the whole picture, which meant it would not yet go to open-unsolved. That in itself felt like a small victory.

Lou DiNova was at home that evening, having just finished dinner with his wife Lucia and his two kids. The boy, Christo (known as Chris), was fourteen, and showing all the signs of adolescence, including a growing resistance to his father's authority. It annoyed Lou and occasionally alarmed him, but he kept a rein on his temper. He had no respect for fathers who abused their position, either physically or emotionally. The girl, Maria, was eleven, and still unaffected by the changes of the teenage years; in Lou's eyes, she was still daddy's little girl.

Now, as he sat in the library reading the evening paper, he enjoyed a cigar. The doorbell rang and he heard Lucia answer it. Normally, their maid-cum-cook Camilla would have answered, but Friday was her evening off. He recognized the voice, and shortly after, Johnny Palmieri appeared in the doorway of the library.

"Evening, Johnny. What's up?" Both DiNova and Palmieri, like most of their generation, spoke fluent Italian, but Lou preferred to use English most of the time. It was a reminder of the need to be seen to fit in with American society.

"Evening, Lou. Sorry to interrupt, but I thought you'd want an update."

"About what, Johnny?"

"You know that guy Deuce? The one you wanted to check out about the L'Heureux kid's shooting?"

"Ah, yes. As I recall, Mickey O'Donoghue was going to pay him a visit?"

"Yeah, that's it. Mickey found the guy and did an extensive interview." Johnny knew the word "interview" didn't really describe O'Donoghue's techniques, but also knew Lou preferred not to be given unnecessary details. "He found the same thing I did. The guy didn't really know shit, but as you suggested, Mickey made sure he wasn't around to confuse the cops." Again, he avoided details. "So, we're square on that score."

"Good. Thank Mickey in a suitable way." Having worked with Palmieri for years, Lou knew he didn't need to give specifics. "But you know, I've been thinking about this—somebody has created a very unpleasant situation for us. The publicity this matter has drawn has been very negative, very bad for business." Lou paused to puff on his cigar. The smoke from his exhalation streamed upward, and he examined the tip to see if the ash needed to be tapped into the ashtray. "I was just reading the *Bulletin*. That reporter who was yelling 'hit' is now saying it's something else. In yesterday's paper, he said the kid's death was related to another murder downtown earlier this week."

"Yeah, I saw the paper. It was some real estate guy in the Weybosset parking garage. Got his throat slit wide open."

"Yes." Lou frowned. He didn't like detailed talk of violence in his home, when his wife or kids might overhear. "The reporter—Osiewicz is his name, must be Polish—he wrote yesterday that the two cases appeared to be connected, and tonight's paper printed the contents of three anonymous notes he received. They don't make a lot of sense, but the last one clearly talks about killing somebody." He puffed at his cigar again. "The reporter didn't come out and say so, but it sounds like one of those nutjobs who kill people randomly." He paused, trying to remember something. "Like that guy in New York several years ago. What did they call him? Son of Sam?"

"Uh, yeah, I think that was it, Lou." Johnny had been in his early twenties and more interested in other things, but took a certain professional interest in killing sprees.

"Well, if that's happening here, I want to know about it. For one thing, the prick is making bad press for us. For another, if he's actually killing people randomly, I don't like it. That L'Heureux kid was only twenty-two; the real estate guy, McIntyre I think it was, had a son in college. I've got two kids, you got kids too. This nutjob, if that's what this is, is a menace. I don't care what the cops do. I want to know what's going on." He tapped the ash off the tip of the cigar and looked directly at Palmieri. "You put the word out, Johnny. Anybody hears anything that might be part of all this, I want to know. Okay?"

"Got it, Lou." The query was unusual, but Johnny never second-guessed the instructions Lou gave. "I'll make sure everybody keeps their eyes and ears open."

"Good. And give Marv Siegel a call. Make sure he understands my concern and acts accordingly." Lou picked up the newspaper again. "Have a good night, Johnny."

A half hour later, Ed rang the bell at Liz's house. Given it was Friday, they had planned to have a late dinner. Liz answered the door and was half surprised to see Ed.

"Hi, Ed. I didn't think you'd be here so early!" Whether surprised by the timing or not, Liz was always happy to see Ed. "Weren't you planning to work out before coming over?"

Ed nodded. "Actually, I did already. But I cut it short." He smiled at Liz. "I couldn't wait to see you!"

"A nice line, Ed, but I know you too well. Something must have happened." It was expressed as a statement, but the inflection indicated it was actually a question.

"OK, you caught me. The workout wasn't going well, so I decided just to head over." He looked at her, then his eyes darted briefly away. "Let's leave it at that for now. Maybe I'll tell you over dinner." His smile returned. "Speaking of which, eat in or out?"

"In. I've already started cooking." It was her turn to smile. "But since you're early, it will still be a while. Come into the kitchen. You can have some wine while you help me finish preparations."

Later, as they sat enjoying the meal—a risotto with asparagus and prosciutto—Liz came back to her earlier question. "So, what's going on, Ed? It's not like you to leave training early."

Once again, Ed looked away, and then back at Liz. "Sometimes I think you know me better than I do myself, Liz. And I'm supposed to be the psychologist!"

"You are, Ed." She put her hand on his. "But you're also human. As much as you see *karate* as a way to enhance self-discipline, you'll never be perfect—or emotionless." She looked at him and smiled. "And a damn good thing too. I'd have no interest in loving an automaton!"

Ed smiled ruefully. "Thanks. You know, Yoshikawa has criticized me in a similar way—I expect too much and it keeps me in my own head." He looked directly at Liz. "And I'm very glad that you're not an automaton!"

"OK, so we've established that neither of us is a robot, and we're happy that way. But that still doesn't tell me what's going on."

Ed looked away for a long moment, his expression pensive. "I think it's the notes Henry Cohen has been getting." He made eye contact, but Liz said nothing, waiting for him to continue. "Did you read today's paper yet? About the two murders they think are connected?"

"Wasn't that in last night's paper? Something about the *Bulletin* thinking there's a link between a couple of recent murders in Providence?"

"Yes, that's it. But I happened to pick up today's paper at CVS after work, and a new story gave the reason why they think they're connected. The story included three notes they've received, one of which talks directly about killing."

"How horrible!"

"Yes, but what gets me is, the notes all make threats about Barton Jewelry."

Liz's eyes went wide, but before she could respond, Karen bounced into the room.

"Hi, guys! Smells like you had a great dinner! Risotto?"

Ed had his back toward the door as Karen entered, but now he turned to say hello. He smiled—Karen was dressed in a form-fitting dress with a short hem, showing off her legs in her high heels. "Hi, Karen. I'm guessing you're not staying home to read a book tonight?"

"Don't you know, Ed!" Karen pirouetted coquettishly. Although she knew Ed and Liz had a solid relationship, Karen still liked to flirt. Thankfully for her, Liz was secure enough to put up with it. Karen turned to Liz. "I'm sorry to interrupt, Liz, but could I please borrow a couple of pieces of jewelry from you? I really want to make a good impression at this club tonight!"

Liz looked at her dress. "Gee, Karen, I don't think any guy is going to notice anything but what's in the dress, but sure, take what you need. You know where my jewelry box is." This was not the first time Karen had borrowed things, but Liz didn't really mind. Karen was always good about returning things, and as far as jewelry was concerned, Ed's connection to Barton meant Liz had more than she would ever need.

"Thanks a lot, Liz!" Karen turned and exited the dining room, calling back, "Have a good evening!" as she headed for the stairs.

Liz shook her head. "Talk about interruptions!" Her smile disappeared as she again focused on Ed. "So, you're saying the paper thinks these notes are related to the murders, and the mention of Barton in the notes makes you think they're related to the notes Henry Cohen has received? Does the content of the notes match somehow?

"No, not directly. From what I read in the paper, it doesn't appear that any of the notes match." He reviewed his memory of the article, and the notes Henry Cohen had received. "But it still seems like more than coincidence that there are two sets of anonymous notes, both talking about Barton and both making threats." He had a further thought. "And the tone of both sets of notes is getting more angry. The last note Henry got said the sender would destroy the company, and it was the last note to the *Bulletin* that directly talked about killing people."

"It all sounds awful, Ed. Does Henry know about the notes the newspaper received? Do you know his reaction?"

"I don't know, Liz. The story about the notes just appeared in tonight's paper, so I haven't been in touch with Henry. But I'm worried. Henry has a family, and I don't think he's told them yet about the notes he's received. Tonight's paper, suggesting the notes are linked to the murders, changes things. Henry and his family could be in danger."

Liz paused to process the information, including Ed's concerns. "Well, it sounds like Henry should be contacting the police, if he hasn't already. But other than maybe phoning Henry, I'm not sure what you can do, Ed." She again reached out to put her hand on his. "In the end, it's not your responsibility." A thought occurred to her. "You said you read the paper before going to the *dojo*? So that's why you gave up on the workout? This stuff was in your head?"

Ed nodded. "Yeah, big time. Normally, if I'm stressed, training clears my head. But this time, it kept intruding in my thoughts." He sighed ruefully. "I even let a brown belt get to me in sparring!"

Liz smiled. "Well, like I said, you're human." Her smile disappeared, and worry lines appeared on her forehead. "I'm not directly involved, but the idea that there's some nutcase out there sending anonymous threats, and maybe even killing people, gives me the creeps."

Ed nodded silently, still thinking about the possibilities, and they sat in silence for several moments. Finally, they heard Karen's heels on the stairs and the front door open. "Thanks, Liz. Have a good night!" The door closed before they could reply.

"Ed, I have to be honest. Ever since you first mentioned the notes to Henry, you haven't been yourself. You often seem distracted and you're telling me you're feeling it at the *dojo*, too, when that's always been the place you go to get centered." She paused, waiting for a response.

"I know what you're saying." He looked down, then looked at Liz. "Hisao took me aside after class recently and said much the same thing. He broke role, talking to me as a friend, and that's something I've never seen him do in the *dojo*. And then he raised it again in the next class." He thought about the class that evening. "And when

I left early tonight, I couldn't even face him to explain. I just bailed." He frowned. "Pretty crappy behavior for somebody who's supposed to be a black belt . . ."

"I think we're both worried about you, Ed. Sometimes you take on too much. And if these notes are really from a killer, this is not something you should be trying to handle."

He said nothing, neither agreeing nor disagreeing.

Liz knew there were limits to giving advice, especially with Ed. "Well, my darling, I hope you can work it out. Unless you plan to phone Henry, it doesn't seem like there's anything you can do right now." Still holding his hand, she gave him a come-hither smile. "Let's clear the dishes and see if we can figure out something better to focus on."

It was one a.m. He had been waiting for over an hour, watching as people came out of the club. He was standing in the darkness of the recessed entry of a store on the other side of the street. From this position, he could observe those leaving as he searched for an appropriate victim. Some people left in couples or small groups, making them unsatisfactory choices. Of the remainder, he looked for a suitable female; with the mild weather, few wore any sort of coat, making it easier to assess possibilities. Twice he saw potential targets, but then they headed in the other direction. Finally, he saw a blonde in a short black dress and high heels, swaying slightly from the alcohol she'd consumed. She turned to wave to a woman exiting the club behind her, her jewelry glinting in the streetlight as she raised her arm. If they stayed together, it would be a problem, but then they separated, the other woman moving in the other direction as the blonde walked toward him.

He felt a surge of adrenaline and his hands involuntarily clenched. He watched her walk along on the other side of the street from where he hid; as she passed his position, she crossed to his side of the street, apparently moving towards her car. His lips tightened in a grim smile. *This is gonna be even easier than I thought.*

Oblivious to the lurking threat, Karen Durant walked slowly down the street, unconsciously humming a fragment of Robert Palmer's "Addicted to Love," which the cover band had been playing shortly before she left. Thinking about it, she wouldn't say she was addicted to love, but admitted she'd been hoping to meet someone. She'd met up with two old friends, Cindy and Marie, and they'd drank, danced, and shared stories. At one point, a guy had bought a round for them, and Karen had danced with him for one song, but quickly decided he wasn't her type. So, love, or even lust, hadn't ended up being part of the evening, but it had still been great to see Cindy and Marie.

As she walked along the empty street, Karen was thinking about the evening. She was a little drunk—enough to feel relaxed, but not enough that she was worried about driving. Absorbed in her thoughts and a bit unfocused, she didn't hear the man come up behind her.

Suddenly she felt a hand cover her mouth from behind, while an arm went across her throat. She was pulled roughly backwards against her assailant's chest, and she felt a well-muscled forearm dig into her windpipe. Shocked and stunned, for an instant, she failed to react. In that moment, the attacker's hand dropped from her mouth to clasp his own forearm, tightening the choke hold.

As fear pumped adrenaline into her veins, Karen suddenly felt completely sober. She dropped her chin, digging it into the attacker's forearm to make it harder to compress her windpipe. In the same moment, she jabbed her right elbow into her attacker's ribs. She heard him grunt, but his hold on her did not loosen. Realizing she had only seconds before she would lose consciousness, she lifted her right foot and stomped downward, trying to hit her attacker's instep. Her first attempt missed, but her heel scraped his shin. He cursed but held on.

Desperate but not yet panicking, Karen tried again. This time, her heel landed right on his instep. Although Karen was far smaller than her assailant, a stiletto heel does a great job of concentrating force. The attacker yelped and loosened his grip, and as he did, Karen simultaneously began yelling and using her own hands to pull his arms away from her neck. Clearly, the attacker wasn't expecting her reaction and he was slow to respond.

From down the street, back towards the club, they both heard a male voice yell, "Hey, asshole! Leave her alone!"

The voice seemed to come closer, suggesting her would-be savior was coming to intervene. The attacker broke Karen's grip on his arms, pushed her forward so that she half-fell, and then ran past her down the street in the direction opposite the club. As she recovered her balance, Karen saw him turn into a side street. She heard the footfalls of the other male approaching, calling out, "Are you OK?"

Then she suddenly felt her stomach surge, and she vomited into the gutter.

Two blocks away, after taking a winding path through several deserted streets, the attacker stopped to regroup. He was breathing heavily, and his instep and calf were both burning with pain. Even through his leather construction boots, the heel had felt like a spike being driven into his foot. *Bitch! How the fuck did she react like that? And why did there have to be a fucking Galahad coming to her rescue? Most people have the brains to steer clear of trouble!*

He was angry that the attack had failed—and angry at himself for his failure to plan adequately. He'd thought a single drunk woman would be an easy target. *Well, I won't make that mistake again.* He considered where things stood in his plan. *Enough of these single attacks. It's time for the big one.*

Removing the cap and jacket he'd been wearing, he tucked them under one arm and walked slowly toward where he'd left his car, limping as little as he could manage.

As he walked, his mind was already focused on the next steps of his plan.

ELEVEN

Monday, May 11, 1987

STAN OSIEWICZ ARRIVED at the *Journal-Bulletin* building at about eight a.m. After running Friday's piece about the notes, the television news had picked up the story and speculation was rampant. Stan figured that if he got to the office before Joe Houle, he would have some time to plot out his next steps.

When he got to his desk, the first thing he noticed was a business envelope, addressed in a now-familiar way: hand-written with a black marker. He briefly considered whether he should turn it over to the police unopened, but then decided he had the right to open it. He wanted to know what it said.

The note had reverted to the style of the first mailing, done with letters cut from a newspaper, but pasted onto a partial sheet of newspaper rather than typing paper. He saw with a mix of interest and horror that the page used was from Friday's paper. The sender had pasted the message over Stan's story about the previous notes!

"So, you finally woke up. Good thing you're not my target. A girl got lucky on Friday night—she didn't end up in the morgue. But next time, luck will run out for Barton and many more. The hand of justice."

Stan read the note, then reread it. It was clear the sender was still fixated on Barton Jewelry and was apparently angry at Stan's handling of the previous notes. But what struck him most was the reference to a girl not ending up in the morgue on Friday—did that mean he'd attacked someone, but she'd somehow gotten away?

Stan looked over at Joe Houle's office, but the editor hadn't arrived yet. His thoughts racing, Stan decided that whatever else he did, he'd better share the note with the police. He took it to the office Xerox machine and made a copy, which he put in his file with the other notes. With the original and its envelope in his pocket, he headed down to his car.

Mike Langan was also in early that day. After Friday's story with the notes and the follow-on by local TV stations, the mayor had taken the unusual step of calling Chief Parker on the weekend. In the typical way that shit flows downhill, the chief had called Briggs and said he wanted to form a task force. Briggs had called Langan and told him to be in his office for a briefing at eight-thirty sharp, without specifying why. Now, Langan was sitting in Briggs's office, along with Francie Weber. The office was not large and three was definitely a crowd.

"Morning, Mike," said Briggs, sipping on a coffee. Weber met Langan's eyes and arched her brows, but said nothing. "Let's get to it. The mayor called the chief last night. He's upset about these news stories about the L'Heureux and McIntyre cases."

"Shit . . ." Langan muttered.

"Yeah, well, whether it is or not, it's been dropped on us." Briggs took a deep gulp of his coffee. "So, here's the word from the chief. He's going to call a news conference later this morning and announce that the department, in response to the 'deeply disturbing reports,' is making these murders the highest priority and committing all necessary resources, and so on—I'll leave it to you to read the release if you care."

"Sure thing. I'll make it my priority at lunch," growled Langan. In his view, every murder was the highest priority, so this was all window dressing.

"Look, Mike, I know how you feel." Briggs stared at him. He knew Langan was both dedicated and good at his job, but also had a low tolerance for politics interfering in his work. Still, Briggs had his own job to do. "In any case, this is how we're gonna do it. The chief knows as well as I do that you two are the best detectives in the force. As of now, you and Weber are on these cases full time. Let's hope no others surface, but if they do, they'll be going to you. If you need OT or other feet on the ground, you let me know. For now, the chief has given us carte blanche." He paused to drink his coffee. "If you need to connect with other departments, you check with me. And whatever you do, you keep me in the loop." He thought for a moment. "And let's hope to hell the feds don't stick their nose in." Like most local police, Briggs held a mix of resentment and scorn towards the FBI, who were viewed as having too much money and too little street smarts, along with a keen interest in grabbing any case that might attract publicity.

"Right." Langan looked at Weber to gauge her reaction, but her face was expressionless. He turned to Briggs. "What about Dunn and Bernstein?" Their regular partners had not been mentioned.

"You leave them to me. This is coming from the chief, and I happen to agree with him. It doesn't hurt that you've each been handling one of the cases. Just read each other in, and if there is some connection, find it. And catch whoever's responsible." Both Langan and Weber knew that "soon" was implied, even if unspoken. Briggs turned to a file on his desk, and they knew the meeting was ever. Briggs was not one for social graces.

Back at his desk, Mike Langan was about to tell Francie Weber to sit when he realized the chair beside his desk was already occupied. He recognized Stan Osiewicz, the reporter from the *Journal* who'd started this whole uproar. Langan nodded at Weber, indicating he'd connect with her shortly.

"So, Osiewicz. Back so soon." Mike sat down heavily at his desk, staring at the reporter. "To what do I owe this visit?"

"Hello, Detective." Stan picked up on the barely concealed animosity and tried to defuse it. "Look, I'm sorry if the stories have made you or the department look bad, but I'm just trying to do my job."

"Right," Mike grunted. "That's why you ran the notes the day after your bullshit theorizing piece."

"Um, look, I don't make all the calls at the paper, any more than I'm guessing you do here. But there's something going on, I'm sure of it."

"Sure. I'll ask the lieutenant to give you a badge so you can join us."

Stan took a deep breath. "Okay, you don't like me—I get it. But before you decide this is all bullshit, take a look at this." He handed Mike the latest note.

Mike quickly read it and his eyes went wide. He looked directly at Stan. "When'd you get this?"

"Just this morning when I got into work, less than an hour ago. It was on my desk."

"Jesus." Mike read it again. "What's this about a girl getting lucky 'cause she's not dead? Do you know what he's talking about?" Both men assumed the sender was a male.

"No." Stan returned Mike's stare. "I was hoping you might know."

"This is homicide, kid. I don't deal with the live ones." For the moment, Mike decided not to mention the task force, which would definitely make this note, and the presumed assault, his business. The note grabbed his attention, but he remained unhappy with the reporter's involvement.

"I know, Detective, your beat is homicide, so this may be off-base." Stan's tone was conciliatory. "But I still figured you might want to see this." He paused, hesitating.

"And if you happen to have anything to share, I'd appreciate hearing about it."

"Yeah, yeah. I get it." Mike decided that the reporter deserved something in return for bringing the note. By noon, the task force would be announced, so mentioning it now would be a cheap payback for the note. "Look, I appreciate you bringing this by so quickly. There may be some news later this morning. If you want, you call me later. Right now, I got murders to solve."

"Right. Talk later, Detective."

When the reporter left, Mike gestured to Francie, who came and sat in the seat recently vacated by Stan Osiewicz. Without saying anything, Mike handed her the note; like Mike, her eyes widened as she read it.

"Shit, Mike, it looks like there is some wacko behind all this." Reading the note again, she asked, "Where'd it come from? And what's this about the girl? Some assault on Friday night?"

"The guy who just left was the reporter, Osiewicz. He said he found it on his desk this morning." A thought occurred to him. "I gotta get in touch with him and find out how the note got there." He thought about the reference to the girl getting away. "It sounds like there was another attack, but the killer messed up somehow." He looked at Francie, but before he could continue, she interrupted.

"Yeah. I'll check with the assaults unit and see if anything was reported Friday night or Saturday morning." She thought about it. "I'm guessing it was a physical assault, not some sex thing. Anyway, I'll get on it." She looked directly at him, her brow furrowed with concern. "Mike, you ever dealt with a psycho? I know I haven't."

"No, not directly, Francie. I guess at some point we'll have to contact some shrink for background. But for now, we got two homicides to deal with, and that's something we've both done. Let's just focus on that and try to find any connections between the cases." He looked at her for a moment. "And Francie, if you don't mind, can I look over your file on McIntyre while you check on the assault angle?" Under normal circumstances, case files were viewed as private, but the task force gambit meant this was not business as usual.

Francie looked at Mike, her lips set in a tight line. Mike guessed she was just realizing he'd already known about the other notes when they'd talked about McIntyre, before Friday's newspaper. Holding back was typical in their job, even with other cops, and he wondered if it was going to be an obstacle to their working together. Finally, she exhaled, and her expression relaxed. "Sure, Mike. I'll get it." She gave a half smile. "I guess we got no secrets now!"

Mike started reading Francie Weber's case file immediately. She was a good detective, and it didn't surprise him that the binder was well organized, the index in the front clearly noting the contents and the date for each addition. Some detectives could be sloppy—they'd put everything in the file, but update the index only periodically, which sometimes led to problems. She was never going to be in that category.

He went first to the medical examiner's report, looking for any information about the assailant. The angle of attack and direction of the slash suggested the killer was right-handed and a bit taller than McIntyre's five foot ten. Mike knew the details of the L'Heureux case almost by heart; while the close proximity of the gun to L'Heureux's head made it difficult to gauge the precise height of the attacker, the killer was probably somewhere in the range of five foot nine to six foot one. The fact that the bullet took a slight leftward direction as it entered the brain made it likely the gun had been in the assailant's right hand. It wasn't much to go on, but the details suggested that both murders had been committed by someone of a similar physical size.

Mike started wondering about the Sanelli case—did that attacker fit the same physical description? He'd been reluctant to abandon the case, and now, with the new task force mandate, he figured he could take another look. Of course, he'd tell Briggs what he was doing—but only after he'd pulled the Sanelli file.

When Weber came back after checking on assaults, Mike shared what he'd noticed about the similarities from the two medical examiner's reports, and his speculation about how the Sanelli case might fit in. Weber agreed with his assessment. She then reviewed what she'd learned about recent assaults.

It turned out there had been three reported assaults on females on Friday night. There had been a domestic assault and a bar fight, but in both those cases, the attackers had been found and charged, and in neither case did the attack seem to have fatal intent. The one remaining incident looked promising: A woman in her twenties had been attacked as she was leaving Joey's, a club near the Civic Center. The attacker had approached her from behind and, according to her report, attempted to choke her, but was scared off when another bar patron noticed and yelled out.

"Did she happen to mention how he choked her?" Mike asked.

"Yeah. He did an arm bar with his right forearm."

"Huh. Fits with what I've been reading about the other cases."

"Sounds like it."

"I'm wondering, though . . ." Mike paused, thinking it through. "In the two, or maybe three, homicides, it seems like the victims had no chance. How does a girl who's presumably been drinking manage to break free? Or did the perp just take off because of the potential witness?"

"According to the report, she had some kind of self-defense training. She stomped on his foot with her stiletto heel."

"Ouch. That's pretty impressive, though. She must be a real together lady."

"I thought so too." Francie hesitated, then said, "I gotta admit, I don't know how I'd react in that situation. Hell, I don't even own high heels! " When Mike gave no response, she continued. "I'm thinking we should try to talk to her. Maybe she knows more than what's in the report."

"Right. Got an address and phone number? Let's set it up for later today. Meanwhile, I'll go pull the file on Sanelli."

"I'm on it. You know, Mike, maybe that reporter was on to something in thinking the cases are connected. But one thing bothers me."

"What's that, Francie?"

"The MOs are all different and the victims don't seem alike. You ever hear of a serial killer where nothing matches? I thought they always had some kind of target factor, and that they always used the same type of attack."

"The same thing struck me." Mike eyes turned downward to the side, and then back up to Francie. "That's why I thought the reporter was blowin' smoke when he first contacted me." He paused again. "But seein' the fourth note, and now the similarities in the attackers in all these cases, it's looking more real. If it is the same guy, there must be more connections—we just have to find them."

"Right." Francie said nothing that indicated how certain she felt about it. "I'll let you know when we've got a meeting with this woman. Karen Durant's her name. In the meantime, how about I look over the L'Heureux and McIntyre files, see if I notice anything you didn't?"

"I haven't finished with McIntyre—just got through the ME's report. But you can scan L'Heureux to get up to speed." He handed her his case file. "Like you said, no secrets now." Francie nodded and headed back to her own desk.

At about the same moment, Ed Underwood was in Henry Cohen's office. After the conversation with Liz on Friday night, Ed had considered phoning Cohen at home to express his concerns, but decided to leave it until Monday at work, when they could talk face to face. Cohen had likely seen the news coverage of the new notes, and if so, had doubtless connected it to the notes he'd previously received. If somehow he hadn't heard, there was no reason to spoil his weekend.

"So, Henry, have the police followed up about the notes you've gotten? Given the recent news, it sounds like this is more serious than we imagined."

Cohen nodded. "I agree. I think I told you, I contacted Chief Parker after the third note and he said he'd have someone look into the situation. But I never heard back. I think it's time to call him again." Cohen scowled, clearly angry. "He may have dismissed it before, but I don't see how he can now."

"Good idea, Henry." Ed thought about the situation. "And I still think you should consider some kind of security, at least for Emily and the girls."

"I'm considering it." Cohen looked out the window, staring at the far horizon of trees coming into full leaf. "But I don't want to alarm them. So far, there has been nothing in the notes threatening them, or even me personally. It's all been about the company." He paused for a long moment, then suddenly said, "Could all this be about some old history? Maybe somebody with a grudge against Ned Barton?"

"I don't know, Henry. It seems unlikely, given how long it's been since Ned died. I think some of the other possibilities we've talked about are more likely—some environmentalist gone off the deep end, or some disgruntled ex-employee or business contact."

"Speaking of which, have you made any headway in checking out ex-employees?"

"I'm working on it. It's complicated, because we have a better system for tracking active employees than for those who quit or were fired, and there's about a ten percent turnover every year." Both men knew the employee complement, and that they were talking about dozens of paper files, if not more. "If it is someone with a grudge, I'm guessing they're more likely to have been fired than quit. But our filing system doesn't sort them that way."

"I understand."

"How far back should I go, anyway?"

"You're the psychologist, Ed. You tell me. How long would somebody sit on a grudge before taking action?"

Ed looked away without comment. After several seconds, he looked back at Cohen. "I don't know, Henry. This whole thing is pretty strange. I'm trying to look at recent terminations as best I can with the way the files are organized. Should I get someone to help me now that the company is already in the news?" Until now, Cohen had resisted spreading any information about the notes.

Cohen shook his head. "For now, do the best you can and see how many possibilities you turn up. If nothing's changed by the end of the week, we'll decide about more help." He stood up, signaling that the topic was finished for now. As Ed headed for the door, Cohen added, "Thanks, Ed. I don't know how I'd handle this without your help."

"No thanks needed, Henry. Happy to do whatever I can."

Ed Underwood left Cohen's office. Thinking about it, he realized that his closing words to Cohen, while well-meant, weren't completely truthful. *There's nothing about this situation that makes me happy—especially being made responsible.*

Chief Parker's news conference was held at eleven a.m. at City Hall. The mayor considered appearing, but decided it was safer to stay in the background in case the situation became even more volatile. News of the task force made it to the midday TV news—the main thrust was that the police were taking significant steps to address two recent murders, but the subtext was that a serial killer was on the loose. Not surprisingly, the *Evening Bulletin* ran the story on the front page, including the latest note, with Stan Osiewicz getting the byline. Beyond what the TV coverage had said, the story noted the newspaper's role in bringing the notes, and the possible pattern, to the attention of the police.

When Mike Langan and Francie Weber met with Karen Durant late that afternoon, at the house she shared with Liz Reynolds. Durant had already heard about the task force. Although they didn't mention the task force when they introduced themselves, she quickly made the connection and her eyes went wide.

"You think the guy who attacked me is this killer the paper's talking about? Oh, God!" She collapsed into a chair in the living room.

The detectives exchanged a glance. Without saying a word, they agreed Francie would take the lead, despite being the junior officer.

"We don't know that, Miss Durant. But if you've heard about the task force, you know that we're taking the situation very seriously. That includes investigating any other incidents that might shed light on what's happening." Unlike Karen, she avoided any reference to a killer. Without mentioning the latest note, or its reference to a girl who "got lucky," she continued, speaking calmly and carefully. "We understand someone assaulted you the other night, and we'd just like to talk with you in case anything was overlooked when the reporting officers took your statement. Is that okay?"

Karen looked up at Francie and took a deep breath. "Um, I guess so. It all happened pretty fast, and I was a bit drunk. I don't know if there's much more to tell."

"You never know. Sometimes the little things are the most important." Francie did her best to offer a reassuring smile. "Can we start with when you were leaving the club? Were you with anyone?"

Francie began taking Karen through the events, being as thorough as possible without unduly upsetting her—and equally importantly, letting Karen tell it in her own words, without being given leading questions. Eventually, they came to the part where Karen broke the choke hold enough to scream, and someone exiting the club shouted at the attacker.

"So what happened when the guy from the bar yelled? How did the attacker react?"

"He . . . he released the choke hold and gave me a push as he let go of me." Karen took a slow breath. "I had been facing away from the club when he came up behind me. Then, after I stomped on his foot and the guy from the club was yelling, he pushed me and ran past, heading away from the club. I tried to run toward the club but after a couple of steps I sort of collapsed and threw up."

"Sounds like a pretty natural reaction, Karen." Francie deliberately used "Karen" rather than the "Miss Durant" dictated by protocol. She waited a moment, letting the girl collect herself. "So did you get a look at the guy during or after the attack?"

"No, I didn't really get a good look. I never saw his face. I got a glimpse of him as he ran past me, but I was pretty panicked." Karen hesitated, her expression tensing as she tried to remember. "He was wearing a baseball cap. I couldn't see much of his hair, but I think it was dark. And he had on a jacket or windbreaker of some kind." She thought some more. "I'd say he was medium to heavy build, and I know he was tall, about six feet."

"What makes you say that?"

"Well, I was wearing four-inch heels, and he had no trouble reaching around my shoulder to choke me, so he had to be several inches taller than me, and I'm five foot five."

Francie was impressed. Karen Durant was clearly not the dumb blonde of clichés. "That makes sense. You may have been afraid, but it doesn't sound like you were panicked."

For the first time, Karen laughed. "Actually, officer, you have no idea."

Francie ignored her use of "officer" rather than "detective." "You're probably right," she agreed. "Do you mind if I ask you something else?"

"No, that's okay. In a strange way, talking about it helps."

"You've described your actions to defend yourself—tucking your chin in to obstruct the choke, elbowing him in the ribs, and using your heel to stomp on his foot. That's pretty impressive. Do you mind if I ask how you knew to do that?"

Karen smiled. "Actually, my housemate's boyfriend is a black belt in *karate* and I asked him to teach me a few self-defense techniques." She smiled again. "He was pretty impressed when I told him what happened."

At that precise moment, the doorbell rang. Liz was in the kitchen, and knowing Karen was occupied with the police, went to answer it.

"Hi, Ed!" She leaned forward to kiss him before he even entered the house.

"Hi to you too!" They prolonged the kiss with a tight embrace.

"Actually, your timing is perfect. Karen is just talking to the police again."

Ed's face became serious. "How's she doing, Liz? She was pretty shook up when I saw her on Saturday."

"I think she'll be okay. Beneath her flirty image, she's pretty tough." Liz frowned briefly. "But still, it was an awful thing."

"Agreed. If I were a clinician, I might be more help. But if she wants, I can connect her with someone who is." His face showed furrows of concern. "You said the police are here? Hadn't they already talked to Karen about the attack?"

"Yes, they did. I don't really know why they're here. They said they were detectives, but didn't explain much when they came to the door. Apparently, they'd been in touch with Karen by phone when she was at work earlier."

Ed crossed the hallway and looked into the living room, but didn't enter. Karen saw him and jumped up. "Ed! It's great that you're here! I was just telling the police about how your self-defense advice probably saved me." She went serious. "They think the guy who attacked me might be the same one that's in the news."

Langan interrupted, trying to cut off speculation. "We don't know that for certain, Miss Durant. Right now, we're really just trying to learn more about what happened to you." He glanced at Ed, but continued speaking to Karen. "And we really appreciate you talking with us." His focus then shifted directly to Ed. "I understand you taught her some self-defense techniques? Would you mind talking with us for a couple of minutes?"

Ed looked at the two detectives, momentarily surprised. In his mind, he was thinking about his earlier conversation with Henry Cohen, as well as the spate of news stories. "Um, sure. I don't know how I can help, but I'll try." He looked at Liz, who had remained in the hallway. "It won't mean dinner's spoiled, will it, Liz?" Liz nodded. "No problem, Ed. I'll be in the kitchen when you're done."

Ed took a seat on the couch, where Karen was patting the cushion beside her.

Mike Langan now took the lead instead of Francie Weber. "Care to have a seat, Mr.—? Sorry, I didn't catch your name."

"Ed Underwood."

Langan offered his right hand, and with his left hand, flashed his badge and ID. "I'm Detective Langan, and this is Detective Weber." He chose not to mention either the homicide squad, or the new task force.

"Good to meet you. Thanks for taking an interest in what happened to Karen." Ed glanced over at her, to see how she was doing. Her face actually looked more relaxed than it had in the past two days.

"We take it seriously," said Langan noncommittally. "I understand you may have had a big part in saving Karen by teaching her some self-defense techniques?"

"Well, I showed her a few things once. But she had the presence of mind to know what to do when she was attacked. At such moments, a lot of people forget whatever they've learned."

"Yes, that's probably so. So, tell me, how did you pick up the techniques you taught her?"

"Well, I'm a black belt in *karate-do*." Many practitioners would simply say "*karate*," but Ed thought of it as more than simply training—it was a Zen path (*do*).

"So, you teach it for a living?"

"No, no, nothing like that! But I've been training for over fifteen years, and it's become an important part of my life."

"Uh-huh." Langan's tone suggested he wasn't overly impressed. "So, what do you do then? For a living, I mean."

"I'm a psychologist. Not a therapist, though. I'm the personnel manager for Barton Jewelry." Ed was a bit puzzled—they seemed more interested in him than the circumstances warranted and it made him wary. "Is there some reason you need to know about me? I mean, I wasn't involved, other than having taught Karen some techniques a while ago."

"No, no, I'm just curious, Mr. Underwood. It seems like your training may have helped save her from serious harm."

Langan's tone was neutral, and it was hard for Ed to read what, if anything, lay beneath.

Langan folded up his notebook to signal that they were finished. "Oh, by the way, I understand you have a relationship with Miss Durant's housemate. Does that mean you were here when she got home after the attack?"

"No, actually. I was here when Karen went out that evening, but I'd already gone home before she came back. Why?"

"Oh, just thinking that if you were here, you might remember something she said that might be helpful." Langan's response seemed deliberately casual. "I figured it was worth asking, if you understand."

"Yeah, sure." In fact, Ed didn't understand at all—the explanation sounded like a rationalization. "Well, sorry I couldn't be of more help."

"Not at all." Langan took out a business card and handed it to Karen. "Well, Miss Durant, we really appreciate your help. I'm sure this has all been pretty difficult for you. If we can do anything, please don't hesitate to call either me or Detective Weber." He glanced at his partner, who nodded in agreement. "And I promise you, we will pursue this very seriously." With another glance at Ed, Langan and Weber left.

Once outside, Mike Langan turned to his partner. "What'd you think?"

Francie Weber understood he was asking about Underwood, not Durant. "He's the right height and build, and he seems to be right-handed. And he's got a connection to both Barton and the girl, and maybe no alibi." She thought it over. "I think we need to look closer at this guy."

"Exactly." Mike was pleased that he and Francie were on the same wavelength. "The only thing that gets me is, why would he risk attacking somebody who could be linked to him?"

"Shit, Mike. If he is the one, who knows what crazy ideas get him going? Maybe it's more of a thrill if it's someone he knows."

"Yeah, could be." Mike laughed shortly. "He must've been surprised as hell when she remembered the martial arts stuff he'd taught her!"

Later that evening, the killer was sitting at home, nursing a beer and thinking. He was still mad at himself for screwing up on Friday night. The idea of killing someone without using a weapon had been intensely appealing, and a woman had seemed like an easy target. But he hadn't figured a drunk dame would react the way she had—or that someone would hear her scream. *Careless*, he thought. *Too damn careless.*

He was worried about being identified but decided the dark street and the cap would have made a real ID nearly impossible. And the guy near the club had been too far away to see much. Still, it was the first time he'd messed up at all—and it had to be the last. *I'm too smart for that kind of shit. Guess I got a little cocky. Well, when I pull off the big one, I'll be damned sure I've got it all covered.*

On the bright side, the notes were finally achieving their goal. Barton was in the news, and the media were cranking up the fear machine, getting people talking about what was going on and why. He smiled at the reports of a police task force being created. *Yeah, right. A couple of homicide dicks. They've been right on top of the cases all along and haven't figured out squat. Fuckin' window-dressing is what they are.*

He reached for a book on the table beside his chair. Opening it, he pulled out the paper on which he had been making notes. *Let them spin their wheels. I got real work to do.*

TWELVE

Tuesday, May 12, 1987

AS HE APPROACHED his office, Stan Osiewicz found himself immersed in thoughts about the serial killer story. (He knew the paper wasn't yet calling it that, but in his own mind, it was.) After his meeting with Detective Langan the previous morning, he'd ended up going to the chief's press conference. The creation of a task force to look at the notes and killings was welcome, and it didn't particularly surprise him that Langan hadn't mentioned it when they talked. Stan knew most cops tended to play their cards very close to the table. This wasn't really a criticism—he usually did the same. Since Langan had claimed to know nothing about the attack mentioned in the latest note, Stan had had to pursue other sources in the police department. In the end, he'd gotten Karen Durant's name but, with Houle's agreement, had left it out of last night's story, which included the latest note.

The creation of the task force justified the direction of the series of articles, away from Stan's earlier theory that the attack on L'Heureux was a hit. With the story gaining momentum, he figured it was time to talk about a serial killer, but doing so would require Joe Houle's okay. To persuade Houle, he would have to make his case clear. By the time he sat down at his desk, Stan knew he needed to have another talk with Dr. Brandt, the psychiatrist.

Luckily for Stan, Heinrich Brandt agreed to meet him over lunch, and the location, the hospital cafeteria, made it clear he wasn't just looking for a free meal. As they started talking, it became apparent that Brandt had been following Stan's stories.

"Your stories about the notes have been interesting, but I notice you aren't saying anything about a serial killer."

"No, not yet." Stan swallowed a half-chewed bite of sandwich. "My editor doesn't want to be alarmist."

"Oh? Isn't that what sells papers?"

"Some would say so." Stan took a gulp of his cola. "I prefer to think that we report what's going on, and a lot of the time, that's bad stuff." Inwardly, Stan chafed at Brandt's remark—he'd gotten that reaction more times than he could count, but in his own mind, he was out to find the truth of every story, and selling papers was never his priority.

Brandt nodded. "Well, there's certainly no shortage of depraved behavior in the world." His father had perished in the Buchenwald concentration camp, and the memory was never far from the surface. "So, do you think it's a serial killer?"

"That's why I'm talking to you." Stan looked directly at the psychiatrist. "Given the latest notes and the failed attack on Friday, it sure looks to me like somebody on a rampage. But my editor wants a professional opinion."

"Of course. Makes it easier to put responsibility for the idea on someone else." Brandt gave a brief half smile. "Or blame." He looked away, thinking about what had been reported so far. "This last attack, the assault on the girl, do you have any details? Have you talked to her?"

Stan shook his head. "I just found out who she is yesterday afternoon. So far, I haven't been able to get her to meet me."

"So, you've got two killings, an attack, and a series of notes about them that also threaten this jewelry company." Brandt looked closely at Stan. "Is there more I should know that hasn't made the paper?"

"Not really. It all began with the notes I got. Then I started thinking about the two recent homicides and wondering if there was a connection. But so far, there's no clear pattern. Don't these guys usually have a pattern?"

"Yes, but it's not always obvious at first. And these things have a way of evolving, of changing as more crimes are committed. The so-called Golden State Killer is believed to have raped over fifty women before he started killing his victims. It's also believed that he did dozens of break-and-enters before the first rape."

"Believed? Don't they know?"

"No. He's never been caught." Brandt paused and took a sip of his coffee. "The robberies started in about 1974, as

I recall, and the rapes a couple of years later. It was apparently another four or five years before he started killing. Nobody's certain of the exact number, but he was linked to at least a dozen murders."

"Shit . . ." Almost involuntarily, Stan's memories of the local student-killer case resurfaced. Even now, years later, it could make his stomach churn. "So, if these guys change their MO, are you saying that's what this latest attack is?"

"Maybe, but not necessarily. Most of the known serial killers have also committed attacks where the victim didn't die. Both Son of Sam and the Zodiac Killer had multiple such incidents. So it could be that the girl who was attacked was just lucky."

"Yeah, that's what the note said. . . ." Stan found he no longer had an appetite for the remainder of his lunch. "So, look, you're the expert. What do you think is going on?"

"Well, technically I'm not an expert on serial killers, but speaking as a clinical psychiatrist, I'd say it sounds like an antisocial personality, what you've called a psychopath. Someone who is very angry, but also very calculating. It's not obvious what their grudge with Barton Jewelry is, but whatever it is, they are willing to go to extremes to damage the company, and in their own mind, that involves killing." He paused, sipping his coffee as he thought about it. "I'd say this is a lot closer to the Zodiac Killer than the Son of Sam. As we discussed last time, David Berkowitz suffered from paranoid schizophrenia, and it was his delusions that drove his attacks. The Zodiac Killer seemed to be much more deliberate, taunting the police with his coded messages. Of course, we can't know for sure, since he was never caught. But in my view, that's the kind of killer at work here."

"So, you're saying you think the attacks are connected, that this is a serial killer?"

"I don't like the phrase, but given the content of the notes and what's been happening, my guess would be, yes, these attacks are the work of a single person. A very dangerous person."

"If the girl was just lucky to get away, then there's likely to be another attack?"

"Probably. These killers seldom stop until they are caught. Sometimes the killings in a particular area stop, but in cases like the Zodiac Killer and the Golden State Killer, we never know whether they may have died without being identified or maybe just moved to another area."

"That's a pretty scary idea," Stan replied, and meant it.

"In this case, as long as notes keep coming, you can assume the attacks will continue. In fact, the failure of his last attack will likely just fuel his rage."

"Meaning what?"

"Hard to say, exactly. It might speed up the timing of the attacks. Or he might change his tactics in some way—as I said, they sometimes evolve. Maybe he'll go for something bigger."

"What's bigger than killing people?"

"Well, all the notes threaten the jewelry company. Until now, it seems he's believed the killings would damage the company. If he decides that isn't working, he might somehow go after the company or its management directly." Dr. Brandt glanced at his watch and rose to go. "I hope this helps. And I'm glad you went to the police with the notes, for everyone's sake. I hope they catch this guy soon."

"Me too, doc. Thanks for your help."

While Stan Osiewicz was talking with Dr. Brandt, Mike Langan and Francie Weber were in the lieutenant's office for the first update on the new task force. Mike didn't relish it—he'd rather spend his time working the case—but he knew the politics of the situation meant he and Weber would be closely monitored. To his surprise, Briggs actually had new information to convey.

"We've found out that the newspaper notes aren't the only ones."

Mike's eyes went wide. "What? What other ones? To who? And what do they say?"

Briggs waved a set of pages, photocopies of the notes that Henry Cohen had received.

"It turns out that the president of Barton Jewelry has also been getting notes. As you can see, they're not exactly the same style, but the threats are similar."

"What's the timeline?" Mike was already thinking about how the two sets of notes were related.

"I don't have all the details. You'll have to talk to Henry Cohen, the president of Barton. But my impression is he started getting notes before the newspaper guy did."

"Shit . . ." Mike was angry that he was just hearing about this now. "So, this guy at Barton gets threatening notes and sees the newspaper stories, and waits a week to contact us?"

"No, no, nothing like that." Briggs swiveled his chair nervously. "It turns out this Cohen guy sent copies to the chief a couple of weeks ago 'cause he was worried, but the chief didn't pay attention till the stories started in the *Journal*."

Mike and Francie exchanged glances. They both knew that however things played out, the chief would want his ass covered—which meant any flak from the delay would end up on them.

"For what it's worth," Briggs continued, "none of these make direct threats like the last two notes to the paper did." He shuffled through the pages, which were copies of the originals sent to Cohen, then handed them to Langan. "The chief has already told the lab boys to expedite looking at them, and also followed up with Cohen. Apparently the guy will be expecting to hear from you." Briggs looked at the detectives. "So what do you have?"

"Well, we're trying to build a profile to see what the cases have in common," Mike said. "After looking over the ME's reports, we discovered the killer in both the McIntyre and L'Heureux cases was roughly the same height, and both likely right-handed. I went back to the Sanelli case, and the physicals match there, too, so Sanelli may also have been a vic. We've also talked with the girl who was attacked on Friday, and while she didn't get a good look at the guy, her description of the attacker also fits."

"Jesus." Briggs thought about the implications. "So you're saying there's probably three vics, not two, and the girl was supposed to be number four?"

"Seems like. Assuming there aren't others we haven't noticed yet."

"Fuck . . ." Briggs rubbed the bridge of his nose and his face wore a pained expression. He stared at the two detectives. "Look, keep me in the loop, and don't go lettin' any of this out till we're sure. We got enough of a shitstorm right now." He looked away, and Mike and Francie took it as a signal they could leave.

Back in the squad room, Mike and Francie talked about the new notes and how to proceed. Both were still trying to work out how the second set of notes fit in. After several read-throughs, Mike led off.

"Well, at least the lieutenant's right that these notes aren't as specific. Still, we've gotta know more about where they fit in the timeline. Francie, how about you talk to this guy Cohen? If the first note to Cohen goes back early enough, it may also confirm our suspicions about Sanelli's death being part of this. In the meantime, I'll check with the lab and see if they've found anything on the Barton notes."

"And light a fire under their asses if they haven't started processing yet," Francie added.

"You know I will." Mike nodded and gave a brief smile. "I also want to talk to a guy in the state police. He was the one who got me looking for a pattern in the cases, and I want to pick his brain."

"Uh-huh." Francie thought about this for a minute. "So, how do we figure out if there's other murders by this guy?"

"Who knows? We didn't think L'Heureux and McIntyre were linked till the notes appeared, so we might have missed others." Mike hated the idea that a case connection had slipped by him.

"Right." Francie nodded, her face compressed in a pained scowl. She resented overlooking something as much as Mike did. "Well, I'm out of here. I'll check with you after I talk to Cohen."

After Francie left, Mike Langan sat at his desk, reading the notes again. He decided they would make more sense after they knew the timeline, assuming Cohen could tell them. For now, he put them aside and called Andy Chow at the state police.

"Constable Chow here."

"Hey, Andy. Mike Langan."

"Mike!" Chow's voice conveyed surprise, but not in a negative way. "Man, it's really hittin' the fan in your department!"

"You got that right, Andy. That's why I'm calling. Remember we talked about looking for patterns beyond the standard MO factors?"

"Yeah, sure. I was saying we could maybe put together a database." Chow paused. "But I don't recall you sending anything over." He sounded puzzled, and maybe a little left out.

"No, you're right, Andy. I haven't had time yet. This whole task force thing just got dropped on me yesterday."

"I get it." Both men knew how things played out when political pressure mixed with police work. "Anyway, I'm happy to put something together if you want."

"Thanks, Andy. I'll try to take you up on the offer." Langan paused, trying to sort out what he was seeking. "You know, I've looked at the files on the two murders and the assault last Friday, and they all jibe. In every case, the attacker was about six feet tall and right-handed. But so far, we don't have anything else to connect them. I'm wondering what you think I should look for." For the moment, he decided not to mention Sanelli.

"Gee, Mike, that's a pretty broad question." Buying time to think, Chow added, "And you know the cases way better than me." Finally, he said, "Didn't you say the notes keep talking about Barton Jewelry? Have you looked for some kind of connection between the company and the victims?"

"Yeah. So far we got nothing, except that the girl who was attacked knows somebody who works at Barton, and that guy fits the physical profile. For the two murders, we"re coming up empty on links."

"Huh." Andy thought about this, and what he knew about criminal patterns. "You know, Mike, I don't buy that the killer is picking victims randomly—not with the way he talks about Barton." He paused again. "I'm no shrink, but I think every perp has a pattern, even serial killers. So I'd lay money there's a connection between each victim and Barton."

"Like I said, we've looked at that and nothing's turned up. Neither vic worked for Barton or did business with them."

"Maybe the connection isn't directly to the company. The company's jewelry is popular, so maybe the link is to their products or their customers? Have you checked what the victims were wearing?"

"You mean jewelry? I dunno, the two homicides were both males. I don't think there was jewelry."

"Well, did they wear watches? Doesn't Barton make some kind of special watchband? There's all those TV ads that show how twisty their watchbands are."

Langan swore under his breath. "Shit. Never thought of that." His mind started racing. "Thanks, Andy. I'll get back to you." He hung up and headed for the property room, his adrenaline pumping at the prospect of a new lead.

Ed Underwood considered Henry Cohen a very calm person, but at the moment, as they sat in Cohen's office, "calm" was not a word that came to mind.

"Ed, what the hell is going on? Why is all this happening?"

"I wish I knew, Henry. From the newspaper stories, it seems the notes involve much more than pranks or harmless threats." Ed thought back to their conversation about the first notes Cohen had received. "Whoever's behind this, they're clearly a bigger danger than I thought."

"Dammit, what did you think was going on?"

"Henry, I'm sorry." Ed felt his body tensing and he took a deep breath to center himself. "As I tried to tell you, this stuff isn't my specialty. And if the paper is right about this being some kind of serial killer, then it's way outside my background."

Cohen exhaled heavily. "I know, Ed. It's just—this is all scary. I'm worried about Emily and the girls. And I thought you would know how to handle it." He paused. "I've been wrong—about the notes, and maybe about you." He added hurriedly, "I don't mean I don't trust you, I just mean you were the wrong person to advise me on this. I should have pushed the police about it much sooner." He looked out the window, his eyes defocusing, and then he looked at Ed. "And Chief Parker might as well be a politician. All I've gotten from him is ass-covering."

"It sounds like a mess all around."

"For damn sure." Cohen paused. After a long moment, he looked at Ed again, his expression more intense. "Well, I've been through messes before, and there's always an answer. We just have to find it." His mouth set in a firm line. "So, where are you on reviewing employee files?"

"Since the story about the task force, I've put everything else on hold. It takes time going through the files, and to be honest, I haven't been sure what to look for. But now I think I've figured out something else to work with."

"What's that?"

"Well, you probably read about the girl who was attacked on Friday, but got away?"

"Yes—it sounds like she was damned lucky!"

"Seems so." He paused briefly. "Actually, you wouldn't necessarily realize from the news reports, but she's Liz's housemate."

"Liz? Your girlfriend?"

"That's right."

"That's horrible!" Cohen's calm evaporated once more. "Then she—how is she?"

"She's doing okay. She's pretty strong emotionally."

"I'm glad to hear!" Cohen thought for a moment. "That's really awful, Ed. It must be very upsetting for Liz too. But tell me, how does this relate to looking for leads in our employee files?"

"See, that's the thing. I happened to arrive at Liz's when the police were there yesterday, apparently doing a follow-up interview with Karen." Ed hesitated, unsure what Henry's reaction would be to what followed. "They started asking me questions and I got the sense they thought I might have attacked Karen."

"You?"

"Yeah. It threw me for a loop."

"But—I can't imagine you doing such a thing, Ed!"

"Thanks for saying so, Henry. I talked with Karen after the cops left, and thankfully she feels the same way."

"I would hope so!" Cohen seemed genuinely dismayed at the idea. "But still, what has this got to do with finding a suspect from the personnel files?"

"It only hit me afterwards, when I was talking with Karen. She told me she thought the attacker was about my height and build, and right-handed, like me. I figured that was why the cops were so interested in questioning me. But what struck me is, these detectives weren't from the assault squad. They were from the task force looking into the notes and killings. So I realized they must think her attack was related to the killings, and if they thought I was a match for Karen's attacker, then they must also think I fit the suspected killer."

"Hmm." Cohen thought about it. "Well, I guess, logically, that makes sense. But Ed, really, thinking you're the killer?"

"It's disturbing, no question. But it made me think, if the police have reason to believe the killer fits my description, then I should be looking for someone similar when I'm looking at the files. I mean, I don't know how they decided on it—and obviously they weren't saying—but if it's on their radar, I should be looking for the same characteristics."

"Sounds reasonable." Cohen got up and extended his hand, signaling the conversation was over. "Well, good luck searching. And please keep me posted." He nodded for emphasis and smiled briefly. "And I'm sorry for getting so angry. This is all so crazy."

"No apology necessary, Henry." Ed returned the smile. "And don't worry, I'll be sure to let you know if I find anything. We both want this to end."

After Ed left, Henry Cohen sat for several minutes, considering the latest revelations. Ed's proposal to look for someone physically similar to himself seemed logical, though disconcerting. Pondering the situation, a dark thought crept into Cohen's mind. *How well do I really know Ed?*

That afternoon, Lou DiNova was having a conversation with his lieutenant, Johnny Palmieri. Like many such meetings, it occurred in the library of his home. DiNova was seated in his favorite overstuffed armchair, and Palmieri was standing, as usual. The *capo dei capi* put down the newspaper on the table beside his chair and looked at Palmieri.

"So, Johnny, you've been keeping up with the news?"

"Ya mean the task force thing, Lou?" Keeping informed of current events wasn't really Palmieri's thing, but he knew DiNova was concerned about the serial killer story. "Yeah, I heard about that on last night's news."

"Yes. The cops finally seem to realize the killing was not us, despite that reporter's stupid speculations." There'd been more than one death, but DiNova was clearly referring to Danny L'Heureux's death. "But I am still concerned about this whole thing. That girl who was attacked on Friday—things like that shouldn't happen, not in our town. If the paper's new theory is right—that some kind of whack job is running loose—then anybody could be a target, even your wife or mine." DiNova scowled, thinking about the possibility.

"Yeah, it definitely sounds like a nut job, Lou." In truth, Palmieri didn't think about such things, but he could figure what DiNova's view was.

"And if the guy is also responsible for the bad publicity we got with that L'Heureux kid, then it has become personal to me. I don't like people who mess with our business." He looked up at Palmieri. "So here's what I want you to do. Find out what the cops know about the assault, because the paper says it's related to the killings. If it is, I want to know what they know. And if they have a suspect, we do our own investigation."

"Sure thing, Lou. I already talked to Marv Siegel. He knows to keep his contacts open. But I'll call him to see about the attack on that girl. If the cops have somebody in mind, we'll know it."

"Good, Johnny. I want action on this. No nutcase is going to shit on our turf." DiNova picked up the newspaper once more. "Let me know as soon as you learn anything." Then, having another thought, he looked up again. "And contact Mickey O'Donoghue. Let him know we may have another job for him."

Things are starting to move along, the killer thought. *The newspaper's finally promoting the story and this shit with the task force is getting people more scared.* Thinking about it, he smiled. *Good.*

He was still pissed about having messed up with the girl, but given the news coverage, it seemed to be playing in his favor. Clearly, they had no leads to identify him and the media circus was adding to the public fear. Now it was time to start the serious planning and get things organized.

He'd already double-checked what materials he would need. Nitric acid and sulfuric acid were both used in the jewelry production process, and he knew he could obtain significant amounts on site. The plant normally also had some glycerin on hand, mostly for use in sand-casting prototype jewelry, but he doubted that there would be enough for his needs. Fortunately, glycerin was used for a variety of everyday purposes and could be obtained from any drugstore. He'd already started buying it from various places, gradually putting together a supply in a way that wouldn't raise questions.

In theory, the process of assembling the ingredients was pretty straightforward—any decent high school chemistry student could handle it. Of course, sometimes theory and reality could differ in a spectacular way. In this case, the real challenge was to assemble the ingredients and blow up the plant without also blowing himself up in the process. Given he would probably need a few hours to assemble things, he figured the best option would be to start in the late evening, so that everything would be ready before the next day's workers arrived at the Barton factory. If he made enough nitroglycerin, he could blow up the neighborhood as well as the plant. *Boom!* He smiled at the mental picture.

He also thought about publicity. He wanted both the company and the public to get more worked up, worrying about what was coming. At the same time, he could not be so specific that it would risk disrupting his plans. It was one thing to threaten an attack on an unnamed individual, but another thing entirely to say he was going to blow up Barton's factory. The note or notes for this purpose would need to be very carefully written, and the timing of their release also had to be just right. He looked at the calendar hanging on his wall.

This is Tuesday. If I do it on Sunday, then I've got a few days. I can probably wait till Thursday or Friday to send the notes. But maybe I should send more than one, to keep things stirred up. So much still to plan . . .

THIRTEEN

Thursday, May 14, 1987

MIKE LANGAN AND Francie Weber met in the squad room, drinking their morning coffee and reviewing where things stood. Mike's trip to the property room had been productive. It turned out that both L'Heureux and McIntyre had been wearing watches with expansion bands made by Barton Jewelry.

"I had to call Sanelli's widow to check on him. His personal effects had already been returned to her," Mike shared. "But my hunch was right. Sanelli wore a watch with the same type of band."

"So, that means we've now got two things that connect all three cases to the same perp," said Francie. "The physical description from the autopsy reports and the type of watchband on the vics."

"Yeah," said Mike, half smiling. "My gut told me the Sanelli case didn't work as just a mugging. Now I know why."

"Right." Francie paused to process this additional information. "Doesn't that mean there might be others? After all, it took us a while to connect the dots on these three."

Mike nodded in agreement. "I thought about that. We now know the first note was received by Barton on April 17. It makes threats, but nothing specific. So I'm guessing that any death before mid-April probably wasn't our guy."

"Okay, I buy that." Francie sipped her coffee, thinking back to April. "The thing is, Mike, the last homicide I recall before Sanelli was at the end of March. It was a domestic that I picked up, so I don't see how it would fit. Or is my memory wrong?"

"No, you're right. We haven't gotten any others in the time frame we're talking about." Mike took a gulp of his coffee and realized it was now cold. He made a face. Not exactly great when it was hot, the brew was now barely worth drinking. "The thing is, if we look at the timeline, there were two weeks between Sanelli and L'Heureux, but only one week between L'Heureux and McIntyre, and about the same between McIntyre and the attack on Durant."

"Uh-huh. So, you're thinking there's another one in between Sanelli and L'Heureux?" Francie drank the last of her coffee, also cold, and dropped the cup in the wastebasket. "But how could that be? Wouldn't we know?"

"Maybe." Mike had been bothered by the same concern. "But what if it wasn't actually in Providence? Who says this guy is sticking to the city limits?"

"Shit. I get ya. So how do we find out?"

"I've already talked to the state cops, and it turns out there's no complete record of homicides across the state. The feds collect some information, but it's always at the end of the year." Mike started to pick up his cup again, then stopped and threw it in the garbage. "So, we've gotta do our own legwork. I figure if there really was another case, it was nearby, so there's no point checking with places like Kingston or Newport. I'd say we divide up the the ones adjoining Providence and start making calls."

"Makes sense. But we've got another loose end—what about Durant? Do we know what she was wearing when she was attacked?"

"Good point. Okay, tell you what. You contact Durant and I'll check with the other nearby departments. There's only five that border Providence. If we come up empty on those, we can always go wider."

"Right." Francie got up to return to her own desk. "Good luck."

Mike Langan began calling around. Rhode Island was a pretty small place, and over the years, he'd developed contacts in most departments. The first four calls—to Johnston, Cranston, North Providence, and East Providence—had come up empty. For the last one, Pawtucket, he called Charlie Bickert.

"Hey, Mike. Good to hear from you." Bickert gave a small laugh. "Boy, you and Weber are hot stuff these days!"

"Yeah, right, Charlie. Happy to trade any time you like!"

"I know, Mike. Actually, you got my sympathy. It's always a pain when the political shit gets into our job."

"You got that right, Charlie." Mike swore under his breath. "Say, look, Charlie, we're working a new angle, and I'm wondering, did you have any new cases in late April?"

"April?" There was a pause that went on too long. "Uh, yeah, Mike, we had a case—you remember, that kid who got killed in a hit-and-run. We've talked about it before."

"Oh. Right." It dawned on Mike that he'd blocked it out, the incident a painful reminder of the death of Mike Jr. He also realized Charlie's pause likely stemmed from the same recognition. Ignoring the past, Mike continued. "So, where's it stand? Did you find the driver?"

"Unfortunately, no. Nobody saw the license plate and the paint chips on the kid's bike were from a blue Tempo. I checked and there's something like four hundred Tempos in Rhode Island and southern Mass. We don't have the resources to run them down, so all we could do was put a flag out to traffic in case somebody stops one with fender damage. 'Course, even if we do, it'll be hard to connect it back to the accident."

"I'm thinking maybe it wasn't an accident, Charlie."

"Huh? Who deliberately runs down a nine-year-old kid?" Bickert's voice revealed his puzzlement. "Wait a minute. You're on this task force thing. Are you saying there really is one perp behind all those homicides? And you're thinking he did the kid too?"

"I dunno for sure. But you can help me check it out, if you don't mind."

"Sure, Mike, anything. But what are you looking for?"

"Can you check his personal stuff and see if he had a watch?"

"A watch? Most kids his age don't have watches. And even if he did, how does that help you?"

"Just check it, Charlie. And if he did, look at what kind of watchband it was." Mike paused, not wanting to say too much at this stage. "Maybe it's nothing. But let me know. Once we find out, I can try to fill you in."

"Yeah, okay. We're nowhere on the case right now, anyway." Bickert paused, probably taking a drag on his ever-present cigarette. "I'll take a look, Mike, and get back to you later today. Okay?"

"That's terrific, Charlie. I owe ya."

It was early afternoon when Sandy DeVito from advertising stopped by Stan Osiewicz's desk with an envelope.

"Hey, Stan. This is for you. Somehow it got directed to our department."

"Thanks, Sandy." As she turned to walk away, he called out to her. "Hey, Sandy. Do you know how this was delivered?"

Sandy paused and turned back. "Gee, I'm not sure, Stan. I think it was in a big envelope addressed to Classifieds." She thought for a moment. "But I don't think there was a stamp or postmark, so maybe it got dropped off at reception."

"Yeah, makes sense. Thanks for bringing it by, Sandy."

"Any time, Stan." She smiled at him in a way that suggested a possible crush and continued on her way.

Stan looked at the white number ten envelope for a long moment without opening it. The writing did not match the previous notes—this was done in very precise block letters with a regular pen. He considered calling the cops without opening it, but his newsman's curiosity got the better of him. *After all*, he rationalized, *it might just be a note from an ordinary reader.*

The note inside was also unlike the previous notes. It was on typing paper and, like the envelope, written in crisp block letters.

Time to end the fun and games. Soon, there'll be no more worries about Barton Jewelry.
The hand of justice

Stan reread the note several times. Apart from the signature and the mention of Barton, the note bore no resemblance to the earlier notes. Could this be a copycat, inspired by the paper's coverage? After all, the stories had not revealed what the earlier notes looked like, only their content, so an imitator would likely get the format wrong. Stan sat thinking for a while, his eyes looking towards the windows, but not really seeing. At last, he decided he should let Mike Langan, the detective on the task force, know—and let him figure out if it was from the real guy.

The phone call was brief.

"Detective Langan? Stan Osiewicz at the *Journal*."

"Yeah, hi. Look, I know I said I'd give you a heads-up, but right now, there's nothing I can share."

"No, that's not why I'm calling. I got what might be another note."

"What do you mean, might be?"

"Well, it doesn't look like the others and doesn't exactly sound like them. I just don't know if it's a copycat or something."

There was a long silence. Finally, Langan responded. "Okay. Whatever it is, I gotta check it out. I'll see you in twenty minutes." The receiver clicked off.

While waiting for Langan, Stan first photocopied the note and then went down to reception to see what he could find out about the delivery. As usual, Paul, the retired cop who served as both receptionist and security for the newspaper, was at the high desk that overlooked the marble-floored lobby.

"Hey, Ozzie, how's it going? Those stories you've been doing are great—real killers!" Paul laughed at his own joke.

"Yeah, thanks, Paul." Paul's use of the nickname grated on him, but at the moment, Stan needed Paul's help. "Say, Paul, do you remember getting an envelope for classifieds today? Maybe one of those big manila envelopes?"

"Uh, I think so. You know, sometimes it's pretty busy here."

"Yes, I realize, Paul, but please try. Can you remember anything about the person who dropped it off?"

"Gee, Ozzie . . ." After a long pause, his eyes lit up. "Wait! I do remember! It was a guy wearing a Pawsox ballcap and some kind of jacket. And he had sunglasses on. I thought that was kinda strange, you know, indoors and all."

"Do you remember anything else? Like how tall he was? Was he thin or heavyset?"

"Uh, he was probably about six feet, pretty solid build."

"What about his hair?"

"Gee, I couldn't see much, with the ballcap. Seemed to be cut short. But if I had to guess, I'd say he had dark hair."

"Did he speak at all?"

Paul scratched the back of his neck. "Probably. You know, something about giving it to the Classifieds department. But I don't really recall." Paul looked directly at Stan. "What's with the questions, Ozzie? Since when has advertising been your beat?"

"It's nothing, Paul. Just curious." Paul gave him a look suggesting he didn't buy it, but there was little he could say. "Anyway, thanks, Paul."

Back in the newsroom, Stan Osiewicz found Detective Langan waiting at his desk—they'd likely missed each other while Stan went to talk to Paul at the reception desk. Langan bore an expression of impatience. "Where ya been, Osiewicz? And where's this note?"

Stan handed it over without comment.

"Shit." Langan read the note several times.

"You think it's legit?"

"Who the fuck knows? There's nothin' about this case that makes sense."

"You said 'case', not 'cases.' So you've concluded the killings are related?"

Langan scowled at Stan. "Yeah, we think they're connected. But I've got no details for you." He waved the note angrily.

"Right. I get it." Stan decided to take a chance. "But off the record, if I suggested the guy was about six feet with dark hair, would I be way off?"

Langan didn't need to speak. His raised eyebrows spoke louder than words. "Who told you that? You got somebody in our department?"

Stan understood Langan's suspicions, but also wanted to make it clear that in this instance there was no leak. "Actually, it was a guess, because that's the description our receptionist just gave me of the guy that dropped off the note you're holding."

"Damn . . . OK, off the record, that sounds like the guy in our two murders and the assault last Friday." Scowling at Stan, Mike added, "But you didn't hear it from me. And if it comes out now, that'll be the last you get from me, got it?"

"Got it. Thanks. And let me know if there's any more about this note."

"Yeah, yeah. So who's this receptionist? I want to ask my own questions."

"His name's Paul--you'll find him in the lobby. " Stan was going to add, "He's actually a retired cop. " Before he could, Langan hurried out the newsroom, note in hand.

After Langan left, Stan rushed to talk with Joe Houle. Houle was on the phone when he approached, so Stan waited impatiently for the call to finish. As he stood there, he looked at his watch and realized the deadline for the evening edition had already passed. *Shit.*

"Come on in, Stan." Houle gestured for him to sit. "What's up?"

"I got another note." He handed the photocopy to the editor.

"I don't get it. This doesn't look like the other notes."

"I know," Stan agreed. "I just talked with Langan, the cop from the task force, and he had the same worry."

"So how do you know it's from the guy? Maybe it's some copycat nutcase."

"Well, I thought the same thing, and Langan and I talked about it." Like a card player, Stan was waiting to play his ace. "But I also got a description of the guy who dropped it off to Paul downstairs, and when I told Langan, he just about dropped. Off the record, he told me it fits the description they're working on for both murders, as well as the assault last Friday."

"You're kidding me, right?"

"No, Joe. Straight scoop. The thing is, Langan won't let me use the description—or at least the link to the cases—in a story."

Houle thought about it for several moments, unconsciously reaching for his bottle of antacid tablets. "Okay," he said finally. "We can't tell what they think, 'cause we don't want to burn the channel. But that doesn't stop us from saying what you found out from Paul. We could spin it as a call to the public, asking if anyone has information." He looked at Stan, reading his face. "You get enough of a description from Paul to be plausible?"

"Yeah, I think so." Stan hesitated. "I mean, you know Paul—he's getting on, and his memory's not always great. But he seemed okay with what he told me."

"Okay." Houle drummed his fingers on the desktop and looked away as if distracted. "You write something up. If I like it, it'll go into tomorrow's *Journal*. Then we'll see what happens."

"Right, Joe, I'll—"

"And Stan," Houle interrupted, "do it without pissing off the cops."

Francie Weber had trouble reaching Karen Durant at work, but left a message, and in midafternoon, got a return call.

"Detective Weber? This is Karen Durant. I understand you were trying to reach me? Have you learned something new about my attacker?"

"Hi, Ms. Durant, thanks for getting back to me." Francie decided to go formal, unlike in the face-to-face interview. "No, I'm sorry, but there's nothing I can say right now. But we are working on it. Actually, that's why I'm calling. I have a couple more questions for you."

"Um, okay." Karen's voice expressed doubt. "Just don't ask me if I thought the attacker was Ed. I heard from Liz that you've been pestering him. Honestly, I can't believe you think it could've been him! I sure as hell don't think it was!"

"I appreciate that, Ms. Durant. Believe me, I'm not in the habit of pestering anyone, including Mr. Underwood. But we have to be thorough, and you'd be surprised how often attacks, and even homicides, are committed by people who know the victim." She paused, hoping the comment would appease Karen.

"Yeah, sure. Anyway, what did you want to know?"

"Do you remember what you were wearing that night?"

"Of course. But I already told that to the original investigators. In fact, I was still wearing the same clothes when they met with me." Karen's tone suggested she was beginning to feel pestered.

"I know. Look, I'm sorry to go back to it—I understand it must be painful—but I want to be sure we don't overlook anything." Francie could read her tone and was trying to keep her calm—not easy to do on the phone. "But the report didn't mention any accessories you were wearing. Do you remember what you might have had on?"

"Accessories? You mean jewelry?" She was silent for a long moment, as if trying to recall the outfit. "Um, I had a gold choker necklace—not real gold, just gold plated—and two multicolored bracelets on my right wrist."

"Thanks." Francie paused, then asked the key question. "Were you wearing a watch?"

"Uh, yeah. It was a Seiko with a gold band, like the necklace."

"A gold band? Like an expansion band?"

"Yeah, that's right. I borrowed it from my roommate. She gets lots of stuff from Ed because he works at Barton. The choker was mine, but I think Ed got it for me from Barton."

Bingo, thought Francie. "Sounds like you've got a generous housemate. And it sounds like Ed Underwood's a good guy to know when it comes to jewelry." In her own mind, the remark cut two ways.

"Yeah, Liz is great, and so's Ed. That's why I don't understand your hounding him."

"It's not personal, Ms. Durant. Like I said, we have to check out all the possibilities."

"Uh-huh." Karen still sounded doubtful. "Look, do you need anything else? I really should be getting back to work."

"No, and thanks very much. I appreciate your patience. As I said, we really are serious about pursuing this."

"Well, I hope you catch the bastard." Without saying goodbye, Karen hung up.

When Mike Langan and Francie Weber reconnected in midafternoon, they were both excited about what they'd found. Francie went first, sharing her conversation with Karen Durant.

"She was a bit hostile. Seems convinced that Ed Underwood isn't our guy and she's angry that we've been checking him out. But it turns out we were right—she had on a watch with a Barton expansion band. Sounds like she was wearing other Barton jewelry too."

"Sonuvabitch!" Mike exclaimed. "Good work, Francie!" After many dead ends, it felt like they were starting to make headway.

"What about you, Mike? Any leads on new cases?"

"Yep—and you won't believe it!"

"What's the scoop?"

"I struck out with the first four calls, but when I talked to Charlie Bickert in Pawtucket, he reminded me they'd had a hit-and-run a few weeks ago, right during the time frame we were looking at."

"Hit-and-run? Wasn't that some kid on a bike?"

"Right, that's the one."

"But I thought he was a little kid—"

"Yeah, he was only nine, but Charlie confirmed he'd been wearing a watch and it had a Barton expansion band." It was Francie's turn to go wide-eyed. "I decided to follow up and called his mother. She told me it was a birthday present. The kid had been really keen to get one."

"Shit . . ."

"You got it." Mike grimaced. "Little guy was hot to have a watch, and it turns out it may be what got him killed. "

"Christ almighty." Francie was a practicing Catholic, but at this moment the expletive felt justified.

"So, the good news is we have a link to another killing. The bad news is Pawtucket's got squat on the case. No witnesses, and the only lead is a paint chip that fits a blue Ford Tempo, of which there are only about four hundred in the area."

"Damn . . ."

"Yeah, and they don't have the manpower to run them all." Mike thought about it. "And neither do we. So the case is almost certainly linked, but it doesn't help us figure out who this whack job is."

"Well, I guess we just gotta keep working it." Francie was distressed that the perp was evidently willing to kill children; any murder was awful, but killing a child seemed outrageous. She was even more unhappy that the day's efforts had not yielded a new lead to go with the new links between cases. She looked at her partner. "We'll get this bastard, Mike. You know we will."

"Yeah, I know," said Mike, frustration obvious in his voice. "At least we know the pattern with the watchbands fits with the references to Barton in the notes." He had a further thought. "And if the perp is somebody connected to Barton, he probably knows their products. That might explain how he picked out Durant when she was leaving the club."

Francie's face lit up. "Yeah! And Durant told me Ed Underwood supplied her and his girlfriend with lots of stuff from Barton!"

"Okay, we've got something to work with. We need to do more checking on this guy." In his haste, Mike almost forgot to give Francie the last piece of new information. "Oh, and what do you think of this?" He handed Francie the note he'd picked up from Stan Osiewicz earlier in the afternoon.

"Is this for real, Mike? I mean, it doesn't look like any of the others."

"I know. That's what I've been wondering too." He looked again at the note, then back at Francie. "But get this—we got a description of the guy that dropped it off, and guess what?"

"He matches our perp? Shit, Mike, that's fuckin' unbelievable! Ya think the guy actually had the balls to deliver it himself?" Francie's eyebrows rose the same way Mike's had when Stan gave him the description. "This thing keeps getting weirder." She remained silent for several moments, evidently thinking about the implications. "Well, if the description fits, then the note is probably legit, right?"

"Yeah, that's what I was thinkin'."

"Okay. So we gotta figure out what he's planning." Francie had a further thought. "You know Mike, I still like Underwood as a suspect, whatever Durant may think.

What say we go to Briggs and see if we can put some surveillance on the guy? If it's him and he's planning something big, we need to be on top of it."

Mike thought about it. "I'm not convinced yet that it's him, and I think we've gotta be careful we don't get tunnel vision on this and end up looking in the wrong direction. But right now we've got nothing better, so it might be worth a try. At the same time, let's keep looking and see if we find another lead. Whoever it is, it sounds like we don't have much time to stop whatever he's planning."

"Right, Mike. You're the lead on this." Francie made eye contact and nodded. "I'll talk to Briggs in the morning about putting a tail on Underwood."

As she started walking away, a sudden thought hit Mike. "Say, Francie, do we know what kind of car Underwood drives?"

"No. I'll check with the DMV." She smiled. "If it's a blue Ford Tempo, I think the lieutenant will be happy to give us guys to shadow him."

When the story broke in the *Journal*, Henry Cohen had felt alarm, followed by a brief sense of relief when the police announced the creation of a task force. Since that announcement, there had not been another note to the company—until today.

Like the earlier ones, the latest note had been sent by mail, and when it reached Cohen's desk, he'd immediately phoned Detective Weber. They'd met on the previous Tuesday, when she came to interview him and pick up the originals of the first four notes. Now, half an hour after calling her about this new note, she was sitting in Cohen's office.

Weber read the note a couple of times and looked at the envelope. The format of this note was like the previous ones, having been assembled from letters cut from a newspaper. In this case, the backing page was from the previous morning's *Providence Journal*, indicating it was newly composed. However, it was the message that really grabbed attention:

> *The time for threats has ended, since nobody seems to listen. That's OK—soon you won't have a company to worry about.*
> *The hand of justice*

"So, it came the same way as the others?"

"Yes, that's right. It came in the afternoon delivery and I phoned you right away." Trying to be helpful, he added, "It's postmarked from Johnston. They've each been sent from a different nearby location. And this is the first one with a signature, if you can call it that."

"Good points. That's the name used in the notes sent to the *Journal*." Weber looked again at the note, and then at Cohen. "So, what do you think he's talking about, this 'won't have a company to worry about' thing?"

"I wish I knew." Cohen frowned. "The previous note talked about making the company a casualty, but there was no mention of how or when."

"Uh-huh. Given this guy's actions so far, I'm guessing he means some kind of violence. And he's talking about 'soon.' Anything special happening in the next week?"

"No, no, just normal business." Cohen threw up his hands. "How can this be happening?"

"Well, we're now pretty certain the recent deaths are related to the notes. And whoever's behind it, they're obviously not playing with a full deck. That don't mean they don't have a reason in their own head, but we're still trying to figure it out."

"But you'll protect us, right?" Cohen's words were more a plea than a question.

"I promise you, we're doing everything we can, Mr. Cohen." Privately, she wondered, *How do we get this guy before there's more killing?*

After making the promise, Weber had left, taking the note with her. Cohen had made a photocopy before she arrived, and now, as he prepared to leave the office, he was tempted to look at it yet again, but resisted.

He'd considered contacting Ed Underwood about the new note, but felt strangely reluctant. In her first interview, Detective Weber had asked a number of questions about Ed, and Ed himself had indicated in their last conversation that the police seemed to be treating him as a suspect. Though rationally, Henry didn't believe Ed could do any of it, emotionally, he felt ungrounded, unsure of what to believe. He was also bothered that since their last conversation on Tuesday, he hadn't heard anything from Ed about the search of the personnel files. All these factors gave substance to the small voice that had been echoing in his head.

What if it is *Ed?*

It was late in the afternoon and Ed Underwood was excited. He'd spent most of his time for the past week going through employee records, trying to find the note sender. At first, it had been a blind search through hundreds of files, with nothing to look for except indications of discipline problems. Since Tuesday, though, he'd realized that he should be looking for a male about six feet tall with a medium build. He was helped in this by the company's requirement for physical exams on hiring, but it still meant going back and starting over.

After two days of searching files for active employees, it had dawned on him that a former employee was more likely to be angry at the company. *What's the saying—you're so smart, you're stupid?* Ed certainly felt stupid as he looked at the file of an employee who had been fired in late March.

Victor Blake had been a foreman in the plating department and had worked for Barton for about ten years. During that time, there had been several incidents that seemed to reflect a combination of impatience and racism—verbally abusing and threatening minority workers who didn't perform as he thought they should. Finally, at the end of March, he actually pushed someone, a young Puerto Rican guy who'd only recently been hired. When the production manager, George Silva, heard about it, he'd decided Blake had to go. According to notes added to the file by Silva, Victor had reacted with intense anger, blaming both the Puerto Rican boy and the company for his fate.

Ed closed the file and sat back, his fingers unconsciously drumming on the cover of the folder. *Could this be the guy?* He considered taking the folder to Henry Cohen and suggesting they tell the police. *But what if I'm wrong? After all, do complaints of racism and verbal abuse really equate to being a killer?* He sat there for several minutes, uncertain what to do. Finally, realizing it was now after five o'clock, he decided he would wait till the next morning to speak to Cohen and use the evening to think about what to do. He planned to go to the *dojo*, and then have dinner with Liz. He was confident that clearing his head by training, and then using Liz as his sounding board, would help him sort out the situation.

Johnny Palmieri was growing impatient. He'd been waiting in the parking lot in front of Barton Jewelry since before four o'clock, and it was now nearly five thirty. His early checks on Wednesday had suggested that it would be easiest to intercept his target as he was leaving work, or, if necessary, follow him until an opportunity for close approach arose.

A handful of cars were still scattered across the lot, which was designed to hold more than a hundred vehicles; an even larger lot was located behind the four-story building. Conveniently, the people high up in the food chain had reserved spaces near the entrance to the four-story brick building, and it was clear that a car, a blue Taurus, was still sitting in the space marked "Reserved for Personnel Manager." The nearly empty lot meant there was unlikely to be an observer if Johnny tried to make contact here, but also made it harder to get near without being spotted by his target. Growing impatient, and not keen to spend his evening following the guy, Johnny decided to make a play here; if he had to bail without making contact, he knew where the guy lived and could approach him there later on. He moved from his car in the far corner of the lot to stand behind some bushes that lined the front wall of the building near the main entrance. Though he'd already determined there was a back entrance for employees, he figured that, given where the guy's car was parked, he'd come out the front door.

He looked again at his watch and mouthed a curse. *This fuckin' guy seems way too dedicated to his job. Makes me think he can't be the one.* He was tempted to leave, but he knew Lou DiNova wouldn't react well to hearing that Johnny hadn't made contact. Hearing the sound of the main door opening, he carefully peeked out from the bushes and saw his man leaving. Underwood's car was parked on the other side of the entrance, away from Johnny's position. *Got ya, asshole!* He grasped the stubby screwdriver in his right hand and moved across the asphalt paving in his rubber-soled shoes.

Leaving work, Ed Underwood was preoccupied with thoughts of Victor Blake, the fired foreman. It seemed too coincidental that the notes and killings had started shortly after he was fired, and that he fit what Ed knew about the physical description of Karen's attacker. *Do I tell Henry or check him out first? His address in our file is probably still OK.* Ed knew it was naïve to think that looking at the man would tell him much, but he was still tempted, especially given the reaction of the cops. Their suspicions about him made Ed reluctant to contact them, and somehow, the idea of checking out Blake himself felt like a way to assert control in a situation that made him feel powerless.

As he approached his car, Ed took out his keys. Just as he did so, he felt a hard object press into his right kidney. A voice said, "Hold it right there, ass—"

Before the word was finished, Ed reacted. He dodged, his left foot moving in front of his right as he pivoted to the side, taking the bulk of his body out of the line of what appeared to be a gun. Simultaneously, his right arm swept around and struck the arm that held the gun. The impact both moved the weapon away from Ed's body and weakened the attacker's grip.

Still turning, Ed jammed his right foot into the attacker's knee, collapsing the joint and throwing the assailant off balance. After striking the forearm, Ed used his right hand to grab the wrist, levering the arm behind and up, as the collapsed knee caused his foe to drop to the ground. Ed followed him down, placing his knee on the attacker's back as he pulled the wrist up towards the left shoulder, his left hand applying further leverage at the elbow. Any attempt to move would result in dislocation of the assailant's shoulder, or worse. The whole sequence had taken perhaps three seconds.

Ed was angry at himself for being caught unawares—it was the kind of lapse that Yoshikawa had frequently criticized. By contrast, his attitude to his would-be attacker was as much curiosity as anger. "Okay, asshole—I think that's what you tried to call me—who are you and what do you want?"

Palmieri was silent for a long moment, struggling for breath after the takedown. Finally he spoke. "Uh, easy, pal. I just wanna talk."

"Talk? That's why you stuck a gun in my back?"

"Nah, no gun. Just a screwdriver." Palmieri's right hand opened, revealing the stubby tool.

What the—? Ed was mystified. After a moment, he repeated, "Okay, so let's try again. Who are you and what do you want?"

"My name's Johnny Palms. I was sent to ask you some questions."

"Johnny Palms? You kidding me? What kind of name is that?"

"It's—it's really Giovanni Palmieri, but everybody calls me Johnny Palms."

"Okay, Johnny. So, who sent you and what did you want to ask me? And don't make me keep repeating myself." For emphasis, Ed levered Johnny's arm further, eliciting a grunt of pain.

"Okay, okay! Jesus, who the hell are you, Bruce Lee?" He hesitated, and then said, "I work for Lou DiNova. He heard the cops were lookin' at you for the attack on that girl last week, and he wanted me to check you out."

Damn! My similiarity to Karen's attacker—was it Victor Blake?—is making things more and more complicated. "DiNova? The mob guy? Why's he care about Karen's attack? He own the club or something, so it's bad for business?"

"I dunno! You'd hafta ask him! I'm just the paid muscle, ya know?"

Ed thought about that for a minute. He suspected he wasn't getting the whole story but wasn't sure about prolonging this situation. If someone else came upon the scene, it would lead to more complications.

"Okay, Johnny. You tell your boss that if he wants to talk to me, he should call me on the phone." Ed considered options—he wasn't keen to let Johnny go, but he also wasn't eager for more contact with the police. "I'm gonna cut you a break. But if I ever see you again, I won't be so nice." He shifted his left arm to come around Palmieri's neck, applying pressure that forced the head back and compressed the windpipe. In moments, Palmieri passed out.

Ed searched the unconscious man, found a set of car keys and threw them across the parking lot. He also checked for a gun—none—and wallet, confirming the name of Giovanni Palmieri. Satisfied, Ed left the failed assailant unconscious on the ground, got in his own car and drove off.

Christ! The mob as well as the cops are after me? That settles it. I need to know if this Victor guy is behind all this, before it's too late.

When he came to, Johnny Palmieri slowly picked himself up and looked around. Underwood's car was gone and no one else was in sight. *Well, at least that much is good.* He started moving towards his car and realized his right knee hurt like hell. *That sonuvabitch! This ain't over!*

Still, he knew any further action would be up to DiNova; he dreaded the conversation that was to come, reporting his fuck-up. He got to his car and reached into his pocket for his keys. *Damn! Did the bastard take them?*

He looked around in panic, and his eyes spotted a glint on the asphalt, toward where he'd confronted Underwood. *Shit!* He grunted as he hobbled to retrieve the keys, even as he figured worse pain was to come when he talked to Lou DiNova.

By the time Johnny Palmieri reached DiNova's house, it was almost seven p.m. His knee injury and the lost keys had really slowed him down. In a way, the timing was good, because it meant he wouldn't interrupt his boss's dinner. DiNova met him in the front room library and, noticing the limp, invited him to sit down.

"So, Johnny. What news do you have? And what happened to your leg?" DiNova had known Palmieri since he was a boy, and his reaction to his lieutenant's condition was almost fatherly.

"Well, Lou, I went to find this Underwood guy, the one the cops are interested in."

"And what did you learn?"

"See, that's the thing. I waited outside Barton Jewelry, where he works, till he came out. He worked late, so it was almost five-thirty. There was nobody around, so I came up from behind to get the drop on him."

DiNova looked intently at Palmieri, but said nothing.

"I got to the guy at his car and started to tell him to stand still. Before I could even finish, he goes Bruce Lee on me. Next thing I knew, I was on the ground and he was choking me out."

"Really? This guy got the better of you? Johnny, that's not like you . . ."

"I'm telling you, Lou, he must be some kind of kung fu master or somethin'. I ain't never seen anythin' like the bastard. He was fast, and he knew what the hell he was doin'."

DiNova looked at Palmieri, and then looked out the window at the gathering dusk. "So, you're saying you never got to question him?"

"That's right. He choked me out, and when I came to, he was gone. The bastard had even thrown my car keys away to slow me down more." On the drive over, Palmieri had decided it was better to present it as a total screw-up than admit that he had told Underwood about working for DiNova.

"Hmm . . ." DiNova thought about it. "Then, to summarize, all we've learned about him is that he works for Barton Jewelry, the company mentioned in the notes the newspaper has published. And we know the cops consider him a suspect in the attack on that girl, and maybe more." *More*, of course, meant the murders, starting with Danny L'Heureux.

DiNova paused to light a cigar, and then continued."It seems we've also learned that he can be a dangerous man to confront." It was by no means a complete picture, and would never prove guilt in a court of law. But DiNova wasn't interested in legalities; he wanted the situation—including the news frenzy—resolved. "Here's what to do, Johnny. You contact Mickey O'Donoghue, tell him I want him watching this guy. He should be there when Underwood wakes up and follow him till he goes to bed.

For now, I don't want Mickey to approach him directly, just keep an eye on him. But if he sees something suggesting Underwood is the guy, Mickey is to make sure he doesn't get to hurt anybody else."

"I got ya, boss." Palmieri gave a grim smile. "And if Mickey needs some extra hands, ya want me to help?" Mentally, he relished the idea of getting even with Underwood.

"No, no, that won't be necessary." DiNova could read Palmieri's mood and didn't want any loose cannons in what was already a disagreeable situation. "You just make sure Mickey understands what I want. And get that knee looked after, Johnny." He shifted focus to his cigar, thinking it would restore the pleasant after-dinner mood he'd been in when Palmieri walked in.

Palmieri limped out, still seething at Underwood.

After the confrontation with Johnny Palmieri, Ed considered going to the *dojo*, as much to clear his head as to do a real workout. At the same time, he was reluctant to go there. Yoshikawa was clearly concerned about Ed, and as close as their relationship was, Ed was avoiding being honest about what was going on, to the point that he'd left the previous class abruptly, without a word to his mentor.

While he considered his conflict, he glanced at his watch. The time gave him an excuse to skip going for a workout. If he went, he would get to Liz's later than he'd promised—and since he knew she was making dinner, he didn't want to be late. Besides, he needed to talk to her about what was happening.

When he rang the doorbell, Karen answered.

"Hi, Ed! Great to see you!" Karen leaned forward to give him a kiss on the cheek, followed by a hug.

"Hi, Karen. Good to see you too." Ed was relieved. He'd been concerned that the police suspicions would push Karen away, but clearly that wasn't the case. "How are you feeling?"

"I'm fine, Ed. You know me, I bounce back when crap happens." She gave a half frown. "I just wish they'd catch the bastard." She made direct eye contact. "And I'm grateful to you, Ed. Without the stuff you taught me, they say he might've killed me." She hugged him again. Almost as an afterthought, she added, "You know, that lady detective called me again today."

"Oh? What'd she want?"

"It was kinda weird. She asked me what jewelry I'd been wearing on Friday."

"Really? Did you remember?"

"Sure, you know me and fashion, Ed! I told her I had on a choker you'd gotten for me with your company discount, and a couple of bracelets, and a watch I'd borrowed from Liz. You know how great Liz is about loaning me stuff."

Ed smiled. "Well, I think she's happy having you for a housemate, Karen."

"I hope so. It sure works for me. Anyway, Liz is in the kitchen. You better go see her before she thinks I'm making moves on you!" Karen danced away and headed up the stairs.

Ed found himself watching her exit. *They asked about jewelry? And it was mostly from Barton?* He put his speculations aside to seek out Liz.

"Hey, Liz!" Ed called as he entered the large kitchen. Liz was at the stove, and turned to embrace him.

"Hi to you too!" Her lips found his for a long kiss. "How was your day?"

"Um, a lot happening. But let's leave it till after we eat." He scanned the kitchen, where the array of dishes and utensils indicated meal preparations were not finished. "Right now, what can I do to help?"

Later, as they sat in the dining room over the remnants of the meal, nursed by a now nearly-empty bottle of Beaujolais, Ed began to tell Liz about the day's events--starting with the encounter with Johnny Palmieri.

"That's awful, Ed!" Liz looked at him closely, as if making sure he was physically okay. "You know, I'm beginning to be grateful for your involvement in *karate.* I mean, first Karen gets attacked, and now you?" She gave a small shiver.

"I'm okay, Liz, and I think Karen is too." He thought about what had happened. "I don't think the guy wanted to hurt me, just intimidate me. Of course, that didn't play out the way he expected." He gave a small smile, like a proud schoolboy. "But what bothers me is, why would a mob boss want to talk to me about Karen? And how did they even get my name?

Liz frowned. "We both know the Mafia has deep roots in Rhode Island. I mean, the mayor of Providence got reelected after a felony charge, and everybody knows businesses that are mob-connected, like that discount clothing store in North Providence where you've shopped.

Half their stuff is hot." His occasional patronage of the store had been a source of friction between them. "So does it really surprise you to think they have informants in the police department?"

"No, I guess you're right. Given the cops' suspicions about me, it easy to see how the mob could find out." Ed looked out the window, frowning, and then back at Liz. "But still, what's their interest in all this?" He shook his head. "I wish I'd asked this Johnny Palmieri more."

"Well, at least you're okay. But Ed, what about telling the police? Shouldn't they know about this?"

Ed grimaced. "No, I'm not ready to do that. I don't like their interest in me, and this could make it worse. For one thing, they'll wonder why I didn't report it right away, or hold the guy, given I subdued him. Worse, the fact that the mob is interested in me may just make them more convinced I'm guilty!"

Liz nodded, but said nothing.

"And besides, Liz, there's this other thing I learned today."

"Oh? What do you mean?"

"I've been going through all the personnel records at work, trying to see if there's somebody who might be behind all this. Henry asked me a few days ago to see if I could find anything." He briefly explained his theory, looking for a troublemaker who also fit the description of Karen's attacker.

"And you found someone?"

"Yes. A foreman we fired in late March. He'd caused problems because of abusiveness and racism.

And his medical records indicate he matches what Karen described."

"Do you really think that's enough?" Liz played the devil's advocate, as she often did in their discussions.

"Well, at the very least, it's a strange coincidence. And don't forget that the file clearly shows resentment toward the company."

"Uh-huh." Liz acknowledged the pattern but was clearly not convinced.

"And there's something else. Karen told me the police were asking her about what jewelry she was wearing on Friday. It turns out most of it was made by Barton—but I can't see how an attacker would recognize that unless—"

"Unless they had worked there . . ." Liz finished the thought for him. "And you think that because the task force cops were asking Karen about this, they think the jewelry is a link in the killings?"

"Exactly."

"But Ed, it's one thing for them to ask about Karen's jewelry, and another to . . . I mean, weren't the murder victims all men?"

"It looks like it, but don't forget, the most popular products Barton makes are the expansion bands. They've got patents on them, so nobody else makes anything similar, and they are made for men's watches as well as women's."

"So, this guy—Victor Blake, you said?—gets fired as foreman, and then takes out his anger on anybody wearing Barton products?" Liz tried to absorb it all. "That's pretty cold, isn't it?"

"Absolutely. But whoever's doing this clearly isn't thinking about morality."

"Ed, it sounds like you should tell the police. Even if Victor Blake isn't really the one, they need to check him out. I mean, if they've been suspicious of you, they should be very interested in this guy."

Ed was silent for several moments. "I hear what you're saying, Liz. And at some point, I will—for that matter, I need to tell Henry too. But with what happened today, it's become personal. Before I let go of it, I need to know more. The cops haven't exactly been forthcoming with me. I think telling them can wait a bit."

Liz shook her head. "I don't know, Ed. This isn't a game. People have died. And you're not the police. What are you going to do, be a vigilante?" She frowned at him, her eyes filled with doubt and concern.

"No, nothing like that." He reached across the table for her hand and tried for a reassuring smile. "Look, Liz, this whole thing has been bothering me since Henry showed me the first note. Now, with what's happened to Karen and this mob guy coming after me, I can't just let it go. But I won't do anything foolish, I promise."

"I believe in you, Ed. And I know you aren't the impulsive type." She looked directly at him and squeezed his hand. "I just hope you don't get in over your head."

They left the topic and went on to other things, but it was one of those discussions where neither felt it was resolved. Ed's thoughts continued to focus on Victor Blake, and Liz, however much she wished to be supportive, was wondering what was driving Ed to act in a way that seemed so out of character.

They talked for a bit longer, then cleared the table and did the dishes together. After that, Ed said he was going to head home. Friday promised to be a busy day at work, and the events of the week thus far had left him feeling drained. It was not unusual for him to leave like this on a weeknight, and Liz made no protest, simply walking to the door with him for a goodbye embrace.

Shortly after, Liz and Karen sat together in the den, watching television—something they rarely did together. On this night, they both felt a need for companionship.

"Liz, how are you doing?" Karen looked over at her housemate as they sat on the couch.

"Me? Shouldn't I be asking you that? After all, you're the one who was attacked!"

"Oh, I'm fine, Liz," Karen replied, brushing aside the concern like a stray lock of her long hair. "But I know the police scrutiny must be hard for Ed—and for you."

Liz was silent, and avoided eye contact with Karen. Finally she spoke, while still looking down. "Okay, you're right. I'm worried about Ed." She frowned, while still not looking at Karen. "It's not just the police. Henry Cohen, his boss, has been pressuring him ever since this whole thing started. And then he was attacked by some Mafia thug tonight as he left work."

"What?! He never said anything when he came in!"

Liz nodded. "I know. He didn't even tell me until we'd finished dinner." She thought about the conversation. "He's okay physically—you know Ed, he's got lots of martial arts training. I'm more worried about his state of mind. Lately he's so distracted, which isn't like him. I know he's really unhappy about the police—"

"I don't blame him!" interrupted Karen. "I think they're way off base! "

Liz didn't acknowledge Karen's defense of Ed, but simply continued her narrative. "Now he's identified a suspicious former Barton employee. I told him he should contact the police immediately, but he refused. I don't know what he's thinking, or what he plans to do." She was silent for several moments, and then said in a low voice, "I'm not even sure I fully believe him. He just seems different."

There was a long silence while Karen processed all that Liz had said. Finally she reached out to put her hand on Liz's knee as they sat on the couch. "Liz, don't let this get to you. I refuse to let the attack rule my life, and you need to support Ed, not doubt him. He's a good person, and you know it better than anyone."

Liz looked up, finally making eye contact with Karen. "Are you sure?"

"Yes, Liz, I'm sure," Karen said firmly. "And you should be, too."

"I guess you're right." She reached out her arms, and Karen gave her a hug to reassure her—but as they hugged, Karen could not see the doubt that still showed in Liz's eyes.

Watching the late news on TV, the killer scowled. *What the fuck? Nothin' in the* Bulletin *or on the news?* He crumpled his empty beer can and tossed it in the direction of the kitchen wastebasket. Not for the first time, he was stunned at how slow the newspaper was to react.

Even so, delivering the note to the newspaper himself had been a real adrenaline boost. Of course, even after planning to do it, he had checked things out—especially the old guy at the reception desk. In the end, he figured the guy was not too sharp and would probably barely remember getting an envelope for the Classifieds department. Even if he did notice, the hat and sunglasses were good cover. It still rankled him that the girl on Friday had gotten away, and he figured she had caught at least a glimpse of him, but obviously nothing had come of it. So, he concluded the risk of making the delivery was more than offset by the pleasure of doing it right under their noses.

In terms of his plans, he'd decided that Sunday was the right day to act. The plant was shut down on weekends, and having extra time would be important. As much as he was confident he could make the nitroglycerin, it was not a process that could be rushed, and mistakes could prove fatal. *So, better to do it when the plant is empty.*

Getting access to the factory might be tricky, especially since he needed to bring in some of the supplies, including the glycerin. He didn't want anyone seeing him and asking questions. From his years working at Barton, the building layout was very familiar. Based on this, he decided that the door beside the shipping dock would be a good entry point—it had a simple cylinder lock with a chain latch on the inside. He figured he could jimmy the lock, and a good shove would be enough to rip out the chain's bracket.

Once he was inside, nobody would be the wiser, even if they walked by the door. He knew that there was only one security guard who watched the building—as a foreman, he'd sometimes arrived early and encountered the guy. *What the hell was his name? Jack? Jock? Jake—yeah, I think that's it.* Although he was supposed to continually roam the four floors of the building, in practice, the guard seldom went beyond the first floor.

"After all," he'd once commented, "who's gonna break in from the fourth floor?"

Just the kind of lazy thinking I like to see.

Satisfied that the trip to the newspaper had gone well, and that his plans for Sunday were in good shape, he settled back with his beer to watch Johnny Carson's monologue.

I love this guy. Ain't it too bad that the people at Barton won't be laughing on Monday.

FOURTEEN

Sunday, May 17, 1987

IT WAS A beautiful Sunday afternoon, and Mike Langan was grateful for the chance to spend it with his wife and son. Clare had assigned him to run the barbecue, and while the coals heated up, he and Jamie were playing catch in the backyard. Not for the first time, Mike was reminded of how good it felt to get away from work. In truth, it never really left him when he was working a case, but for a few moments, he could pretend. Homicide was a dark domain at the best of times, and the task force work was worse than most cases. But at least for today, he could put it aside—after Francie Weber had gotten approval from Lieutenant Bickert to tail Underwood, they'd been doing twelve-hour alternating shifts with Dunn and Bernstein. Thankfully, Mike and Francie had this afternoon off.

"C'mon, Dad, you can throw harder than that! I can catch 'em!" At four, Jamie was enthusiastic about everything he encountered. It made him free in a way that Mike no longer was.

"You got it, champ. Heads up!" Seeing Jamie's grin, Mike reflected that the real beauty of life was in the small things.

"Mike, is the barbecue hot yet?" Clare stood in the half-open door to the kitchen. Her expression was questioning, but not negative. Mike was grateful that their marriage continued to survive amid the stresses of his job.

"I'm on it, honey! If the burgers are ready, the coals should be good to go!" Mike made one more toss to Jamie and set down his glove. *Life could be a lot worse,* he thought.

Ed Underwood's Sunday afternoon was not as enjoyable, as he sat in his car watching the building where Victor Blake lived. It was a brick apartment building, a four-story walk-up, and he knew from the personnel records that Blake lived in unit 302. Ed had walked through the building the day before—the front door was always unlocked—and knew that Blake's apartment was on the back side, facing an alley. That was helpful for keeping tabs, as the parking spaces for the building were also in the alley.

Now, Ed sat at the end of the alley, sweating even with the open window on a warm May afternoon, hoping that Blake would emerge. Since starting his observations on Saturday, he had not laid eyes on the ex-foreman. Even if they were to meet face-to-face, Ed doubted that Blake would recognize him, since their jobs hadn't intersected, and the plant production manager had done the firing, not Ed.

When he'd talked with Liz on Thursday night and told her he wanted to check out Blake himself before notifying the police, she had expressed serious doubts. And then, when he told her on Friday that he'd be busy all weekend, she immediately figured out the reason and made it clear she was unhappy about it.

He'd had a similar encounter with Yoshikawa on Saturday morning. Thinking a workout would help him focus, he'd finally gone back to the *dojo*. Not surprisingly, Yoshikawa had recognized that something was wrong, but Ed lied and said he was simply worried about Liz's housemate having been attacked. The *sensei* had looked at him impassively, but clearly didn't believe Ed's explanation. Thrown off equilibrium, Ed tried to regain his focus, but in the end had cut his workout short and quickly left the *dojo*. He wondered how he had gotten to the point of lying to the two most important people in his life. *I'll have some fence-mending to do after this, that's for sure.*

For now, he intended to continue his surveillance, hoping to at least lay eyes on Blake. In *karate*, he'd learned that you can tell a great deal about an opponent simply from the way they stand and move—and even more from their eyes and face. More generally, his experiences in sparring had confirmed that the unconscious mind can often perceive what the conscious mind misses. His psychology background would explain it simply by noting that much human communication is nonverbal. But while Ed was educated to favor rational analysis, he no longer believed it was always the best approach. And though he was reluctant to admit it, he felt he had something to prove—that he deserved to be a black belt, that his intuition and judgement were correct, and that both the police and his loved ones were wrong to doubt him. And Victor Blake held the key to his redemption.

As Ed sat in his car, sweating and thinking, he was unaware that he was also being observed. A block down the street from the alley was a battered Chevy, the kind of car that is so commonplace as to go unnoticed. Inside sat Mickey O'Donoghue, doing as he'd been ordered by Lou DiNova—watching Ed Underwood.

Surveillance was not O'Donoghue's normal work—he was a "fixer" who normally fixed things by ensuring that his target ended up dead. In some cases, this meant staging a very public demise in order to send a message to others. About a year ago, he'd shot a wayward mob underling, then dragged the body behind his car and dropped it in front of the man's house.

Normally, though, it meant getting rid of someone in a way that would go unnoticed, as he'd done with Deuce Washington. O'Donoghue considered himself a craftsman, not a simple goon, and he prided himself on careful preparation of the jobs he handled. That often meant tailing a target to determine their routine and points of vulnerability. So, while he had not been given a green light to kill Underwood, he was content to watch, knowing his observations would serve him well if the moment came for action.

He'd begun following Underwood late Friday, noting his visit to his girlfriend's house, and the fact that at the end of the evening, he went back to his own place. O'Donoghue had picked him up again early on Saturday morning, when Underwood had headed for a martial arts studio on Mineral Spring Avenue. O'Donoghue had heard about Johnny's run-in with Underwood, and while he had refrained from commenting on it, it had given him a red flag. He knew he needed to be particularly careful in his surveillance and try to avoid dealing with Underwood up close. His mind went to the guns he carried in the trunk, as well as his ankle holster containing a snub-nose .32 caliber revolver that he called the "peashooter," and he gave a thin smile. *No kung fu moves on me, pal.*

As he followed Underwood on Saturday, O'Donoghue had noticed that his target had another escort—the cops. In Mickey's eyes, the black Dodge Diplomat with blackwall tires stood out as if it were painted florescent orange, screaming "plainclothes cops." Mickey always preferred to keep back from his quarry, and when he'd spotted the Diplomat outside Underwood's home on Saturday morning, he made a point of being even more cautious than usual. He risked losing direct contact with Underwood but knew he could always follow the followers. At least he could if the cops were half-decent at their tailing. After all, they could afford to stay closer, since they had the authority of their badges to justify them. Now, while the two detectives sat halfway down the block between himself and Underwood, O'Donoghue watched with binoculars, confident that the cops were so intent on surveilling Underwood that they wouldn't even notice him. *Just the way I like it.*

It was late afternoon when Victor Blake left his apartment and drove off in his car. He wasn't expecting an entourage, so he didn't notice Underwood, the cops, and Mickey O'Donoghue. Still, he was cautious, and when he neared the Barton Jewelry building, he did not go directly in. The building faced onto Park Avenue, with the parking lot accessible via a short street that ended at the back of the property. He circled past the front entrance, ignored the street that led to the parking lot, and went down the next side street, circling back around via Pontiac Avenue, which completed a triangle around the property and its neighbors.

Seeing nothing amiss, and noting that Barton's front parking lot was empty, he did another circuit and turned down the side street to reach the rear parking lot and loading docks. This area was also empty, but he looped through the lot without stopping, and again exited onto Park Avenue, Despite his caution, he was still unaware he was being followed.

On his next loop, Victor again went into the rear parking lot and this time stopped by the loading dock. He got out, looked around and, seeing no one nearby, took a large cardboard box from the trunk. He swiveled his head to check again, then stashed the box behind a pile of wooden pallets beside the loading doors. Satisfied that he had not been observed, he got back in his car and exited the lot back out to Park Avenue.

Victor again circled away from the Barton building, continuing on to Pontiac Avenue. He picked a spot that enabled him to cross to the factory on foot through adjacent properties—the area was mostly commercial buildings, essentially deserted on a Sunday afternoon. Reaching the loading docks, he looked around again, then pulled a trowel and screwdriver from his pocket and used them to jimmy open the primitive lock on the door to the shipping room. Once it was open, he retrieved the box he'd stashed and entered the plant, closing the door behind him.

Ed had also parked on Pontiac Avenue, and cautiously followed Blake as he walked to the back of the Barton plant. Not wanting to get too close, Ed couldn't see clearly, but it looked like Blake had somehow forced open the door and entered with a large cardboard box. Ed stood there, debating what to do; finally, he hurried back to his car, drove to the front parking lot, and used his keys to enter the front door. Intent on watching Victor, he didn't notice the detectives or Mickey O'Donoghue further up the street. From the air, the scene might have looked like some sort of parade.

Inside, the building was quiet. Ed knew there was a back stairway near the loading area, so Victor could be anywhere in the building. Ed was unsure what Victor was planning to do, but he knew that the fired foreman had no business being in the building. He briefly thought about going to his office and calling the police, but decided he wanted to know more before doing so. Rather than attempt to find Victor Blake immediately, he started looking for the lone security guard. He found Jake Hansen sitting in a small room equipped with an ancient wooden desk and a telephone; it appeared Hansen had also added a radio. Startled at seeing Ed appear in the doorway, Hansen scrambled to his feet.

"Uh, Mr. Underwood, sir! What brings you in today?"

"Hi, Jake. Don't worry, I'm not checking up on you!" Ed gestured for him to sit down again. Ed had become familiar with Hansen over the years; he knew the man was honest, though perhaps not too meticulous in his duties. "Tell me, have you heard any noises in the last little while?"

"Noises? What kind? I haven't noticed anything."

"I saw somebody break into the loading area. Have you heard anyone moving around?"

"Breaking in? Shit!" Hansen jumped up again and started to head out the door.

"No, no. Sit, Jake."

Hansen looked at him quizzically, but sat back down.

"Do you remember a production foreman named Victor Blake?" Ed asked.

"Uh, yeah . . . Tall guy, dark hair?"

"That's him. Well, we had to fire him, but he came back today. That's who was breaking in." Ed neglected to mention why he was watching Blake, and Hansen didn't ask.

"Huh. Why would he do that? He coulda rung the bell and I'd 've come."

"Well, the thing is, since we fired him, he shouldn't be here at all."

"Crap. Should I call the cops?" Hansen started reaching for the phone.

"No, please don't. At least, not till I find him. I'd like to know why he's here."

"Shall I go look?" Hansen started to rise again.

"No, it's okay, Jake. I'll find him." Hansen gave him a blank look, clearly confused. "Here's what I'd like you to do, Jake. I'm gonna go look for him and see why he's here. Once I do, I'll come back to find you. If I don't come back within an hour, you should call the police and explain the situation. But whatever you do, don't go looking for him on your own. Okay?"

"Gee, Mr. Underwood, that doesn't sound—"

"It's okay, Jake. I know what I'm doing. Please, just do what I say."

Hansen's face expressed clear doubts, but he responded, "Well, okay, Mr. Underwood. It don't sound quite right, but you're my boss."

"Good." Ed gave a smile meant to be reassuring. "I don't have time now, but I'll explain it all to you later." Without waiting for further response, Ed exited the office, intent on finding Victor Blake and discovering what he was up to.

While Ed Underwood was talking with Hansen, there was also activity outside. The detectives following him—Frank Dunn and Lenny Bernstein—had hung back to avoid being spotted, and so had not seen Victor Blake force his way into the building. Instead, they'd seen Underwood stop on Pontiac Avenue, walk through an adjacent property, and then reappear in the back parking lot of Barton Jewelry. He'd gone up to a loading dock door, which, for some reason, seemed to be unlocked, then went back to his car, drove to the front parking lot at Barton, and entered through the front door using his keys. They waited, uncertain what to do. Finally, after fifteen minutes had passed and Underwood had not reappeared, they radioed dispatch and told them to contact Mike Langan at home, updating him on the situation.

Langan had mixed feelings on getting the call from dispatch. He was dismayed at the interruption to a Sunday afternoon with his family, but juiced at hearing about Underwood's actions. He knew from the notes that something big was supposed to happen soon, and this sounded like it. He told dispatch to contact Francie Weber and tell her to meet him outside Barton Jewelry, where Dunn and Bernstein were waiting. He briefed Clara on the need to go to work, gave Jamie a hug, and headed out in his car.

Mickey O'Donoghue was perplexed. Like the detectives, he'd seen Underwood's circuitous route and eventual entrance through the front door. A large sign near the roof told him the building belonged to Barton Jewelry, and he knew Underwood worked there. He'd also read the newspaper stories and knew the note-writer had threatened Barton. DiNova had given instructions that he was to watch Underwood without taking any action—unless he seemed to be a threat. Though he hadn't directly observed Victor Blake, Mickey was savvy enough to suspect that Underwood's meandering path meant he was watching somebody. The question was, was that somebody a target or something else? If a target, did it mean Underwood was about to attack? If something else, why was Underwood so intent on following the person? Seeing the cops stop on the side street, in view of the front entrance where

Underwood had entered, O'Donoghue decided to circle past again while he decided what to do.

Once inside the building, Victor Blake carried his box through the shipping area, his footsteps softly echoing in the large space. The layout of the building was very familiar to him, and he easily made his way past the company lunchroom to the stairwell that connected all floors, and then to the plating department on the second floor. There, he paused at the door from the corridor to listen, ensuring that his entrance had not drawn the attention of the security guard. From past observations, Victor felt confident the guard would not venture outside his office.

Satisfied that his entry and movement had not drawn any attention, he moved to a desk along one wall; it had been his when he was foreman. He began removing the contents of the box—a ten-gallon glass aquarium with a smaller five-gallon one nested inside, a half-gallon bottle of glycerin, two bags of ice, and a variety of hoses, measuring cups, and other items.

After unpacking his supplies, Victor went to the storage closet situated along the same wall as the desk. The door was locked, but the lock was even more basic than the one at the loading dock and he easily pried it open. He flipped on the light switch and scanned the room, which contained a variety of materials used in plating jewelry. Anchored to the floor was a safe, which he knew contained small amounts of silver and gold, used for plating some of the higher-quality items. Victor didn't care about the safe or its contents; he had bigger goals. Instead, he found the shelf that contained bottles of nitric acid and sulfuric acid, used for cleaning and etching the jewelry pieces. One at a time, he carried several of the bottles, which were marked "Danger! Corrosive acid!" in large letters, to the desk where his other supplies awaited.

Victor knew that for the best result, he should use acids with the highest possible concentration levels. The acids used by Barton Jewelry were lower concentrations—sufficient for the needs of jewelry-making and safer to handle in an industrial setting. Even so, he had calculated he could still produce a sufficient quantity of decent nitroglycerin. Most people know that nitroglycerin can be tricky to transport or even handle—temperature variations, vibrations, and even some types of impurities can cause it to unexpectedly explode. Alfred Nobel had addressed this by combining the explosive oil with diatomaceous earth; the resulting gel, which he dubbed "dynamite," was far more stable and made him a substantial fortune. Victor had thought carefully about the difficulties, and had eventually worked out a plan that made the volatility work to his advantage. Of course, things could still go wrong—but if they did, he figured he wouldn't survive to worry about it.

Now, with the materials collected, it was time to start the mixing process.

After leaving Jake Hansen, Ed had begun a slow search of the deserted building. His task was doubly difficult because he knew neither Victor Blake's goal nor his destination, only that he had brought a box with him. Additionally, in his role as personnel director, Ed had only limited familiarity with the production areas of the building. The reality was that Blake, as an ex-foreman, likely knew the plant much better than he did. Knowing that, Ed was even more cautious; if the guy really was the killer, Ed didn't want to be surprised by him. He thought of his recent lapses in focus when sparring in the *dojo*. They reflected poorly on his status as a black belt, but even so, that was only sport; if Victor Blake was a killer, the stakes here were deadly.

Am I really up to this? He was not reassured to realize he did not know the answer.

Slowly, Ed worked his way through the first floor, which had a reception desk and elevator by the main entrance, along with a showroom, a few offices for sales staff, a company lunchroom, and the shipping and receiving areas. As he proceeded, it was still daylight outside, and many areas had enough windows to allow him a clear view; however, the lunchroom had only a row of windows near the ceiling, and the tables and counters cast long shadows as he strained to scan the room, slowing his progress. The loading dock area was even worse; Ed considered turning on the lights, but decided not to. Finally, he got to the large roll-up doors and the adjacent conventional door, which, he'd seen from outside, had been jimmied open. *But where had Blake gone? And what was in the box he carried?*

Ed quickly reviewed his options: It had taken him more than twenty minutes to go through the first floor, leaving two floors of production areas and the top floor of administration offices still to be checked. He remembered his instructions to Jake Hansen and was now regretting the one-hour deadline. Since he was near the back stairs, he decided to go up to the fourth floor, which was very familiar to him; if, after that, he still hadn't found Blake, he could go back to Hansen and maybe further delay the call to the police. Not wanting to waste more time, he headed up the stairs—the same ones Victor Blake had used.

Outside, Mike Langan and Francie Weber had both arrived and were getting an update from Frank Dunn and Lenny Bernstein. The latter two had been tailing Underwood since six a.m. They'd been waiting when he emerged from his apartment and drove across town, only to sit at the top end of an alley for several hours. They recapped the drive to Barton Jewelry, complete with several loops around the block, and a brief episode where he parked nearby and seemed to head to the back of the plant on foot, only to then return to his car, park near the main entrance, and go into the Barton building through the front door. By their calculations, he'd entered about forty minutes earlier.

Mike was frustrated. His gut told him something was up, but he wasn't sure what.

"I don't like it, Francie. What's this guy up to, coming here on a Sunday afternoon?"

"Got me, Mike. But it don't smell right." She thought for a moment. "Think we got probable cause?" All four detectives knew that without a warrant, they had to be careful before making the decision to go in.

"I doubt it." He turned to Dunn, who was still sitting in the plainclothes car with the window down. "Hey, Frank, you sure he used a key to get in? He wasn't breakin' in?"

"We both saw him take out a key, Mike." Dunn nodded toward Bernstein. "But, uh, you know, we weren't real close. Maybe we were mistaken."

Mike shook his head. "No. We fuck that up and we could lose everything." A tainted search would make everything it led to inadmissible—an outcome he did not want. "I want this guy, and I want it to stick." He paused, thinking about the options, and finally said, "Okay, let's give it a little while. Frank, how 'bout you circle the building and keep an eye out in the back? If nothing happens in the next half hour or so, we'll call the lieutenant—let him make the call on goin' in."

As Mike Langan debated going in, Mickey O'Donoghue was facing his own decisions. He was parked near the side street, where he could watch both the front of the Barton building and the driveway into the back lot without drawing attention to himself. He had observed Langan and Weber arrive, and realized things were getting more complicated. He was a pro and prided himself on always completing a job. In general, he didn't worry about cops, though his preference was to handle things in ways that avoided direct face-offs. Now, he was concerned that Underwood might be up to something, and Lou DiNova had told him to stop him from committing new attacks. At the same time, the presence of four cops on the scene required caution. When O'Donoghue saw Frank Dunn head towards the back of the building, while the other three stayed by the entrance to the front parking lot, he made up his mind. *Better to be inside, and see what Underwood is up to than sit out here watching the cops.*

O'Donoghue drove down Park Street past the Barton factory, turned onto Pontiac Avenue, and parked close to where Underwood had briefly stopped earlier. He then followed Ed Underwood's path, cutting through the back lots of commercial buildings, and approached the back of Barton Jewelry. There were some bushes on the edge of the property, which let Mickey pause to survey the scene. He had arrived just as Frank Dunn rounded the corner at the other side of the building and made his way to the loading docks. Dunn looked at the stacked pallets and pulled up on the handles of the two roll-up bay doors.

Moving quietly on rubber soles, O'Donoghue moved towards Dunn, screening his approach by keeping the tower of wooden pallets between them. Dunn was now at the loading door, and he reached out to give a tug on the door handle. Just as he did so, O'Donoghue came up behind him. He punched Dunn in the side of the head, and then used a choke hold. The cop collapsed, unconscious.

It wasn't his preferred play, but O'Donoghue couldn't have the cops going in ahead of him. Putting on a pair of thin gloves he carried with him, he used Dunn's own handcuffs to bind his hands behind his back, took off the cop's shoes and socks, and stuffed the socks in the inert man's mouth. He then searched Dunn's pockets, removing his walkie-talkie and gun, both of which he placed on the pile of pallets, knowing that when Dunn awoke, he wouldn't be able to reach them while cuffed. He tossed the keys to the cuffs across the parking lot. When Dunn did wake up and was able to talk to the other cops, he would likely assume Underwood had been the one who attacked him.

Satisfied that these actions would buy him some time to find Underwood inside the factory, O'Donoghue went in through the loading room door and closed it behind him. He looked around for something to secure the door; finding nothing better at hand, he used a roll of shipping twine to tie the door closed. He took the .32 pistol from its ankle holster and stuffed it into his belt; using it would be a last resort, but it was better to have it handy. Taking a quick glance at his watch, he figured he had about twenty minutes before the unconscious cop was able to raise an alarm—at which point, things would likely get busy in the factory.

While Mickey O'Donoghue began his search for Ed Underwood, Stan Osiewicz was sitting at home, watching the end of a Red Sox game on TV. It was the top of the tenth inning, and Boston was tied three-three with Detroit at Fenway. Getting to watch a game was a rare treat for Stan, who often had to give priority to work over leisure pursuits. As the 3-2 pitch was delivered, with two out, the phone rang. Stan groaned to himself but reached over to pick it up.

"Hey, Stan, how ya doin'?"

Stan recognized the voice—it was Joey Rivera, one of his contacts in the Providence Police Department. "Hi, Joey. I'm good. Just watching the Sox. What's up?"

"I heard a call come through on dispatch. Frank Dunn was at Barton Jewelry, and he wanted Mike Langan and

Francie Weber to join him. I dunno what's goin' on, but with you writing stories about the task force and all, I figured you'd wanna know."

"You got it right." Stan thoughts started racing—was this about the attack on Barton that the notes had threatened? "Do you know how long ago the call came in to dispatch, Joey?"

"I think maybe half an hour or so? I've been busy, so I ain't quite sure."

"Well, I appreciate the heads up, Joey. I owe you."

"Sure do, pal. See ya soon." Rivera hung up.

Dunn called them in on a Sunday afternoon? Whatever it is, I need to check it out.

While Stan had been talking, the batter had struck out, and the Red Sox were now coming up, with the chance to win the game. Reluctantly, he turned off the TV. *Shit. Of all the times. I hope this is worth it.*

Intent on the delicate process underway, Victor was unaware that others were in the building, or outside. He had partly filled the larger aquarium with water from the washroom nearby and then placed the smaller tank within it. The smaller tank rested on small spacers, which he had placed at the corners to create a gap both under the inner tank and on the sides. He then added some ice cubes so that the outer tank would provide a chilly bath for the contents of the inner tank. Carefully, he measured out the required amount of sulfuric acid and poured it into the inner tank. After giving it a few minutes to cool, he slowly began pouring nitric acid into the sulfuric acid.

Because the nitric acid used in the factory was not as pure as what might be found in a chemistry lab—it didn't need to be, and was safer to handle for use in cleaning jewelry blanks—the reaction produced both heat and fumes. He had clamped a glass thermometer to the wall of the inner tank so he could monitor the temperature, ensuring that the reaction did not overheat. As he continued, he added more ice cubes to keep the inner vessel sufficiently cooled.

After about fifteen minutes, he had added all of the required nitric acid, and the temperature of the resulting acid was stable. *Now comes the tricky part.* He measured out the required amount of glycerin into a graduated cylinder, which had a thin pipette valve at the bottom so he could precisely control the flow of glycerin into the acid solution. The introduction of glycerin led to the creation of nitroglycerin, but the process also generated considerable heat. Unfortunately, excessive heat was one of the factors that could cause the compound to explode. Thus, he had to add the glycerin very slowly, while monitoring the temperature of the tank and, if necessary, adding more ice cubes as he proceeded.

A further problem was that nitroglycerin was denser than the acid bath, and as he slowly added drips of glycerin, the resulting blobs of nitroglycerin would settle to the bottom of the tank rather than forming a new solution. This meant he needed to very gently stir the tank of acid to promote a more efficient reaction. Unfortunately, if he stirred too vigorously, the vibrations could trigger an explosion of whatever amount of nitroglycerin had already formed.

A further concern was that impurities in the nitric acid could trigger an unexpected reaction and a premature explosion. Victor had thought about this risk, but knew he had no real control over it. It wasn't a possibility that he relished, but he proceeded anyway, accepting it as an inherent limitation of the overall scenario.

As the minutes went by, more and more blobs of nitroglycerin formed in the tank. He could not be sure of the exact quantity, or its purity, but he knew that even the equivalent of a few tablespoons would likely destroy the room he was in. That was okay, but he wanted a larger quantity—ideally, enough to destroy the whole building. When it happened, he intended to be far away. . . .

Drop by drop, the reaction continued. Victor had arranged a stand to hold the jug of glycerin over the tank, and as it slowly oozed out, he concentrated on gently stirring the tank and continuing to add ice to keep the temperature low enough. After about fifteen minutes of this painstaking and nerve-wracking process, he figured there was probably about two ounces of nitroglycerin in the tank. His supply of ice was beginning to run low, but not all of the glycerin had yet been added. He had expected this to happen and, in fact, had included it in his plans. He gave a final gentle stir, slightly closed the valve on the glycerin flask, and added the remaining ice to the cooling bath. His plan was to allow the reaction to continue, unmonitored, while he exited the building. At some point, the ice would be exhausted, the temperature of the continuing reaction would rise to the danger level, and—boom! *Bye-bye Barton*. But by then, he would be long gone.

Smiling, he headed for the stairs, intending to leave the same way he had come.

Ed Underwood had completed his search of the fourth floor offices and decided to next check the third floor, which held the assembly machinery for making watch-bands and stamping jewelry parts. His exploration of the fourth floor had been guided by his familiarity, but he also attempted to open his mind. In *karate*, he'd often sensed an opponent's intention by the intuitive sense, *haragei*. That, of course, was just in sparring in the *dojo*, not a situation that could be life or death. Now he paused before descending the stairs. Taking a slow deep breath called *sanchin*, he tried to detect Victor's presence--but sensed nothing. *Am I really ready for this? Maybe Liz was right. What am I trying to prove?* Unable to answer, he nonetheless moved forward.

Ed did not know the production areas well, but fortunately, the third floor was divided into two large areas, which, apart from support pillars, were fairly open. Thus, it actually took him less time to move through this floor than it had the fourth floor, and his mind raised no alarms about unseen enemies. Having found nothing amiss, and no Victor, Ed headed back towards the rear stairwell. Just as he reached the landing, he heard the fire door on the floor below him open. He froze and tried to peer down through the metal steps to the dimly lit landing below. He saw a shadowy figure—Victor!

Moving carefully, trying not to alert his target, he started down the stairs.

At the same moment, Mickey O'Donoghue was moving through the loading docks toward the staircase, which was marked by a sign above the door. Hearing something, he opened the door slowly—and spotted someone on the stairs, who had frozen at the squeal as the door opened.

O'Donoghue drew his pistol and aimed. "Hold it right there, Underwood!"

Ed was startled to hear his name. He couldn't see the person two flights below, but assumed it must be the police.

In a startled voice, Victor yelled,"My name's not Underwood—"

"But mine is!" Ed turned the corner on the landing above Victor Blake. Closing the gap, he grabbed Victor's arm, quickly putting him in a submission hold. Still thinking the stranger down below was a cop, Ed suddenly realized he'd had a feeling of being followed since he'd left home this morning.

"Okay, you both freeze, unless you wanna die!" Mickey O'Donoghue knew what Underwood looked like and realized he was speaking the truth. *But who the hell is this other guy?* "Look, I know you, Underwood. But who's this guy?"

"My—my name's Jake! I'm the security guard here. I stumbled onto Underwood—he's got some kind of bomb upstairs. He must be the one who's been writing those notes and killing people. I was just on my way to call the police. He must have spotted me and come after me. I'm glad you found us." Almost as an afterthought, he added, "You're a cop, right?"

O'Donoghue looked at the two, keeping his gun leveled at them. *Bomb? What the fuck?*

Before O'Donoghue could speak, Ed interjected, "Don't believe him! His name's Victor Blake. He was a foreman here until we fired him two months ago. I know, because I'm head of personnel. He's the one the papers have been writing about! I discovered him breaking in, and—"

"Wait, hold it." O'Donoghue waved the barrel of the gun for emphasis. He looked at the two, uncertain who to believe. Finally, he spoke to Victor. "What's this about finding a bomb? What kind of bomb?"

"It's in the plating department, on the second floor!" There was a thin sheen of sweat forming on Victor's forehead. "Look, you gotta arrest him—and we gotta get out of here before it blows!"

"How do you know it's gonna blow? If Underwood made it, why would he want it to blow while he's still in the building?"

"I—I don't know. It just looked like he'd finished working on it!" The comment came out rather lamely, but it was clear Victor was agitated.

"I ain't a cop, but I am the one with the gun." At first impulse, O'Donoghue would have been inclined to simply kill them both. But that would be messy, especially with the cops nearby, and it didn't fit with his instructions from Lou DiNova. After a long moment, during which he kept the gun pointed at the two men, he continued, "I'm thinking your story don't make sense, pal. The only thing I know for sure is that he's Underwood. If he's right about who you are, you must be the one making bombs—if there really is one. If he's lyin' and you're some security guard, you don't need to worry, 'cause the cops are gonna be here soon." He saw surprise register in both faces. "So, I ain't hangin' around to sort this mess out." He backed towards the fire door from the stairwell to the first floor. Going through the door, he told them, "If either of you tries to follow me, you'll get a bullet."

When Frank Dunn woke up, he was lying on the ground on his side, his hands cuffed behind his back. He momentarily gagged on the socks in his mouth, but as he got to his knees and stood, he was able to push the gross gag out with his tongue. Without attempting to put on his shoes, he stumbled toward the front of the building, where Mike Langan and the others waited.

"What the hell happened, Frank?" Mike was stunned at the sight of the barefooted Dunn, who was gingerly moving across the asphalt parking lot.

"Somebody sucker-punched me, just as I was about to go in through a door that looked like it had been jimmied."

"Underwood?"

"I dunno. Never got a look at 'im. Hit me in the side of the head, then choked me out."

"Shit . . ." Mike quickly evaluated the situation. "Well, now we've definitely got probable cause. Francie, you and Bernstein go to the front door. Pound on it, see if maybe there's a security guard to let you in. If not, maybe the noise will drive the guy to us. Frank, you and I will go in through the door you saw." As he spoke, he used his key to unlock Frank Dunn's cuffs.

"Yeah. I want this bastard. And I'll get my friggin' shoes."

Langan and Dunn headed to the back of the building, Dunn still walking gingerly in his bare feet. He picked up his socks where he'd spit them out, put on his shoes, and retrieved his gun and radio from the pallet where his attacker had left them. The two approached the door, guns drawn.

Mickey O'Donoghue had reentered the loading area, while listening for the squeak of the stairwell door, in case Underwood or the other guy tried to follow him. Instead, he heard a sound come from the loading room door. Quickly, he ducked out of sight behind some boxes.

In the stairwell, Ed Underwood continued to keep Victor Blake in a submission hold, levering his arm up behind him, while with his other hand he held Victor by the belt. After the guy with the gun had disappeared, he decided they should head to the security room. If the guy had been lying about the cops coming in, Ed could have Jake Hansen phone them, assuming he hadn't already—it must be almost an hour since they'd spoken.

Mike Langan and Frank Dunn entered the loading area and looked around. They were aware that it was a big building, and that considerable time had elapsed since Dunn had been attacked. Underwood probably knew the building layout well, and could be anywhere. On the far side of the loading area were two doors, both open. They looked at each other, nodded, and each headed toward a different one. They passed the area where Mickey

O'Donoghue was hiding without noticing him. After they disappeared through the doorways, he quietly made his way to the exit. For him, the job was done—Underwood and the other guy would be grabbed by the cops, who could then sort out the guilty one.

Mike found himself in some kind of lunchroom, with a door at the far side that was marked "To Stairs." As he moved towards it in the dim late afternoon light, he bumped a table. To his surprise, he heard someone yell, "Hey! Are you the cops? We're over here!" The voice sounded like Underwood. Drawing his gun, he headed towards the voice.

Jake Hansen was getting worried. Ed had said that if he didn't return within an hour, Hansen should phone the police—and time was just about up. More than once, he'd debated leaving his office to look for Ed, but he was unarmed and had never felt like a hero. *Better to do like Ed said.*

As he was about to pick up the phone, he heard what sounded like Ed's voice, coming from the corridor leading to the lunchroom. He couldn't make out the words, but jumped up from his desk to find Ed. As he reached the corridor, he heard pounding at the front doors. *Which way do I go?* Hesitating momentarily, he went to the front doors. There, he found a man and a woman banging the doors and shouting. They wore street clothes, but one was flashing a police badge. Francie Weber and Lenny

Bernstein hurried in, explaining that another officer had been assaulted at the back of the building and that two officers were entering from the back.

"Gee, I was just about to call you guys. My boss is here and said I should phone if he wasn't back within an hour."

"Your boss?"

"Yeah, Ed Underwood, he's the personnel manager. He came in earlier, saying he'd seen somebody breaking in and he was gonna look for the guy."

Weber and Bernstein exchanged glances, but said nothing.

"And I just heard him calling out. I was gonna go look for him, but heard you at the doors."

Francie took the lead. "Where'd the voice come from?"

"Toward the back, where the lunchroom is."

"Okay, show us."

Mike Langan and Frank Dunn met up in the hallway off the lunchroom, and together headed for the stairs to the second floor. Once in the stairwell, they found Ed Underwood. To their surprise, he had some guy in a submission hold and was pushing him toward the first floor..

"Hold it right there, Underwood." Langan and Dunn, both with guns drawn, confronted the two men coming down the stairs.

"Sure. I'm glad you're here!"

"Yeah? Why's that?"

"This is an ex-employee. I saw him break in at the back and he's saying something about a bomb upstairs that's about to go off."

“That so?” Having been regarding Underwood as a suspect, Mike wasn’t quite ready to believe him.

“He’s right about the bomb—but he planted it, not me! I was about to call for help when he grabbed me.” Victor seemed to be spinning the same story he’d told Mickey O’Donoghue. Unfortunately for his story, at that moment Jake Hansen turned the corner, accompanied by Francie Weber and Lenny Bernstein.

“What’s all this, Mike? We miss the party?” Francie stared at Ed and, seeing Mike with his gun drawn, drew hers.

“Hey, Francie. Just in time.” He looked at Victor. “Okay, you, who are you? You got ID? And Underwood, let him go. Whatever’s going on here, we got it.”

Victor Blake rubbed his shoulder when Ed released the submission hold, trying to buy time to think. *How do I get out of this?* He’d always prided himself on good planning and felt he was smarter than most people, but this situation had gone totally sideways. He decided the first thing was to survive, and that meant getting out of the plant before the nitroglycerin exploded. “Okay, okay. I’ll tell you whatever you want to know. But first, we need to get out of this building before the whole thing blows up.”

“So that stuff about a bomb was real? ” The first cop, referred to as “Mike” by the new arrivals, did the talking, and everyone present reacted as if he was in charge. “Where is it, and what kind? Don’t you have some kind of remote detonator?” “It’s up on the second floor, in the plating department.

There's enough homemade nitroglycerin to level this place-, and it's getting more unstable as we stand here. I don't know when it will blow, but it'll be soon. I would've been far away by now, except for this asshole." He nodded at Underwood.

Mike's eyes widened and he turned to Francie. "Francie, get outside and take everyone with you. Call the bomb squad, tell 'em it's urgent." He turned to Victor. "You, bomb boy, what's your name?"

"Victor Blake," Ed answered for him. "Victor, why is it getting more unstable if there's no detonator?"

Victor grimaced. "The nitro's still being created. We don't have time for a chemistry lesson, but there's an ice bath to cool it and the ice is melting. When it's all gone—boom." He looked at the detective. "Now, can we get out of here?"

"Not till you show me, so I can tell the bomb squad."

"But it's—"

"Quit talkin' and get moving." The cop cuffed Victor's hands behind his back and pushed him toward the stairway.

"Wait, Detective." As Ed spoke, the others turned to look at him. "If ice will stop the reaction, there's a refrigerator in the lunchroom. There should be some trays of ice cubes. Let me grab them."

Mike looked at Ed speculatively.

"After all, this is where I work. If it blows, I won't have a job." Ed smiled at the poor joke.

Mike turned to Victor. "Will more ice help?"

"Probably, but it depends how far things have gone. It could blow as we walk into the room." Victor was very unhappy at the idea of going back upstairs, but since the cops weren't giving him a choice, the sooner they went up—and then got out—the better.

"Okay. Let's move, everybody!" Francie and Lenny had already started for the front door, closely followed by Jake Hansen.

With the discussion ended, Frank Dunn turned to go, then stopped. "I'm coming, too, Mike. If it's gonna blow, we'll go together." He and Mike Langan had been partners for years and it didn't feel right to bail now.

As they headed for the stairwell, Victor leading the way under close watch, Ed dashed into the lunchroom to grab the ice. By the time they reached the second floor fire door, he had rejoined them.

Victor gingerly opened the fire door from the stairwell. He stuck his head in the room, looking toward the desk along the wall where the bomb sat. "There.," he pointed. "Can we go now?"

Ed pushed past him, carrying the ice trays. As he approached the desk, he shuffled his feet slowly, trying to avoid any vibration. He could see the jug of glycerin above the tanks. It seemed nearly empty, but a slow drip of the viscous liquid continued to flow, drop by drop, into the tank of acid. Reaching the apparatus, Ed could see that there were only a few small bits of ice left in the cooling bath. He reached out and gingerly closed the valve on the glycerin flow, and then pried an ice cube from one of the trays.

"Whatever you do, don't get any water in the inside tank—that'll make it blow!" Victor urged, still peering around the edge of the fire door. Langan and Dunn stood on either side of Victor.

"Understood." Slowly, one by one, Ed placed the cubes into the water of the outer tank, taking pains not to make a splash or shake the tanks. By the time he had added all the ice, the glycerin was no longer dripping from the valve, and the side of the outer tank definitely felt cooler. He placed the empty ice trays gently on the desk, turned, and began shuffling toward the stairs.

"Good work, Underwood." Mike clapped him on the shoulder. "Pretty ballsy."

"Well, if it blew, we all would've gone with it, so you guys are as brave as me."

"Yeah, yeah." Victor was less impressed. "Can we get the hell out of here now?"

"Sure," Mike replied. "But don't worry—we've got lots to talk about with you." As he urged Victor down the stairs, he noticed that Victor and Ed were the same height, and both had dark hair. *So that explains. . .*

When everyone was outside, Stan Osiewicz appeared. There was no police tape, so he felt entitled to approach Langan. Victor Blake had been placed in the back of Langan's plainclothes car, pending the arrival of a patrol car to transport him to the station. Seeing who was present, the reporter correctly guessed it was related to the task force investigation.

"Hello, Detective. Looks like you've been busy. I'm guessing you've arrested a suspect for the task force?"

"Hi, Osiewicz." Mike was annoyed at the reporter's presence, but also knew he had been instrumental in the case, so he reined in his irritation. "Look, we're kinda busy right now, and this is a crime scene—and it ain't over yet. So, do us both a favor and take off. If you do, I promise you, you'll be the first one I talk to outside the department."

Stan was unhappy at the brush-off. "Can you at least confirm you have a suspect?"

Mike hesitated, then responded, "Off the record, we got a guy. But until he's processed, I got nothin' else for you."

"Fair enough." Stan knew when not to push. "Congrats. I'll look forward to talking to you." He walked slowly back to his car, unaware that the whole building could blow up.

Suddenly tired, Ed Underwood wanted to leave. Almost as an afterthought, he realized his car was parked in its usual space, near the front entrance. *If the building goes, my car will go with it.* He approached Mike Langan.

"Look, Detective, this has been quite a day. Were you planning to hold me for some reason, or can I go?"

"Uh, you can go, Mr. Underwood." After the events of the previous hour, Langan's view of Ed seemed to have shifted considerably. "I still have questions, and we're going to need a formal statement about what happened, but that can wait till tomorrow. I'll give you a call." He offered his hand. "And thanks for what you did upstairs."

"Sure." Ed shook hands. "You can call me at the office—assuming the building's still here tomorrow!" He gave a small smile and headed to his car. *Liz will not believe all this . . .*

FIFTEEN

Monday, May 18, 1987

MONDAY MORNING FOUND Mike Langan and Francie Weber once again in Lieutenant Briggs's office for an update—though this time, there were big developments. They outlined what had happened the previous day, starting with the tail of Ed Underwood and ending with the events at the Barton factory.

After his brief admission about the bomb when they were in the factory, Victor Blake had been interrogated at the station and had ultimately given a full confession. He admitted to all four murders, starting with Sanelli and ending with McIntyre, as well as acknowledging the attack on Karen Durant.

The bomb at the factory was obviously his doing, which he also described in his signed statement. Interestingly, he seemed to take pride in his actions. He was particularly pleased with the design he'd developed for the nitroglycerin bomb, including the use of acids from the factory's own supplies. At this point, he was being held in the cells and was scheduled to be arraigned in the afternoon.

At first, Langan had been flummoxed by Blake's willingness to talk, suspecting that he was using it as a ploy to hide other crimes, including possibly murders. However, the four murders were sufficient to get him multiple life sentences, and at this point, they had nothing else to pin on him. Beyond having nothing more to lose, Blake's taking credit for unsolved murders was also a known phenomenon among serial killers. David Berkowitz, the Pawtucket student-killer, and others had readily confessed when brought in for questioning—even to crimes unknown to the police.

"Jesus . . ." Briggs remarked when Mike had finished. "So, this guy actually killed four people, tried to kill another, and almost blew up the Barton building?"

"Yeah. That's about the size of it." Mike nodded, still incredulous.

"Well, good job to you two—and to the bomb squad. I gather they were able to get the bomb out and destroy the nitro?"

"Uh-huh, though if it hadn't been for Underwood, it might've ended badly." Mike had already explained Ed Underwood's actions with the ice to Briggs, but felt it was worth noting again.

"So, you're saying the guy you thought was the perp actually led you to the real perp, and also figured out how to keep the place from blowing up before the bomb squad could get there?" Briggs thought about that and shook his head. "Man, what a crazy case."

"You got it." For Mike, it had been the most bizarre in his career—and he hoped it would remain so. "But we also have to remember that reporter, Stan Osiewicz. I hate to admit it, but if he hadn't pushed the link between L'Heureux and McIntyre, we might still be spinning our wheels and this wacko would be running loose."

"Well, don't go saying that in public." Briggs knew the chief and the mayor were going to want the credit for themselves—and maybe give a little to the homicide team.

"Right, Lieutenant. But off the record, it did get us going. And I owe the guy an update because of that." However he felt about the press, Mike liked to keep his word.

"Okay, but you make sure he doesn't upstage the chief's press conference after the arraignment." In general, Briggs didn't like the politics, but his main concern was to avoid problems for himself. "So, is that it?"

"For now, as far as we know." Mike looked to Francie for confirmation, and she nodded.

"Great. So, good work, and tell Dunn and Bernstein they handled the tail well." Mentioning Dunn prompted another thought. "What about what happened to Dunn? It sounds like Blake was busy building the bomb, and from what we know now, it seems unlikely Underwood attacked him—so who did?"

Mike and Francie looked at each other and shrugged. "We've got no clue. Underwood said some other guy was there, who he thought at first was a cop, but the guy took off before we got inside. Underwood said he has no idea who he was, but we'll get a description when we take his formal statement today."

Briggs nodded and gave a short laugh. "Shit, that thing with the socks in his mouth and no shoes—that's priceless! Uh, but don't tell him I said that." They all knew the story would make the rounds, and soon the whole department would be secretly laughing about it—everyone except Frank Dunn. "Anyway, you're still on task force duty till the chief tells us different. Make sure you get your paperwork done on this, but for now, you got a breather." As an afterthought, he added, "And stick around in case the chief wants to show you off at the press conference."

"Right. Thanks, Lieutenant." Mike and Francie rose to go back to their desks. It wasn't anything like a vacation, but solving a case—especially one as weird as this one—always felt good. In their job, that was enough.

Stan Osiewicz was at his desk first thing on Monday. He planned to speak to Joe Houle about Sunday's events and the paper's strategy for reporting the story. As yet, no word of it had leaked, though he'd heard Chief Parker of the Providence Police Department was calling a press conference for twelve-thirty. Stan figured it was about the case, and hoped Langan would call him before that happened. For now, all he could do was talk to Joe Houle and try to sketch out an angle without actually knowing any details.

Stan knocked on the open door of Houle's office, noting that for once, the editor was not on the phone. He looked up and waved Stan in.

"C'mon in, Stan. What's up?"

"Morning, Joe. I think the serial killer story is about to break open." He sat down, eager to fill Houle in on Sunday's visit to the Barton plant.

Houle nodded, and for once, did not reach for an antacid tablet. "You figure that's what the press conference is about?"

"Uh-huh. See, I got a tip from inside the PD yesterday that something was happening at the Barton building. So I gave up on the Sox game and headed over there. When I arrived, the task force cops were there and they were just putting someone in cuffs into a plainclothes car. I talked to Langan." Stan looked at Houle to make sure he was following. "He wouldn't say anything on the record, but off the record, he said they had a suspect." That got Houle's full attention. "He said that it was still an active scene and that I should leave. I didn't want to push him too much, but he did promise he'd get in touch with me before any other version of it broke. I'm hoping it'll be before the press conference."
"Right. The press conference is set for twelve-thirty, so it's obvious the publicity flacks want it to make tonight's paper. They wouldn't do that if it was bad news."

"Makes sense, Joe. So, I don't know the whole score yet, but I'm guessing there'll be enough for a story tonight." Stan looked at Houle questioningly.

"Should be." Houle looked out the window, as he often did when thinking. "Okay, Ozzie, tell you what, you work out what you'd like to include, assuming we're guessing right, and give me a look. Depending on how things play out, I can probably give you some space on the front page."

Stan nodded but said nothing. He'd been hoping Joe would see it this way, and it was as close to a guarantee as he'd get.

"If it's what you think," Joe continued, "it'll be big news. Let's hope the cop gets in touch in time for us to take the lead on it." He started to go back to the work on his desk, but then looked up again. "Great work, Ozzie. When this is over, you should be a good candidate for a Pulitzer. After all, it was your reporting that led to the task force."

Stan went back to his desk and reviewed the file he'd built up on the story. Though he didn't consciously acknowledge it, his attention was mostly on the phone, hoping Langan would call soon. He made some rough notes on a yellow legal pad, but it was mostly an activity to pass the time. Until he knew the details of Sunday's events, he couldn't be sure how the piece should go.

Finally, at about ten-thirty, the phone rang.

"Osiewicz? This is Detective Langan." Mike's tone was business-like rather than friendly. Though he appreciated Stan's contributions to the case, he had an inherent aversion to being chummy with reporters. Still, he intended to keep his word.

"Hi, Detective. Thanks for getting in touch." Stan's mind was racing, both with the many questions he had and concern as to how much Langan was willing to say—after all, given the upcoming press conference, this was really leaking the story. "Look, it's pretty obvious there's been a break in the task force work, given what I saw yesterday, and the press conference the chief has called. So what can you tell me?"

"Yeah, you got the basic picture. We arrested a suspect yesterday and he goes to court for arraignment this afternoon."

"So, who is the guy?"

Mike hesitated for several moments. Finally, he replied. "Anything I say now is off the record until after the chief's talk. You can do your write-up or whatever, but if anything gets out beforehand, you can consider yourself dead in this department. Got it?"

"I've got it." Stan knew this was the necessary trade-off, but it meant he could still have a story ready to go in the evening paper and hopefully he'd have some details the chief wouldn't touch on. He repeated his question. "So, who's the guy?"

"His name's Victor Blake. He used to be a foreman at Barton but got canned a few months ago. He was at Barton yesterday trying to blow up the whole building but we got to him before he could set it off."

"What kind of bomb?"

"Homemade nitroglycerin. Apparently, he knew most of the chemicals were available in the plant. You'd have to talk to the bomb squad—later—to get the technical stuff, but apparently he made enough to take down a big part of the building, and maybe more."

"Shit, really?"

"Really. But that ain't the best part. There's a guy at Barton who was on to Blake and had followed him yesterday. He not only stopped him, he also stopped the bomb from going off before the bomb squad got there."

"You're kidding me, right?"

"No, it's for real." Mike paused. "And the chief hasn't been briefed on it. He's gonna say we stopped the guy and the bomb squad did their thing."

"OK. I won't put anything in that'll embarrass the chief. We can put this in a follow-up—shit, this story will be front page all week." Stan was making notes as he talked, highlighting what wouldn't be in the press conference. "So, who is this guy? I'm gonna want to talk to him."

"Um, I don't know if he'll be willing to talk to you. He hasn't even come in for his formal statement yet." Mike thought about how much he should say. "But if he does, you'll probably find out something else—until yesterday afternoon, he was number one on our list. We were tailing him and that's why we were at the plant when we got the real perp."

"What is this, some bullshit? You don't expect me to buy that, do you?"

"Believe what you want, Osiewicz." Mike's tone suggested he was getting irritated. "If he decides to talk to you, you'll see."

"Okay, okay. Look, I'm not saying you're blowing smoke, Detective, but this is all pretty way out compared to any story I've covered."

"Yeah, you and me, too."

"So, what's his name?"

"Ed Underwood. He's the personnel director at Barton. Also happens to have a black belt in *karate*."

"Is that why you liked him as a suspect?"

"No. He matches the physical profile we'd developed, based on the medical examiner's reports and that assault case." Mike paused. Connecting the dots, Stan realized the detective was embarrassed to admit they'd been focusing on the wrong guy. After a long silence, Mike continued. "Look, I'm not filling in all the blanks. You talk to the guy, put it together. You still got questions, you call me—and I'll see if I'm willing to answer."

Stan realized the conversation was about to end. If he were in Langan's shoes, he wasn't sure he'd reveal even this much. "I appreciate you calling—I know it's a big deal. And I'm sure you've still got lots of details to tie up. Can I ask one more question?"

"What?"

"What's Blake being charged with?"

Mike snorted. "That's the damndest part. When we grabbed him at Barton, he started admitting about the bomb 'cause he was afraid the building would blow up with him inside. But then when we got him to the station, he not only admitted the bomb plan, he also copped to the assault on Karen Durant and—get this—the two killings you were writing about, plus two others we had no solid evidence for." Mike paused to let that sink in. "Of course, it's up to the district attorney what charges to lay, but Blake's statement includes it all. If I were you, I'd wanna be in court this afternoon."

"Yeah, yeah—I will." Stan was stunned. It was not unheard of for a suspect to claim credit for additional crimes, but this was still a wild story. "So, you're saying this guy got fired and then went on a rampage against Barton?"

"Yep. In addition to the notes he sent you, he'd been sending notes to the president of Barton, starting at the time of the first murder."

"Jesus." Stan was writing furiously. "But wait a minute, what was the link to the victims? I didn't think they had any tie to the company."

"Get this—they had the bad luck to be wearing Barton watchbands. You know, those twisty ones they advertise?"

"Uh, yeah, I think so." Stan tried to make sense of it all. "But I don't get it—how did he think that would hurt Barton? Is he some kind of schizo nutcase?"

"Don't ask me, Osiewicz. Explaining that shit ain't my job." He made what sounded like a cross between a snort and a grunt. "From what he said when we got his statement, it sounds like Blake thought when people figured out the link between the watchbands and the attacks, it would hurt Barton's sales." He paused, then added, "I guess it's like that case where somebody put cyanide in bottles of Tylenol."

"The one in Chicago about five years ago? Yeah, I remember—they figure the goal was to ruin the company."

"Seems like this guy had similar ideas." There was a silence as Mike waited for more questions. When Stan didn't speak, he continued. "Anyway, I think you got more than enough. However you write it, you make damn sure you keep our deal."

"Right, you can be sure I—" Before Stan could finish,the line went dead.

Stan sat there for several minutes, looking over the notes he'd taken and thinking about the many bizarre elements that Mike Langan had shared. He glanced at his watch and figured he had time to update Joe Houle before the chief's press appearance. This was going to be a busy day, and there would certainly be follow-up stories. He thought about Houle's last comment.

It might even get me a Pulitzer!

As expected, the information Stan Osiewicz had received from Langan, along with the press conference, made the top of the news that day in both the *Evening Bulletin* and other media. When Lou DiNova read the front page story, it helped to complete the picture he'd been forming after learning of Mickey O'Donoghue's presence at the Barton factory. Now, sitting in the library before dinner, he spoke with Johnny Palmieri, who had appeared shortly after the newspaper arrived.

"So, Johnny, it seems that Mickey O'Donoghue made the right choice yesterday." DiNova lit a cigar, a habit when he wanted to focus his thoughts. After a couple of puffs, he continued. "It seems Underwood was not the killer after all and it would have been very messy if Mickey had killed both men."

"Yeah, well, you know, Lou. Mickey's a pro. That's why we use him."

"Indeed." Lou puffed slowly on the cigar. "Well, I expect the killer won't be causing any more problems. And the false stories about our involvement in all this should also be finished." He almost seemed to smile—a rare event for a man whose approach to business was seldom emotional. "Thanks for your part, Johnny." DiNova started to turn back to the newspaper, but then added, "And Johnny—don't be thinking about payback for your experience with

Underwood. I wouldn't want a local hero suffering harm for his efforts."

Ed Underwood had gone to the police station in the afternoon to give a formal statement about Sunday's events. While initially he was a bit uneasy due to the police's earlier suspicions, he found the interview was actually a positive experience. It allowed the detectives to complete their chronology of events, but also let Ed explain to them the reasons for his actions. Inwardly, he recognized that it felt good to no longer be treated like a suspect. In fact, Langan had been genuinely grateful for Ed's actions in stabilizing the nitroglycerin. As a result, the taking of the statement, while consuming more than an hour, provided Ed an unexpected sense of closure—the first of several emotional loose ends he needed to address.

Ed had also met with Henry Cohen, who was extremely relieved to know that the note-writer—and killer--had been apprehended, and also very appreciative of Ed's actions. "We'll talk later about how I can reward you, Ed, but for now, you have my thanks. You've done the company, and me personally, a huge good deed." He told Ed to take the rest of the day off after his visit to the police. "It's the least I can do for you, Ed."

Now Ed was on his way to Liz's. They'd talked last night, and by phone a couple of times earlier in the day, but he was looking forward to a quiet evening to decompress from the recent events. Liz remained anxious and told him she would be leaving her teaching at RISD early to meet him. So, just before four p. m., he was approaching Liz's front door.

To his surprise, the door swung open as he mounted the front steps. Liz stood there, a look of concern on her face.

"Oh, Ed! Are you okay? I've been so worried!"

"I'm fine, Liz." He gave a half-smile and then hugged her, followed by a long kiss.

"When you called last night and said there'd been a problem at the factory, but it turned out okay, I didn't know what to think. And you said you were too tired to come by last night, and that seemed unusual. Then I heard on the news that they caught a suspect, and—" The rush of words stopped. She scrutinized him for a long moment, then drew him close for another embrace. When she finally relaxed the hug, she held him at arm's length, her look of relief replaced by a scowl. "You, you—I don't know what you are, Ed Underwood! You lied to me about what you were doing this weekend, and then you risked your life confronting this madman, and, and—" Her words ended with a sob.

Ed held her for a long moment without saying anything, letting her emotions flow. Finally, he spoke. "It's all okay, Liz. Let's go inside and I'll tell you the whole story."

They went to the living room and sat facing each other on the couch. He realized the significance of lying to her about his decision to keep an eye on Blake for the weekend. Their relationship had always been based on honesty, and it had required a real effort to resist sharing with her. He had rationalized that if she knew, she would be worried and object to his plan to follow Blake, so it was easier not to discuss it. Now, with Blake in custody and the situation seemingly resolved, he was willing to share all the details in an effort to make amends for his dishonesty.

Liz listened without comment, though at some points her eyes went wide and her brow furrowed with concern. When Ed got to the events at the plant on Sunday afternoon, however, she began interrupting to ask questions.

"So, you saw Blake break in, but rather than call the police, you decided to look for him?"

"Actually, he'd broken in through the back door of the shipping department, and I went in the front. I knew the security guard would be there. I briefed him on the situation and told him to call the police if I didn't check back in a hour."

"An hour? Blake might've killed you both in that time—or, given what the news reports say, blown up the whole building with you in it!"

Ed gave what he hoped was a reassuring smile. "Remember, Liz, I know the building pretty well, and I knew Blake was there, but he didn't know about me." Liz's expression expressed clear doubt. "And don't forget, I'm a black belt in *karate*. I can take care of myself."

At that moment, Karen came down the stairs and entered the living room. "I know you're a black belt—and it's sure as hell helped me!" She came up and gave him a big hug, along with a chaste kiss on the cheek. "I thought I heard your voice, honey. I'm guessing you're telling Liz about your part in capturing the wacko who attacked me. Can I join?" Without waiting for an answer, she sat down in an easy chair beside the couch.

"Sure, Karen—er, you okay with that, Liz?"

Liz gave a fake pout. "Okay. After all, when have I ever been able to keep you out of something, Karen?" Her expression relaxed. "But I get to ask most of the questions!"

Karen nodded, and Ed waited for Liz's response to his previous narrative.

"So, you're in the plant looking for Blake, and you don't know where he is, or what he's planning." She thought about the situation. "That's a pretty big building, Ed. How could you be sure you wouldn't miss him? You know, he comes, does his thing, and leaves before you can find him?"

"Honestly, I couldn't be sure. But as I looked around, I just had a gut feeling he was still there. I've talked about *haragei* in terms of the *dojo*, and I really wasn't sure it would help me. I still can't explain it, but at some point, I just felt he was nearby." Whether this was the truth, or an after-the-fact rationalization, even Ed didn't know.

"Uh-huh. Go on." Liz was doubtful, but knew better than to challenge Ed on his *karate* training.

"So, I'd gone through the top two floors, and was just heading down the back stairs when I heard someone enter the stairwell from the second floor. It was Blake, and I was able to grab him from behind and put him in a submission hold."

"You actually caught him?" Karen couldn't resist interjecting.

"Yes, but then this other guy came up the stairs from the first floor, pointing a gun at us. At first, I thought he was a plainclothes cop. I'd had a feeling they'd been watching me. But then he took off when we heard other people in the building—the real cops, as it turned out."

“So who was he, then?”

Ed shook his head. “I’m not sure. He never said—and don’t forget he had a gun on us. If I had to guess, I’d say he had something to do with that Mafia goon who tried to blindside me at work the other day.” He paused, thinking about it. “But he seemed concerned about what Blake and I were each doing—like he wasn’t sure who the real criminal was. His uncertainty turned out to be a good thing, because it led Victor to talk about the bomb. Of course, he tried to claim I’d planted the bomb and that he’d tried to stop it. I knew the truth, but the guy with the gun didn’t seem to care either way—he just took off when he heard the cops.”

“What about if the cops hadn’t come just then? Did he threaten you?” Liz’s face expressed worry again.

“Honestly, I don’t know. I’d like to think he’d have believed me, not Blake, but I really can’t say.” He paused. “I guess it’s good I didn’t have to find out.”

“I’ll say!” Karen chimed in.

“Anyway, a few moments after the guy took off, I heard voices entering the stairwell on the first floor. At that point I was still holding Blake on the stairs between the first and second floors. It turned out to be Detective Langan, followed shortly after by three others, along with the Barton security guard. At first, Langan seemed to think I was the guilty one, but thankfully, Blake was worried about the bomb going off, so he started blabbing about how we needed to get out. Meanwhile, when I’d gone looking for him, I hadn’t even known there was a bomb.”

“So what was it? Was he really trying to blow up the whole building?” Liz frowned. Meanwhile, Karen sat mute, her mouth hanging half-open.

"Yes. He'd used some of the chemicals from the plating department, along with things he'd brought in, and was making nitroglycerin to—"

"Nitroglycerin! Isn't that pretty unstable?"

"Apparently. He was actually counting on a temperature increase to make it blow after he left the building. From what I gathered from talking to Langan at the station this afternoon, the bomb squad people say it would've been crude, but might well have brought down a big part of the building."

"Oh my God!" Liz's face showed shock—and then anger. "Ed, what the hell were you doing? This guy was a killer, and nitroglycerin is dangerous, and—"

"It's okay, Liz. I'm okay." Ed reached over to hug her. They held the position for several moments. Karen, sitting in the chair, partly stretched out her hands and leaned forward, seemingly wishing to join the embrace. When they broke the hug, Ed continued. "They got the guy and the plant is safe." He ventured a half-smile. "And Henry Cohen is thrilled—the company is safe, no more threatening notes. He'll probably give me a big raise!"

Liz lightly slapped his hand in rebuke. "Ed, you had no business taking such risks!" She frowned again.

"Well, then I guess I shouldn't say anything about disarming the bomb."

"*What?*" The exclamation came from Liz and Karen simultaneously.

"While we were still in the stairway and Blake was raving about the bomb going off, Langan managed to get him to explain how a rising temperature would trigger the explosion, and that the ice he'd brought to cool it was nearly gone. I remembered there was ice in the refrigerator in the lunchroom, and Langan forced Blake to show us where the bomb was. As long as we kept him in the building, Blake's life was in danger, too, so he cooperated. All I did was get the ice and add it, to buy time for the bomb squad."

"'All I did,' my ass!" Liz seldom used vulgar language, but Ed's story was incredible. "All you did was capture a serial killer and stop the building from blowing up. Never mind Henry Cohen—the city should give you a medal!"

"Absolutely!" Karen chimed in. "And don't forget that if it weren't for what you taught me, I might be dead now!' Impulsively, Karen jumped up, embraced Ed, and gave him another kiss—this time a long, lingering kiss on the lips.

"Okay, Karen. Time to come up for air!" Liz finally interrupted, but without taking offense. "Ed, I need a drink to calm down from hearing all this, but then we're going out to dinner—my treat. And Karen, you can come too, if you want."

"For sure! And let me pay half!"

Ed smiled at the two of them, relieved that Liz was no longer angry. He realized how much he loved Liz, and that Karen was like a stepsister, flirty but caring. He took a deep breath, regaining his center. He still hadn't fully dealt with every detail of events—including talking to Yoshikawa-*sensei*—but in this moment, he was fully alive, and life was good.

Everything else could wait.

Acknowledgements

Like every creative project, this book reflects the contributions of many people besides the author. While the storyline is fictional, the places, and some of the ideas, reflect three major influences: My experiences growing up in Rhode Island, my years as a professor of psychology, and my pursuit of Zen and *karate-do*. Among individuals, I wish to acknowledge, but cannot directly thank, two people who sadly are no longer living: my long-time friend, David Lisker, who by sharing his extensive experience in the costume jewelry industry helped me provide what I hope is a sense of authenticity to the story; and Dr. Burt Konzak, *karate sensei*, sociologist, and friend, whose passion for the martial arts inspired and challenged me for more than sixteen years of training. Grace Bogaert, a friend and author, and members of the Victoria Creative Writing Group have provided both motivation and technical guidance, which have been valuable in many ways.

I also wish to thank several people who provided both encouragement and helpful comments on earlier drafts of this book: Marilyn Shanman (my sister), Birgit Brand, Dana Williams, and two friends who read early portions, but sadly are not here to see the end result: Gerry Lin and Isaac Engel. I also want to thank the team at Friesen Press, especially Leanne Janzen, for their guidance, support and patience in bringing this project to completion. To all of these, and others unmentioned, my grateful thanks.

One note about accuracy: many descriptions of places and situations are intended to enhance the sense of verisimilitude, but the discussion of nitroglycerin is deliberately inaccurate in some details, to deter those whose motivations might be other than entertainment.

CPSIA information can be obtained
at www.ICGtesting.com
Printed in the USA
LVHW050220100122
708132LV00014B/1625

9 781039 128798